Panic clutched at my throat; I glanced around, looking for anyone out of the ordinary, but everyone appeared normal—except for their confused looks. The homeless guy slipping into the alley behind the Media station barely registered in my brain.

A man's voice spoke through the vert system. *"This moment of silence has been brought to you by the Resistance. In quietness, people can think for themselves. Which is just what the Governing—"*

A loud electronic screeching cut off the words, causing half of the people on the street, Sandy and me included, to slap their hands over their ears.

Just when I thought I couldn't take the piercing tone any longer, there was a crackle, and then, *". . . the End-of-Wars extravaganza sale ends at midnight tonight. Don't battle for bargains, shop Sale-o-rama, where every deal is a good deal."*

Several police had arrived on the scene. Some were conferring with the Media repairmen while others questioned the drivers involved in the accident.

Traffic picked back up and Sandy and I clicked our PAVs back on. Passing by the cops, I dipped my head down. Pretending to examine a spot on my jeans, I glanced down the alley where the homeless guy had disappeared. It was empty.

OTHER BOOKS YOU MAY ENJOY

Faithful	Janet Fox
Fat Kid Rules the World	K. L. Going
Impossible	Nancy Werlin
Looking for Alaska	John Green
Matched	Ally Condie
The Rules of Survival	Nancy Werlin
Sunshine	Robin McKinley
Willow	Julia Hoban
Wintergirls	Laurie Halse Anderson

XVI

Julia Karr

speak

An Imprint of Penguin Group (USA) Inc.

SPEAK

Published by the Penguin Group

Penguin Group (USA) Inc., 345 Hudson Street, New York, New York 10014, U.S.A.

Penguin Group (Canada), 90 Elington Avenue East, Suite 700, Toronto, Ontario, Canada M4P 2Y3
(a division of Pearson Penguin Canada Inc.)

Penguin Books Ltd, 80 Strand, London WC2R 0RL, England

Penguin Ireland, 25 St Stephen's Green, Dublin 2, Ireland (a division of Penguin Books Ltd)

Penguin Group (Australia), 250 Camberwell Road, Camberwell, Victoria 3124, Australia
(a division of Pearson Australia Group Pty Ltd)

Penguin Books India Pvt Ltd, 11 Community Centre, Panchsheel Park, New Delhi - 110 017, India

Penguin Group (NZ), 67 Apollo Drive, Rosedale, North Shore 0632, New Zealand
(a division of Pearson New Zealand Ltd.)

Penguin Books (South Africa) (Pty) Ltd, 24 Sturdee Avenue, Rosebank, Johannesburg 2196, South Africa

Registered Offices: Penguin Books Ltd, 80 Strand, London WC2R 0RL, England

First published in the United States of America by Speak, an imprint of Penguin Group (USA) Inc., 2011

1 3 5 7 9 10 8 6 4 2

CIP Data Is Available

Speak ISBN 978-0-14-241771-3

ACKNOWLEDGMENTS

I do not want to be the Oscar winner who's dragged offstage still reciting names of every person they ever thought had anything to do with their accomplishment. In the spirit of not being that person, this will, hopefully, be brief.

I have to thank my sister, Sarah, for teaching me to read when I was three. It was probably self-preservation on her part, so she wasn't stuck reading to me all the time. But, thanks to her, I have been a voracious reader and ardent lover of books ever since. In the present, she's been my constant cheerleader and support. My co-worker, Betty Myers, deserves much thanks, too, for countering every muttered word of doubt and discouragement with "keep the faith." Of course, she did get to hear me "SQUEE!!!" when *XVI* sold.

Through the Society of Children's Book Writers and Illustrators (SCBWI), I found my critique partner, Marybeth Kelsey (also an author), and through her, my other critique partner, Marcy Skelton. Without their friendship and amazingly kind ways of saying, "This part sucks," *XVI* would never have been agent-ready.

Which brings me to my fabulous agent, Kate Schafer Testerman of kt literary. Wow! Oh! Wow! She is one hundred kinds of awesome! Her industry savvy, perseverance, and confidence are what got *XVI* to exactly the right editor—the amazing and insightful Jennifer Bonnell. The very first time I talked with Jen I knew she "got" my story. Her spot-on editing had me arranging, cutting, adding, and tweaking what I'd written in the very best of ways.

Much gratitude goes out to my personal and online friends who were there for me in all my angsty-ness. And I am indebted to all the associates at Puffin/Speak whose support, talent, and expertise brought about this amazing finished product.

The powers-that-be are tugging on my sleeve to wrap it up, but . . . there are two more people (the most important ones) who had more to do with me writing than anyone except myself—my daughters. When I started out, Amy said, "If you write a page a day, in 365 days you'll have 365 pages." And, Melissa said, "Don't stop, Mom." So, I didn't.

A huge "Thank You!" and a heart full of gratitude to each and every one of you that helped make this dream of mine a reality. I love you all!

XVI

I

"**N**ina, look." Sandy jabbed me in the ribs.

I glanced up at the AV screen expecting to see the latest vert of back-to-school fashion for sixteens.

"No, there." Sandy jerked my arm, bringing my attention to the doorway.

Four guys approached us, lurching and swaying through the moving express. They sat across the aisle, immediately crowding together in a knot. A low buzz of unintelligible words, accompanied by the occasional rowdy snort, rose from their cluster.

"They're eighteen," she whispered. "I bet it's that one in the middle's birthday. He's cute!" She wriggled in her seat.

By the way he kept admiring the tattoo on his wrist and fingering the Band-Aid behind his ear, where his GPS had been, I knew she was right. I involuntarily touched my own tracker. The tiny grain-sized pellet embedded beneath the skin barely registered on my fingertips. What would it be like to be able to go someplace where you were untraceable?

Before my thoughts went any further down that path, Sandy said, "They're going into the city to celebrate. I wish—"

"No, you don't." My stomach turned at the thought of

eighteenth celebrations. We'd heard all about them, particularly the Angel affair. I quickly blocked the images from my mind.

Sandy "humphed" back into the seat, crossing her arms over her chest. "Those stories can't be true. Guys wouldn't do stuff like that. I mean, look at them . . ." She leaned toward me conspiratorially, but I saw her peeking at the boys from under her bangs. "Someone that cute could never do those kinds of things. Listen . . ." She fished around in her bag and handed me a rapido. "You're the one who took all those art lessons. Draw the tattoo. Okay?" She stuck her wrist in front of me.

"Sandy!" I pushed her hand away. "We could get arrested!"

One of the guys, not the birthday boy, must've heard us and looked over. He ogled Sandy the way I'd seen her stepdad do when he thought no one was watching. I grabbed her wrist and thrust it toward him, showing the absence of the obligatory XVI tattoo. He shrugged and turned back to his friends.

"Hey!" She pulled her arm away from me. "He was going to talk to me."

"It's not talk he wants, Sandy. Those stories aren't all made up. Ginnie said that ever since they started the tattooing twenty years ago, girls aren't safe. She thinks that—"

"She's your mom. What do you expect?"

"I dunno." I shrugged, letting it drop. Sandy was so caught up in all things sixteen that there was no reasoning with her. Her mother and mine were galaxies apart in just about every way possible. Mrs. Eskew not only allowed, but encouraged Sandy's sex-teen ways. She was even prepping her for FeLS. My mother, Ginnie, on the other hand, was doing everything she could to keep me from applying for the program, even though it was about the only way out of our tier-two status. When I tried talking about it with her, she'd say not to worry. I wouldn't be a low-tier forever. But she never told me how I'd move up. It wasn't like I wanted to join FeLS, but outside of marrying some upper-tier guy, I didn't have many options.

Sandy snatched a retractable zine chip from the rack on the back of the seat in front of her. She let go and it snapped back in place. She grabbed another, doing the same thing. I sighed. If she'd reached for a third, I would've stopped her. Sometimes I felt more like Sandy's mother than her best friend.

Her mood suddenly changed, thank goodness. "Scoot over," she said. "We're almost to that big farm and I want to see the cows. Can you believe people used to eat meat? Makes me want to puke just thinking about it."

Sandy's almost as crazy about cows as she is about boys. Truthfully, we're both animal lovers. That's one of the reasons we got to be such good friends. When Ginnie moved me and Dee out of the city and into Cementville, I didn't think I'd ever find a friend. But the first day of school, I met Sandy. We were both wearing the same shirt, with a horse on the front; and after school she got off the transit at the same stop as me. It turned out that we lived right next door to each other. We've been best friends ever since. Even if she does get on my last nerve sometimes.

The dull monotony of suburbia and Cementville finally gave way to an oasis of rolling hills and clumps of trees. As the express approached Mill Run Farm, Sandy and I both pressed our noses to the window like little kids. A herd of black-and-white cows was grazing in the distance. Two horses appeared, racing along the white board fence.

"They're so beautiful," I whispered.

Sandy gave my hand a squeeze. "Nina, I know you don't want me to do anything stupid," she said softly. The farm faded into the distance, and we settled back in our seats. "Hey, did you get all your homework done?"

"Yep," I said. "Regional Government and Twentieth-Century Literature. Love the Lit. Hate the Gov."

We both laughed.

"I'm dying in Lit," Sandy said. "You have to help me out. Promise?"

"Of course." She always depended on me to explain books to her, and I didn't mind. It wasn't like she couldn't or didn't read, she just didn't get the deeper meanings. I don't always either, but Ginnie talks with me a lot about what I read and helps me work through it.

"So. Are you going to take the FeLS prep?"

"Sandy, you promised." I half glared at her.

"Sorry, I forgot Ginnie won't let you." She tickled me. "Come on, don't be mad."

I couldn't help laughing, and I didn't want to stay angry with her—so I didn't.

"Are we going to your gran's first, before we meet up with Mike?" she asked.

I nodded.

"You know your grandfather freaks me out." She dug into her pocket, retrieving a small bag. "Want one?"

I stuck the frosted lemon drop into my mouth, rolling it around on my tongue until the rough sugar smoothed into puckery sourness. I sucked on the candy. "Yeah, Pops is a little strange. But I'd think you'd be used to him by now."

Sandy put several drops in her mouth and the bag back in her pocket. "No way," she mumbled, arranging the pieces with her tongue so she could talk. "I don't get a lot of what he says, and it creeps me out when he takes his leg off."

"I'll try to keep him under control," I promised, chuckling to myself. As if anyone could control Pops. "Maybe we should go to the zoo. It's probably the only way we'll get Mike away from all the new verts downtown."

"We are going to Gran's before we meet up with him, right?"

I laughed. We both knew that if Mike came with us, he'd talk Pops into taking his leg off. Mike was fascinated by the prosthesis. "Sandy, it's just an old GI leg."

"GI-wha?"

"For the billionth time, microbrain . . ." I tapped her head. "Government issue. Remember back in the 2000s the soldiers were called GIs because everything they had was issued to them by the government? That's where Pops got his leg after the accident, from the government. He says that's why it doesn't work right. It's cheap. Like something from Megaworld or Sale-o-rama."

"Hey, come on! These jeans are from Sale."

"I meant that when rich people get body parts, they get the good stuff, bionic, acts like the real thing." We both shopped the discount stores, like everyone else who was lower tier. "And," I added, "I love those jeans."

Sandy smiled and ran her hands around her waist. "Thanks," she said. "They fit good, don't they?"

Her clothes fit her a lot better than mine fit me. As Gran would say, "She's built like an MK lunar pod." Which I'm sure is why her stepdad looks at her the way he does.

The men I knew were either crazy, like Pops; half creepy and weird, like Sandy's stepdad; or mean cheaters, like Ed. He's Ginnie's married boyfriend, who also happens to be my little sister Dee's dad. I had no idea what it was like to have a father, real or otherwise, since mine died the day I was born. All I had was an old photo chip and the stories Gran used to tell me about him. Sandy pulled a mirror out of her purse and fluffed her hair, pouting at her reflection.

"Do I need more lipstick? Mascara?"

"Come on, Sandy, we're just meeting Mike and Derek—you know, friends." That's how I preferred guys, as friends. Any other way freaked me out. Sometimes I wondered if I was some kind of freak myself. Most every girl my age was getting primed for turning sex-teen. I had my reasons for never wanting to have sex. I just didn't have anyone to talk about my reasons with. Especially not Sandy or Ginnie.

Sandy sighed and put her mirror back. "You never know who might be looking at you." She gazed longingly across the aisle.

The guy who'd noticed her earlier glanced at me, quickly taking in all the important details. He cocked one eyebrow and licked his lips. I held my breath, scared he was going to speak, but the other guys drew his attention back into their huddle. I exhaled. At least for a few more months I was fifteen—and safe.

II

t was late September, blue sky, crisp air—not at all typical fall weather in Chicago. I wondered if this was how the country felt, clean and fresh. Sealed up in the express from Cementville to the city, you couldn't experience it. I glanced at Sandy, doubting she ever gave the weather a thought, unless it mussed her hair or forced her to wear a coat over some new outfit.

"Let's walk." I took off down the street, Sandy next to me.

On State Street, the verts were so constant and annoying they bombarded us from every store. *"Get the latest Personal Audio/ Video, virtually invisible in your ear, compatible with any omni-PAV receiver, only $29.95 . . . Visit the Dark Side—moon shuttle special—buy one ticket and a companion travels free, Sunday through Thursday . . . Mars burgers, for a taste that's out of this world."*

Sandy and I talked via our PAVs so we could hear ourselves over the verts. We were plotting out the day's events when there was a loud bang, followed by two more. Three trannies had slammed into each other right in the middle of the street. All the other traffic stopped. We clicked off our PAVs. Not one vert was blaring. There was total silence. Which was more jarring than the crash of the accident.

Sandy stared at me, her eyes grew huge. For a moment, I thought she was going to cry. Instead, she whispered, "NonCons."

Panic clutched at my throat; I glanced around, looking for anyone out of the ordinary, but everyone appeared normal—except for their confused looks. The homeless guy slipping into the alley behind the Media station barely registered in my brain.

A man's voice spoke through the vert system. *"This moment of silence has been brought to you by the Resistance. In quietness, people can think for themselves. Which is just what the Governing—"*

A loud electronic screeching cut off the words, causing half of the people on the street, Sandy and me included, to slap their hands over their ears. A dual trannie squealed up and two men armed with tool kits jumped out and rushed over to the Media station.

Just when I thought I couldn't take the piercing tone any longer, there was a crackle, and then, *". . . the End-of-Wars extravaganza sale ends at midnight tonight. Don't battle for bargains, shop Sale-o-rama, where every deal is a good deal."*

Several police had arrived on the scene. Some were conferring with the Media repairmen while others questioned the drivers involved in the accident. I overheard one of them say, "Officer, I don't know what to do. It was so quiet, all of a sudden like. I figured it was some kind of emergency. So, I hit the brakes . . ."

Traffic picked back up and Sandy and I clicked our PAVs back on. Passing by the cops, I dipped my head down. Pretending to examine a spot on my jeans, I glanced down the alley where the homeless guy had disappeared. It was empty.

"Two weeks ago, when Mom and I came into town, the same thing happened. Not the accident, but the silence," Sandy said. "It freaked me out then, too. Mom says it's happening more often." She frowned. "Damn NonCons. How dare they say that people don't think for themselves?"

I wasn't about to say that I liked the silence, NonCons or not. The constant bombardment of verts really didn't give anyone a chance to think. Ginnie always taught us that thinking for yourself is the most important thing. When I see how Sandy blindly follows whatever the latest Media-induced frenzy is—I know my mom is right. But it's hard being the only person who thinks like me. Sometimes I wish I could just be like everyone else my age and not think at all.

We were almost to Gran and Pops's, so I changed the subject. Pointing across the Chicago River at their building, I said, "The reflection's pretty cool, huh?"

Sandy barely looked up. "Yeah. That broadcast better not have messed with this." She tapped the face of her new chronos all-in-one. "Says it's eleven-thirty, the temperature is sixty-two and we're on the corner of LaSalle and Wacker." She squinted up at the street sign. "Guess it's okay."

While we waited for the light to change, I stared at the shimmering wall of glass caused by sunlight bouncing off the water. It reminded me of a painting I'd seen on a field trip to the Art Institute.

Inside, the lobby hardly resembled art: subsidized housing for retirees and disability pensioners like Pops; decorated on the blech side of ugly in lifeless beige and gray, standard government building colors. Gran often threatened to make a sneak attack on the lobby with a can of rainbow spray paint just to get some life in there.

I wondered again, like I've done all my life, what our lives would've been like if Pops hadn't had that accident. He'd been on his way up tier, on his way to becoming Corporate, before it happened. Everything would be so much different, maybe my dad would even still be alive ... if only—

"Hey, Nina, what planet are you on?" Sandy tapped my shoulder. "Light's changed."

I shook my head back to reality, determined not to let myself get caught up in wishful, impossible thoughts. We hurried across the bridge.

At the entrance, I flashed a cheesy grin into the security panel and put my hand on the auto-recognition pad announcing, "Nina Oberon and guest." I grabbed Sandy's shoulders, pointing her face at the panel—she grinned, too.

"Did I tell you last week was Gran and Pops's anniversary?" I steered her into the revolving door and got in the next compartment. "Thirty-eight years," I hollered through the glass. Before she could exit, I spun us around a couple more times. We finally whirled out the other side in a fit of laughter. "Most of the time Gran and Pops kind of pick at each other—you know, like those chickens at the zoo." I picked Sandy's sleeve and she smacked at my hand, giggling. "But they really love each other."

"Just because people are married doesn't mean they're in love. If Ed loved his wife he wouldn't be with your mom."

"Don't." I gave her a sideways glance.

"Sorry."

She knew I hated Ed. More times than I could remember, Ginnie would send me and Dee over to Sandy's when Ed was coming over. That way we hardly ever saw the full force of his rages. Although I always had a front-row seat for the aftermath. Mostly, I did my best not to think about him. Especially not about him and my mother, together.

"Anyway," Sandy said, "my mom and dad were in love. I remember how they used to laugh and dance around the house when I was little. Daddy would twirl Mom and then swoop me up with them." Her face darkened and she jabbed the elport button. "Stupid forays."

I thought I'd dodged the subject of NonCons after the Resistance's announcement—guess not. I knew better than to say anything. Sandy's real dad had been a policeman. When she was five, he and his partner were on a foray in the tunnels under the Chicago River searching for NonCons. Police had been tipped off that there was a pocket of the Resistance living in an underground city hidden in the ancient storm drains. An overflow door got jammed open (on purpose, the Media said) and water poured into the room the cops were in. They all drowned.

Ginnie was sure it was a setup to make it look like NonCons were responsible; she knew they weren't killers. She might be right, but I'd never say that to Sandy. Besides, Ginnie's just a cafeteria cashier at Cor-Cem Works, so how would she know something about NonCons that the rest of the world doesn't?

'd barely pressed the buzzer when the apartment door swung open and there stood Pops leaning on his crutch—holding the GI leg in his hand. "Damn thing, ain't good for nothin'!" He waved it in our faces and Sandy shrank back into the hallway.

"Pops." I lowered his arm and whispered, "Please, don't, you're scaring Sandy."

"Huh?" He stopped brandishing the leg and stared at me, confused. I smiled back, waiting for his brain to catch up with his eyes. It took a second. "Little Bit!" He hugged me as best as he could considering the circumstances.

I took the prosthesis and shook it back at him, grinning. "Little bit more than you." Out of the corner of my eye I saw Sandy looking everywhere except at us. I lowered the leg and urged Pops inside. "Let me help you get this on." Guiding him to his favorite chair, I asked, "What were you doing at the door like that?"

"Foray. Cops all over the building; I thought you were them again." He eased himself down onto the cushion. "Didn't have time to get my leg back on." Pointing at the top of it, he said, "There's something irritating there."

There was always something there. The whole leg was just uncomfortable, from what Gran said. I knelt down beside him and brushed off the nonexistent offending particle—then inspected his stump. "Looks good, Pops." I handed the prosthesis back to him. "There was a vert silence downtown and a Resistance announcement. That must be what the foray's about."

"Guess so." He snorted. "Supposed to be a NonCon in the building. We're all too damn old to be NonCons." He jerked the straps of his prosthesis into place. "Not that I wouldn't be, mind you, if I had the body parts. Someone needs to put the GC in their place. World's gone to hell in a—"

"Pops, stop." If surveillance was aimed at the apartment, those cops would be back in a second. Besides, I didn't want Sandy to hear him go on about wanting to be a NonCon. She was uncomfortable enough around him as it was.

Fortunately, he noticed her still standing in the hall. "Sorry, little missy, didn't mean to scare you."

"I'm fine, Mr. Oberon." She came inside, but left the door open.

She had on her dutiful face—expressionless with wide eyes. The same one I use when I have to listen to her mother go on and on about her weight and whatever new diet she's trying. It's what best friends do—try to ignore the crazies in each other's family.

"Where's Gran?" I asked.

"She'll be right back. Harriet called her after the checker heads left."

Oh, Pops! Why did he have to insult cops in front of Sandy? He knew about her dad. I snuck a peek; she must not have heard.

"No school today, Little Bit?"

"It's End-of-Wars Day. We had a choice to take it or Moon Settlement Day off. The class chose today because everything's still open and there's plenty to do."

"Plus"—Sandy finally shut the door behind her—"on MSD we have a big party at school and the AVs tune into our sister school on the Dark Side. My aunt's a teacher there. It's the only time I get to see her."

Pops made a funny half-cough, half-spew sound and grimaced.

He doesn't think we should have settled the moon, says it's sacrilegious. I didn't see anything religious about the moon, or anything else. Religion went out with automobiles, except for people like him and Gran. Sometimes they would go to a tiny church near Grant Park. Gran even reads the Bible. But everyone knows that's mythology. Although sometimes when I see how good it seems to make Gran feel, I have to wonder if there's some truth to it.

"I like Moon Settlement Day, too." I glared at Pops and he averted his eyes, like a little kid who thinks you won't see him if he isn't looking at you.

"Moon belongs in the sky without people tromping around all over it." He pushed his crutch out of the way and hobbled to the window. "When I was a boy . . ." His shoulders slumped and he leaned his forehead on the glass. "Eh . . . everything's changed," he muttered.

Sandy gave me her I-told-you-he's-weird look. I feigned indifference, but my insides clutched. He looked so wretched.

The door opened behind us and in came Gran. I rushed into her arms, burying my face in the crook between her shoulder and neck. Enveloped in her warmth, I felt five again, when her hugs fixed everything. Part of me could've stayed there forever.

"How's my favorite granddaughter?"

"Fine." I gave her cheek a peck.

Gran motioned Sandy over and hugged her, then held her out at arm's length and said, "Does your mother know you're wearing that? It's too revealing. It's not safe."

"Mom doesn't mind. And I can take care of myself. Besides, I'm almost sixteen." All the same, Sandy pulled her sweater closed over her slide top and zipped it partway up.

"Sixteen's not everything the Media makes it out to be, hon." Gran shook her head. It wasn't the first time she'd tried to say something to Sandy about her obsession with all things Media. I could have told her it was a hopeless cause. Sandy was practically a walking sex-teen vert; her clothes, her hair, the way she was insane about boys—exactly the way girls were supposed to be. "And aren't you applying for FeLS? I was under the impression that the candidates had to be virgins."

"I'm a virgin." Sandy looked the teeniest bit hurt at the implication.

"I know you are, dear." Gran gave her a hug. "It's just that dressing like that gives boys the impression that you don't want to be."

Before Sandy had the chance to confuse Gran with her convoluted reasoning about FeLS and sex-teen, Pops, who had hobbled back to his chair, said, "How's Harriet?"

Gran shook her head. "It's her son, Johnny. The Bureau of Safety and Security took him. Found some kind of transmitter, or so they said . . ." She must've noticed Sandy's expression, and cut her sentence short.

"B.O.S.S.? If I was thirty years younger . . ." Pops snorted.

"You'd still have only one leg and not a lick of sense in that head of yours." She gave him a look that could only be interpreted as Don't-say-another-word. Pops shut up.

"Gran," I said, "we can't stay. I just wanted to come by and say hello to my two favorite people."

"See there? You scared 'em off with your ridiculous antics and whatever nonsense you were spouting." She swatted at him with a news zine from the end table.

Pops ducked, squawking when a corner of it caught his shoulder.

I planted a kiss on his cheek; his whiskers poked me like a thousand tiny needles. Sandy waved her fingers at him. She was already halfway out the door.

"You girls be careful." Gran stuffed something in my back pocket and gave me a good-bye squeeze. "Watch out for Sandy," she whispered. "I worry about her."

Yeah, I thought, *so do I.*

At the elport, I pulled out the card Gran snuck me from my jeans. It flashed five credits. "We've got lunch."

Sandy peered over my shoulder. "Your gran's so ultra."

"Between this and what your mom gave you we can eat at TJ's. If Mike's bust we'll have to go some place cheaper, though, like Tofu Heaven, 'cause I'll have to pay for his. And you know how he likes to eat."

"Yeah, no kidding. Typical welf."

"Sandy!" I hated that word. I never used insulting slang—Ginnie would have killed me if I did. And everyone has feelings, no matter what tier they are.

Mike's dad didn't work and his family got free food from the government store over on Clark. I'd eaten at his house a couple of times when we were little. That stuff tasted like the containers it came in, and I didn't think it was because of his mom's cooking. Ginnie claims welfare food is low on nutrition and high on additives to keep welfare recipients overweight, unhealthy, and dependent on the government for menial jobs, like Bio-testers. Ginnie says a lot, but I figured she must be right because Mike's family is all of those things.

"Sorry, you know I like Mike okay." She shrugged and two seconds later changed the subject. "I wish we'd been there when the foray happened. Policemen are so cool."

Maybe if I'd known Sandy's dad I'd feel differently, but I didn't know him and I'm not sure I'd really have wanted to anyway. Ever since the time I saw a couple of cops ignore a group of eighteens beating up a homeless person, my opinion of police had been much closer to Pops's.

When we reached the ground floor, there was a circle of cops standing at the entrance. As we walked by, one of them tipped his checkered hat to Sandy. The officer next to him, an older guy, scrutinized us. I mentally ran through everything about me at that moment. I looked like a typical teenage girl, although not as blatant as Sandy. We weren't doing anything wrong. Why did I feel guilty? Then I remembered Pops's tirade upstairs. Had they heard? Did they know?

The officers approached us, and my palms began to sweat. I felt a blush rising. I'd never been stopped in my life. Ginnie's stories about false arrests and being thrown in jail zinged through my head. If they had an emo-detector, I was in trouble.

How would I explain my reaction? Out of the corner of my eye, I saw Sandy flouncing her hair. Crap! Didn't she think about anything except guys?

"Girls," the older cop said, "let's see your ID."

I'd watched enough AV to know the routine. In unison, we presented the back of our left hands to the officer. He ran the scanner over them.

"Wrists."

We turned over our arms, so they could see we weren't tattooed. It took everything I had to keep mine from shaking off my body.

"Nina Oberon," the older one said, examining my ID on the scan screen. "You live in Cementville. What are you doing here?"

"Visiting my grandparents." I fought to keep the trembling out of my voice.

"Oberon." He scrutinized my face, looking like he was trying to retrieve a memory. All I could do was quake inside.

Meanwhile, Sandy had launched into the whole story about her father with the other cop. Turned out that he knew someone who knew someone who'd known her dad. After a few moments, and lots of sweating on my part, they warned us about the NonCon activity in the area and advised us to report anything suspicious. Like we would know what "suspicious" was. Moments later we were outside.

I took a deep breath. "I really—" I was going to say hate cops, but caught myself just in time, covering with, "I wonder if Johnny really is a NonCon? He's always been nice to me."

"If he is," Sandy replied, with a look of pure hate in her eyes, "he'll get what he deserves, reassimilation by B.O.S.S. It's what they do to criminals. Remember Mr. Dunbar."

I shuddered. I would never forget Mr. Dunbar. He had been my seventh-grade Ethno Customs and Languages teacher—and one of my favorites. He'd been a friend of Ginnie's, too.

Before they took Mr. Dunbar away, he was fun—cracking jokes, taking us on field trips, and telling us stuff that wasn't in our text chips. A month after they took him, he returned. But it might as well have not been him. No more jokes, no more field trips, and he never deviated from our chips again. There were all kinds of rumors about actual reassimilation, but no one really knew the facts about it. That was one thing they didn't teach us in school.

Anyone who knew Johnny Pace would know he's no criminal. The last time Ginnie and I were in town together, he and Ginnie got to talking about the government. But that was just *talk*. It didn't mean they were NonCons. But if people thought Johnny was a NonCon, what would they think about Ginnie? What if she were mistaken for a NonCon . . . ? I didn't want to think about that now. It wasn't like the thought had never occurred to me. It had, and often. But I knew I had to stop myself now, because whatever I didn't want to think about is what I couldn't stop thinking about.

"Wish they'd had an emo-detector," Sandy said, cocking her head at me. "You would've been off the meter. I saw how red you were." She laughed.

"It's not funny, Sandy." I could feel myself starting to blush again. "What if they had had one, and ran me? What if the Bureau of Safety and Security took me? Huh?" How could she not realize what could have been? My temper was rising.

"Oh, come on, Nina. Everyone knows that sixteens are emo wreckage. Cops hardly ever ED them, for that reason alone." She hooked her arm in mine and I started breathing a little easier. "I was just kidding, okay? I wouldn't have let them do anything to you. Besides, it's not like it was B.O.S.S. They were just local police."

We headed north on LaSalle, toward my old neighborhood. I vaguely listened as she babbled on about how cute the younger cop had been. Even though the sun was bright, my mood wasn't. Those eighteens on the express, forays, NonCons, cops, and then setting my mind running worrying about my mom—well, it could ruin anyone's day.

IV

"There's Mike," Sandy said. "Derek's with him."

The guys sauntered down the street toward us, Mike gesturing like crazy and Derek laughing. Just seeing them started lifting the cloud on my mood. They were such opposites. Mike was short and round. Derek was at least a foot taller and skinny as a temo shaft. I'd known them both since the first day of kindergarten; other than Sandy, they were my best friends.

Before they got to us, Sandy turned to me and asked, "What happened to Mike?"

He had the scabbed-over remains of a gash across his forehead, left eye, and down his cheek. "His dad," I whispered. "Those government experiments sometimes make him crazy. Don't say anything, okay?"

"Sure."

They joined us and we headed down the street as a group. Verts blasted out from every store, hoping that in the five seconds or so it took for a person to walk by they'd hear something that would lure them inside. They were the most annoying form of advertising I could imagine. Everywhere you looked downtown, there were flashing signs, moving displays, and audio sales pitches. It made me dizzy. As always, I clicked on my PAV to listen to some music and ignored everything else.

Sandy pressed her nose to the window of every clothing shop. "Come on, Nina . . . just this once?" She'd been sucked in by a group of mannebots in the window at Mars 9.

Their vignette was about one girl and three guys in a school hallway. One of the guys was supposed to be the Tylo, who was the hottest teen vid star ever. The girl-bot sported a XVI tattoo and an ultrachic outfit that I was sure cost more than what Ginnie made in a month. The guy-bots were circling around her like Saturn's moons, but she only had eyes for the Tylo.

"We can't even afford to breathe the air in there," I said, dragging her away from the display. "Let's go eat."

***

An hour later, we were sitting in a booth at TJ's fiddling with the remains of lunch.

As usual, Mike didn't have any credits, but Derek was full up. He'd been playing music on the streets in his neighborhood. I joked that people only gave him money to keep him quiet. The truth is he's a good musician. When he covers Van Stacy's "Girl's Gone to the Moon," it makes me cry.

"You gonna finish those fries?" Mike asked Sandy.

"Take 'em." She shoved the plate catty-corner across the table. "I'm not a big fan. Besides, I'm watching my weight." She patted a nonexistent belly bulge.

"Oh, puh-leese," I said. "Your mom is who's watching your weight. You look fine. You know you can eat anything and not put on a pound."

"Mom says—"

"Your mother is totally obsessed with your food intake." I reached over and grabbed a fry. "There is nothing wrong with the way you look, and you know it. But you can give me those, I'm not watching anything."

"Want more?" Derek asked. "I'll get you some."

"Huh?" I wrinkled my brow at him. "No." Leaning on the table, I rested my chin on my hand, staring at a small rip in the plasticene seat between him and Mike, avoiding Derek's eyes. He'd been acting strange lately. I'd been doing my best to ignore each little incident, like him buying me Astro-Lite's latest music chip for no reason, but they were piling up. I had to put a stop to it, but I wasn't sure how, and it was making me kind of mad.

I loved Derek, but not as his girlfriend. I didn't want to be anyone's girlfriend and Derek knew that. Better than almost anyone.

He knew that I'd much rather stay fifteen. Everyone knows what's expected of a girl when she turns sixteen. They don't call it "sex-teen" for nothing. We're all supposed to be so excited about sex and willing to do whatever with practically any guy who asks. But the whole sex thing was definitely not what I wanted. I'd seen more than just the Health and Sociology vids at school. I knew girls hadn't always been treated like that, making me wish I'd been born one hundred years earlier.

The thought of Ed crossed my mind and I shoved the fries away, shutting down those images. I was so wrapped up in my own head I didn't notice Mike sneaking his hand across the table until he'd knocked my elbow out from under me.

"What the . . . !" I managed to catch myself before my face smacked onto the tabletop.

"On the moon, Neenie-beanie?" He grinned at me. Sandy laughed out loud.

I glared back at both of them, ignoring my grade school nickname and trying to recover some dignity. Derek opened his mouth to say something, which I was afraid was going to be an overly concerned *You okay?* So I went for a quick comeback before he had the chance.

"For your information, Mikey, I was thinking about my birthday this December and how I'd just as soon not turn sixteen."

"Not an option," Sandy said. "I'm looking forward to it myself." She tossed her bangs to the side and glanced around the restaurant, most likely looking to see if anybody was checking her out. Two boys were sitting across the restaurant. Sandy unzipped her sweater, exposing the slide top that barely hid anything.

I sighed. Gran was right. Sandy needed watching over.

"I can't wait until selection day. I plan on being chosen." She squirmed around, trying to get the guys' attention. "I wonder if the FeLS rep will be cute."

"I don't think that matters. It's probably the only time you'll see him." Twice a year, a man from the Governing Council's Liaison Department came to select sixteen-year-old girls for training as Female Liaison Specialists. All tier-one and -two girls—the lowest of the low—were required to fill out applications when they turned fifteen. Upper-tier girls never went into FeLS. It wasn't even an option for them. It was the only option for us low-tiers: the government had set up the program so that only the bottom two tiers were eligible.

On selection day, the FeLS rep—everyone called him the Chooser—interviewed everyone and made his picks. The GC sent the girls who were chosen to an education center on one of the space stations where they were trained for diplomatic service.

"It better not be your mom's boyfriend." Sandy wrinkled her nose. "He's gross."

"Yeah." No way could I argue with that. "You don't really want to go into FeLS, do you?" I was 99 percent sure I didn't want to. Ginnie certainly made her opinion on the matter clear. I'd filled out my application, but only because it was mandatory. The idea of moving up in the world was certainly attractive, but the program didn't sound all that great. The worst part of it was you couldn't have any contact with your family for the entire two years you were in the program.

"Yes," she answered, but she wasn't paying attention to me. One of the guys had noticed her. "It's the only way for girls like us to get into the upper tiers."

"You could study harder and try to get a scholarship," I said. "Then you wouldn't need FeLS."

She shrugged her sweater off one shoulder, smiling at the guy looking at her, and completely ignoring me.

"Sandy"—I hoped to appeal to her obvious sex-teen-ness— "you know you can't dress like you do now if you're a FeLS. I heard you have to wear uniforms. Plus, you'll be out there in space, and who knows if there are any guys there?"

"Of course there are guys." She shot me a look like I'd just said two plus two was five. "Guys are everywhere. And"—she paused; for effect, I guessed—"you've seen the verts . . . in your free time, you can dress any way you want, go anywhere you want, and do anything you want. Anything, except *that*." She could tell I was not impressed. "Well, you can go anywhere on the station. Guess you can't really sneak off of it." She laughed, shaking out her hair, and the other side of her sweater slipped down, too. "Hey, Mike, isn't Joan a FeLS?"

Mike was staring across the booth at Sandy's practically naked chest. "Huh?" he grunted.

"Joan." I snapped my fingers under his nose. "Your sister? She's in FeLS?"

"She is?" He was struggling to focus somewhere besides Sandy's breasts.

In order to help, I yanked her sweater closed. "Joan?" I kicked him under the table. "FeLS?"

"Oh, yeah." He snatched up a fry. "She was."

"Maybe I should talk to her," Sandy said. "She could tell me all about how to get chosen, right?" She propped her chin in her hands, leaning toward Mike. "Can you arrange that? Please?"

"Nope. Sorry. Haven't talked to her since she left."

"Wait, isn't her two years up?" I said.

"I guess. Mom gets chips from her, I think," Mike said. "Heck, I dunno. My dad says she probably thinks she's too good for us now."

The guy who'd been watching Sandy motioned her to show her wrist. Reluctantly, she did. He shook his head and turned away.

"Oh well." She flipped her hair, scanning the rest of the tables with no success.

"You gotta be a virgin to get into FeLS, don't you?" Derek said.

"Of course." Sandy rolled her eyes. "Everyone knows that. Why does everyone keep asking me if I know that?" She turned her attention to me. "I wonder what it's going to be like, really? Can you believe those 'how-to' vids? We've watched like, what, one a week since school started? I mean, sex has got to be the most ultra thing in the galaxy! I wonder what the guys get to see when we're watching our vids?" She looked over at Derek. "I don't know why they separate us, we're going to be doing it together, so, duh—"

"Will you stop?" It was bad enough that Derek was making moon eyes across the table at me. I didn't need Sandy saying anything that might encourage him to think about me and sex in the same thought. "No wonder guys think when girls are tattooed all they want is to get laid."

"Don't they?" Mike gave me his biggest wide-eyed innocent look.

A part of me knew he was joking, but the part that didn't said, "Shut up." I paused, knowing the reaction I'd get if I said what was on my mind. I couldn't stop myself. "Look at what happened to Angel."

Suddenly, it seemed the remaining ketchup on Mike's plate was the most interesting thing he'd ever seen. Sandy began digging around in her purse. Derek glanced at me for a second and then looked out the window. Nobody wanted to remember. I should have felt bad for bringing it up, but I didn't. I was sick and tired of the constant sex talk, and teasing. Couldn't my friends at least try to understand that maybe all girls—like maybe *me*—don't want to have sex?

Angel Cordoba had been in Mike's older sister Joan's grade, just a couple of years ahead of us. She was cute and nice, and we'd all hung out at Oak Street beach two summers earlier, before Joan went into FeLS. Right after Angel got her XVI, a couple of guys invited her to a party. It was an eighteenth and she was the only girl there.

The guys got off with six months' community service for the "accident" with the lighter fluid. There were no rape charges. They convinced the prosecutor that she'd wanted it—that happened a lot when the girl was a sixteen. All the Media news stories said Angel was just another oversexed sixteen, that she got high, accidentally lit herself on fire, and then blamed the guys after the fact. But anyone who knew her knew that was a lie. No one had the nerve to say anything, except her brother. He started an antitattooing, antigovernment vlog, but it got shut down and he disappeared. Rumors were he became a NonCon. Ginnie'd told me she thought he was dead.

Angel had five operations total. She almost looked like herself afterward, but looks weren't everything. She hadn't been the same person since.

"Sorry. But Angel didn't want sex, did she?" I dropped the card Gran had given me on the table. "That covers mine. I'm going for a walk."

"I'll come with you." Derek started to get up.

"No. I'll catch up with you guys at the Water Tower at one."

***

I always found downtown streets overwhelming. Sometimes I felt like the combination of verts and people would drown me or swallow me whole. My stomach tightened and my breathing quickened, and I had to keep myself from breaking into a run. Once I was out of the worst of it, I hurried over to Lincoln Park, to my favorite place.

A bigger-than-life-sized holographic statue of Lincoln stood at the park entrance. He'd been a president of the United States, which hadn't existed for years. Ever since the End-of-Wars treaty, the Governing Council had ruled the Americas, the moon colonies, Venus, and the ocribundan mines on Mars. Except for the Great Oil Deserts, which no one cared about now that ocribundan was the Earth's main fuel, and some islands off the Greater United Isles, the rest of the world was ruled by councils run like the GC.

I shielded my eyes from the sun, peering up at the statue. Lincoln was ugly, but there was something in his eyes that seemed kind. I pressed the info button and the image began reciting the Gettysburg Address. I should take time to learn more about what Lincoln believed in—freedom and equality for everyone. Between school and art classes and life, I barely had enough time to study anything except homework, and I didn't always get that done.

Before the recording ended, I'd forgotten about Lincoln and everything else. My attention was drawn to the scene in front of me and I shuffled off through the brilliant fall colors. The trees looked like giant candles. Their fiery leaves were sparks flying wherever the wind took them. I crunched through the ones on the ground, reveling in the crackles and snaps and the earthy aroma that filled my nostrils. I felt lighter, freer. Being in any kind of natural setting did that for me. If I didn't look beyond the trees to see the buildings, I could imagine I was a million miles from the city. Maybe out at Mill Run Farm with the cows and horses; I wouldn't worry about anything then.

Before long, I was at the grassy mound that I'd always called "my mountain." There was a weird animal-like noise, and for a moment I was scared. *Oh, come on,* I thought, *what kind of animals would be loose in the park? Squirrels? Chipmunks?* Not exactly terror-worthy. But the noise got louder and I realized that something wasn't right. I strode to the top of the mound and looked down the other side.

Three guys were beating up a fourth who was curled into a ball, arms wrapped around his head. I could tell he was homeless by his clothes.

I should've turned and left, but I didn't.

V

"Stop it!" I yelled.

The three boys, college athletes according to their letter jackets, stopped kicking the guy and turned around.

One of them, a beefy guy with slicked-back brown hair and piggish eyes, leered at me. "You sixteen?"

"No," I squeaked, holding up my wrist for him to see. That's when I realized the danger I was in, all alone in a secluded area of Lincoln Park facing three 'letes who were primed for trouble. My being underage wouldn't matter to them. 'Letes could do whatever they wanted. There was no way I could outrun them, so I stood my ground, hoping the meanest glare I could muster would hide my terror.

The tallest of the three yanked on Pig Eyes' sleeve. "Come on, Coach'll bench us if we're late again."

Pig Eyes shook off his grasp, and locked eyes with me. Then his gaze traveled downward. "Oh, baby, I'd love some of that." He grabbed his crotch and thrust his hips at me before turning to follow his friends. I wanted to vomit.

On their way past the guy on the ground, Pig Eyes kicked him one more time.

They finally disappeared behind the trees. I was shaking so hard I was afraid if I tried to walk I'd collapse in a sobbing heap. The homeless guy still lay there like a giant tattered baby. I should have gone; anyone else would've left him.

Homeless are no better than river rats, maybe even worse. They get beaten and killed without anyone noticing. No one in their right mind has anything to do with them. But I guess at that moment my mind wasn't quite right. Even though my knees were like rubber bands, I took a deep breath and scrunched through the leaves to the moaning heap of ragged clothes.

"You okay?"

All I got back was a grunt.

"Hey, can I do anything?"

Rolling onto his back, he groaned.

"Shit." He spat out some blood and touched the split on his lip from where it was flowing. "How stupid am I?"

"I dunno." I stared at him. He looked almost as bad as Ginnie after one of Ed's rages. "You look more hurt than stupid."

I was surprised—the face that glanced up at me wasn't a man's, old or otherwise. He was a boy, my age. "That was rhetorical," he snapped, dabbing at his lip with a filthy sleeve.

"Here." I offered him a rumpled napkin from my pocket, ignoring his attitude.

Holding it on the cut, he squinted in my general direction. "You're not afraid to talk to me?"

"No." That wasn't entirely true. I was terrified. "You homeless?"

He sat up, clutching his stomach. "Man, that really hurts," he muttered, not to me in particular, so I didn't comment. Shading his eyes with one hand, he looked up at me. "Does it make a difference if I am?"

"Well . . . uh . . . I, ah . . ."

I couldn't shake the impulse to help him. It seemed that the older I got the more I believed that everyone, homeless or not, deserved to be treated at least like a human. I knew it was my mom's influence. She always says everyone has a right to live. Just because the homeless don't want to take handouts from the government because of what they have to do in return doesn't mean they're subhuman.

This guy looked so vulnerable, all I could think of was Ginnie after a go-round with Ed. For ten years I've seen this—I'd try to help her clean up afterward, but she looked so awful I would cry and that would upset my little sister, Dee. I'd choked back so many tears, they'd become a lake of sadness in my belly.

"Well?" His voice brought me back to the present. "You got a problem with that?"

"No."

"Yeah, right, Little Miss Burbs." He looked me up and down, but not the way Pig Eyes had. "I bet you don't."

My jaw dropped. As if I would lie to some guy I'd risked my life to help? And the slam about the suburbs? It hadn't been *my* choice to go from our tier-five apartment in the city to our tier-two existence in Cementville. Any compulsion to help him flew right away like a swirl of autumn leaves.

"Seems like you're fine now." I stepped around him "Keep the napkin."

A tiny part of me wanted to kick him, too, not because he was homeless, but because he was a judgmental asshole.

"Hey," he called after me. "Sorry. I'm not usually . . . well . . . the circumstances, you know."

That stopped me. I did know. Sometimes when Ginnie'd come home beat-up, she would lash out at me. Not ever physically, but she'd say mean things. She needed to share her pain, so I took some of it. I'd do anything for her, no matter how much it hurt. I turned around.

I sat on the ground across from him. "Where do you stay? Is there someone I can call?" I pulled my PAV receiver out of my pocket. "Do you need—"

"I'm not homeless. I live over there." He jerked his head to the west. "Ow!" He grabbed his neck and rubbed it. "I'll be fine, it'll just take a sec." He wasn't homeless? I started to ask him why he looked like he was, when he said, "What about you? Where do you live?"

My cheeks reddened, remembering his earlier slam. "I do live in the suburbs." I held my chin up. "But I used to live here, on Wrightwood."

"What's your name?"

"Nina."

"Nina what?"

Why did he want to know? I wasn't sure I should tell him my last name. The earlier terror I'd felt had subsided, but this interest in me made me nervous. I shook it off. What would it hurt for him to know my name? It's not like he could get my PAV number. (I shoved the receiver back in my pocket, just in case.) "Oberon."

"Oberon?" He dropped his hand from his neck. "Nina Oberon," he repeated, scrutinizing my face, which made me even more uneasy.

"What's yours?" I felt the heat rising up my neck again. Damn blushing. I averted my eyes.

"Sal Davis."

I glanced back at him, and he looked away. A bit of napkin clung to the blood that had dried on his lip. Even though he was sitting, I could tell he was taller than me, and he was skinny, but not in an unhealthy way. Thick dark lashes rimmed his eyes. His longish black hair was wavy and there were leaf bits randomly sticking out of it. *He's kind of cute,* I thought, which didn't make me any less uncomfortable.

"You're a mess." I pointed to his head. As he reached up, I took a deep breath and asked, "How come you're dressed like that if you're not homeless?"

"No one notices me that way." He brushed the leaves off his head.

"Why don't you want to be noticed?"

Sal leaned back and looked at me. "You sure do ask a lot of questions. What's up with that?"

Me? He'd asked just as many questions, maybe even more. Whether it was his attitude again or the stress of the whole situation, a stupid tear chose that moment to trickle down my cheek. I wasn't fast enough to wipe it away before he noticed.

"I'm hurt and you're crying?" He started laughing.

"You know what?" I jumped up and jabbed my finger at him. "I came down here to help you. I was trying to be nice."

I marched to the top of the mound, and looked over my shoulder, at not-homeless Sal Davis, leaves stuck to his ratty clothes, eyes shaded by a hand that was still clutching the tattered, bloody napkin. "Thanks, Nina Oberon."

I kept on walking until I got to Michigan Avenue. I was almost glad to hear the verts, *"Celebrate Moon Settlement Day on the Dark Side. Only Four hundred and fifty round-trip . . . ,"* *"Maria Corcoran fashions, straight from the runway in Milan . . . ,"* *". . . Stacy's latest hit, 'City of Tears' . . ."* They drowned out Sal's voice saying my name.

VI

"You gotta listen to this one, Neens." Mike dragged me toward a sporting-goods store. "They're talking about how balls feel—it'll crack you up."

I pulled my arm away. "Cut it out."

"First you stomp off and now you're acting all weird. What's gotten into you?" Sandy gave me a sideways look.

"Nothing," I said. *Everything,* I thought.

"Here." Derek handed me a little box. "Maybe this'll help."

He stood there watching while I lifted off the lid. Inside was a little silver horse charm nestled in a bed of fluff.

"Wow, Derek! It's beautiful. Why'd you do this?" I looked up at him. "My birthday's weeks away."

He shrugged. "I was playing music in front of a store the other day. The guy said I was good for business and filled me—twenty whole credits. This was in the window. I knew you'd like it. No big deal."

I should have given it back. I could tell it meant more to him than just a token of friendship, but it was so beautiful. I didn't have many beautiful things.

"Thanks." Sitting down on the curb, I took off my necklace

and laced the horse between my other two charms. One was the number seven, which Gran had given to me on my seventh birthday. The other was from Pops, the letter T for "Truth." He says that the truth can't stay hidden. Derek's true feelings sure weren't. Not anymore.

Sandy sat down next to me and admired the little horse. "Cute! Good call, Derek."

He stuck his hands in his pockets, grinned at me, and shuffled over to Mike, who was busy looking at travel posters and listening to their verts.

"Here." I handed the necklace to Sandy. "Hook this for me, okay?" I turned my back to her and held up my hair so she could clasp it around my neck.

She fastened the necklace and I sat for a moment longer, people-watching. Two girls walked by, one had her view wrap on and was giving the other a blow-by-blow description of whatever it was she was watching. A kid on a zoom board careened around the corner, nearly hitting some guy. I thought for a second that the guy who dodged him was Sal. He wouldn't have followed me, would he? I hadn't told anyone what had happened—I didn't want to hear it from the guys. But I also didn't want to keep it to myself.

"The weirdest thing happened at the park." I proceeded to tell Sandy what happened on the mound. I had hardly finished the story when she pounced on me.

"Are you crazy!?" she asked, her eyes big as Chrometers. "Helping homeless?"

"Sandy, I'm *fine*. And he said he wasn't homeless."

"You don't know that for sure, do you? What is the matter with you, Nina? You want to get arrested?"

She was right. He could've been lying. It didn't matter now; I'd already helped him. "They can't arrest you for talking to someone." Could they? I wondered. "Besides, he was hurt. You know how I am about people getting hurt."

She knew. She'd been over after Ginnie and Ed's fights.

"But you could have . . . those 'letes . . . they could've—"

"But they didn't." For once, Sandy was the protector and I was the reckless one. She was right, though. I could've ended up like Angel, maybe even worse. I shuddered, staring at the little veins trailing greenish blue right under the skin on my wrist. "If I was sixteen, they could've done whatever they wanted, and no one would have cared."

"It's not going to be like that, Nina." Sandy hugged me. "You just need to not do stuff like helping homeless anymore. Sixteen will be fun, you'll see."

"I hate that we have to get tattooed." I rubbed the imaginary Roman numerals off my skin.

"Nothing we can do about it. We'll get 'em and then we can have sex—"

"I thought you wanted to go into FeLS. Besides, how can you worry about what some guys might've done to me, when it's exactly the thing that you can't seem to wait to have happen to you?" Sometimes I didn't understand her at all.

"Of course I want FeLS. And I don't want some guy, or three, forcing me to have sex. I just can't wait to have all the guys wanting to have sex with me. Can't you see it now? Just like in the verts.

Me, surrounded by Orie and Brek and Jude, all looking at me like . . . oh, you know." She tilted her head back, eyes shut and a big smile on her face. "What's cool is that when you're sixteen you can do it, if you want."

"It won't be Orie, Brek, or Jude if you're off on some space station learning how to be a diplomatic specialist."

"I mean after getting out of FeLS." Sandy bolted upright. "You know what?"

"What?"

"Even though he's a galactic-sized skiv, I bet your mom could get Ed to find out who the Chooser is and they could pick both of us! Then we could go to training together."

"I've told you a gazillion times, there's no way Ginnie would let me be a FeLS. Besides, I have to be around to take care of Dee." I had never been completely honest with Sandy about FeLS, never told her that I really didn't want to go. If FeLS relied on some guy like Ed, a former GC spy, to choose girls . . . well, anything that he's involved in couldn't be something I wanted to be in, no matter what.

"I could have my mom talk to her," Sandy offered. "It would be so much fun! 'Cause you know I'm going to miss you when I go." She squeezed me.

"You don't even know if you'll get chosen. Think of how many girls in our school are turning sixteen."

"Yeah, but I bet less than half of them are virgins." Sandy scrunched her eyebrows and nodded. "Yep, I'm sure to get chosen. I'm still a virgin and I look like a FeLS." She pushed up on her breasts and then smoothed her hands down her torso. "Just like on the cover of *XVI Ways*, right?" She studied herself in the store window, turning and twisting around like a model.

"Right." A part of me had dreamed about being chosen for FeLS once. The FeLS graduates who came to talk to us at school were all tier five or above. They got good jobs after their FeLS time. I'd figured when I was out of training and making lots of credits, I'd have enough so I could move Ginnie and Dee back to Chicago into a higher-tier place. Ginnie wouldn't have to see Ed anymore and we'd be happy, like we'd been when I was little.

Sandy was right—there were strings that could be pulled. If she wanted to, Ginnie could get Ed to make sure I was chosen. But after I turned twelve and was eligible for the extra-credit FeLS prep classes, Ginnie told me outright that she'd never allow me to go. Even if I did get chosen, Ginnie said she'd buy out my contract, somehow. She enrolled me in a Creatives' art class instead. I don't know that I was ever that disappointed to not go the FeLS classes—I loved art, and sketching came naturally to me. I was just like Ginnie in that way.

I glanced over at Sandy, who was still prancing and preening. "That's the other thing, Sandy—I'm not pretty enough to be chosen."

She reached into her bag and pulled out a smaller bag filled to overflowing with makeup. "I can fix that!" She sprayed something on my hair. Teasing out some strands, she styled away, patting and combing. Then she said, "We could stuff your bra, no one would ever know." She jammed her hand back in the bag and produced a handful of tissues. "Here."

Fortunately, Mike and Derek interrupted us at that moment. I pressed the tissues back into Sandy's hand and ran my hands through my hair so it was back to normal. Glancing in the window, I checked to make sure I looked like me again.

"Ready? To the zoo," Mike announced, pointing northward.

We tromped down the street, and on the way, I glanced down every side street and alley, half expecting to see Sal. They were mostly empty except for a few homeless who melted into the alleyscapes like ghosts.

VII

Since Mike volunteered at the zoo, he had a digital code by his ID that allowed him access to restricted areas. He let us all in, then took Sandy to the cow barn to see the baby calves while Derek followed me to the horse barn. We both grabbed a handful of treats from a dispenser and got into the petting line.

"I hope you like the charm." His eyes got a kind of dreamy look and his arm brushed up against mine and he stayed close.

"I love it." I stepped back, glancing down the row of waiting people. "Not too busy today. It won't be long before we get to the front."

He moved closer again. "I know how much you like horses, and—"

"Yeah, you do, too." No way was I going to let him say something stupid if I could help it. "Hey, look, it's Pepper." I pointed to the horse being petted by a couple and their little girl. "Cool! She's my favorite."

Derek reached for my hand. "You're my fav—"

"Derek—" I pulled my hand away and stuffed it into my pocket and faced him square on. It was not the time to be subtle. "We're friends, right? Like Mike? We're best friends."

"But I—"

Pepper bumped me, demanding her treats. I gave her some grain pellets, barely noticing her velvety nose nuzzle my hand, which was always my favorite part.

Looking up, I spotted Mike and Sandy through the open doorway. "Hey, let's go." I ducked outside, narrowly missing a head-on collision with someone. "'Scuse me," I muttered, keeping my head down, intent on escaping any more one-on-one conversation with Derek.

"What's your hurry, Nina?"

Sal. I spun around. I might not have recognized Sal in his regular clothes, but there was no mistaking the voice. Or the green-and-purple bruises. Was he following me? It must have been him I'd seen on Michigan Avenue. This was not a coincidence. My heart started pounding faster. I was actually relieved when Derek caught up to me.

"Nina—hey, who's this?" he asked.

"Derek, this is Sal." Glancing over Sal's shoulder in the direction of the cow barn, I yanked on Derek's arm. "Come on." I nodded at Sal. "We gotta catch our friends. See ya."

"Mind if I tag along?" Without waiting for an answer, Sal fell into step with us.

"Okay," Derek said, looking at me.

I ignored both of them and walked faster toward Mike and Sandy. They were behind the barn, hanging on the fence, mooing at the pasture's inhabitants, who were completely oblivious to them.

Sandy saw us coming and hopped down. When she spotted Sal, she shook out her hair. I thought she looked like a horse when she did that, but guys seemed to like it. At least *XVI Ways,* the most popular teen zine ever, said they do. There was even a vid showing how to shake your head properly, for maximum effect. Sandy'd rehearsed the move from the *XVI Ways* Nonverbal Cues guide every day. I thought it was stupid—but still I'd sit there watching while she practiced. It wasn't nearly as impressive with my short dark hair.

"Who's this?" she asked Derek. "Someone from your band?"

"No, he's a friend of Nina's."

I could see she was about to say something else, so I stepped in before she had the chance. "This is Sal."

Mike pointed to the bruises on Sal's face. "What happened to you? Kiss a trans?"

"Might as well have." Sal laughed. "I walked into a door."

"Hey." Derek had been staring pretty intently at him. "I know you. You go to Daley. My locker's across the hall from yours."

"Oh, yeah," Mike said. "You're the guy whose parents died in that leviton crash."

Leave it to Mike to get straight to the heart of things, no matter how tactless.

"I am," Sal replied.

"That's awful," I said. "I'm really—"

"My dad's dead, too." Sandy slipped closer to him, flashing her sweetest smile. She started twirling a lock of her hair.

More Nonverbal Cues guide. Sandy was acting so typically sixteen; it didn't matter to her at all that her birthday was still a month away. I shouldn't have been surprised that she brought up her father being dead to connect with Sal. She was so desperate for guys' attention, for any kind of connection. That was the last thing I wanted to do, so I kept my mouth shut about my dad.

I'd hoped Sal would leave, but it appeared he was staying. And I wanted to stop Sandy from looking like a fool, throwing herself at him. It seemed like small talk was my only choice. "So who do you live with?"

Sal's eyes met mine. I hadn't anticipated the effect those deep brown eyes would have on me. My pulse sped up and I felt my heart banging against my chest. I dropped my gaze to the ground and toed lines in the gravel.

"My brother, John, took me in after our parents died. I help him out repairing transports and city transits. My sister-in-law says it pays my expenses."

"You work on trannies?" Mike said. "That is so cool. I saw one the other day that I really want. It's an early-thirties cruiser; comet-tail red, with Orion pin-striping and chromax levelers. Man, what I wouldn't give to have something like that."

"Have you got your own?" Derek asked. It appeared he was as impressed as Mike. The pressure was off me, at least for the time being.

"I got my license last year. But John won't let me buy one until I'm eighteen. He says young drivers have too many accidents. Sounds just like my dad used to. I do get to drive his 260G Perseids sometimes. Man, it's as fast as a tri-leviton express."

Almost instantly, the guys were deep into discussing the pros and cons of personal versus multitransits and what models were the best. Sandy tugged me over to the fence.

"That's him, isn't it?" She kept her eyes glued on Sal. "He's really cute. You didn't tell me he was really cute." She cut her eyes at me for a second, quickly looking back at Sal.

"He's okay, if you like tall and skinny. And what happened to my being in danger for talking to a homeless?" I didn't say what I thought of his looks, and I didn't dare confide the effect he'd had on me. I wasn't looking for a boyfriend, least of all some guy who snuck around in rags and had a raging case of attitude. I did feel bad for him about his parents.

"Oh, he's definitely not homeless." She eyed him in a way that made me blush. "And I prefer to call it lean and lanky. Ultrayum!"

"Cut it out, Sandy. You're as bad as those eighteens on the express." The way she said it was like Sal was nothing more than something to be devoured. It shouldn't have reminded me of the pig-eyed 'lete, but it did. I shook it off, putting it down to me thinking too much about Angel and what could have happened. "Speaking of the express . . ." I pulled her wrist over, checking the time on her chronos. "We'd better leave soon. I have to be home by six."

The guys were still talking trannies. "Hey, we gotta go," I said. "I'm watching Dee tonight."

"We'll walk you to the station," Derek offered.

"No, you guys hang out. See ya."

Sal pulled out his PAV receiver. "Hey, Nina, I accidentally deleted my list. What's your number?"

Before I could reply, Mike blurted it out.

Sal ticked it in, grinning at me the whole time. "I'll call you later."

My heart beat faster, but this time out of anger. I started to tell him not to call until I noticed everyone looking at me. Sandy's I-could-kill-you glare stood out like a beacon.

"What?" I glared right back at her. "Later, guys." Sandy charged off down the sidewalk.

Derek looked from me to Sal and back again. "Yeah, later, Nina," he echoed.

By the time I caught up to Sandy, she wasn't speaking to me. Unfortunately, that didn't last long.

She stopped in the center island on State Street, planted her hands on her hips, and lit into me. "What do you think you're doing, giving Sal your number? You knew I thought he was cute and wanted to hang out. We could've taken the later express. Do you want him for yourself? I didn't think you wanted a boyfriend."

It seemed like a million transits whizzed by us while she went on—berating and blaming me. Finally, I grabbed her sleeve. "Sandy, stop!"

She yanked her arm away and stared at me. "Well?"

"Well what? *I* didn't give Sal my number, *Mike* did. I don't care whether he's cute or not, or whether he likes you or not. And you're right, I don't want a boyfriend. Between you and Derek . . . hellzit . . . one minute you're my best friend and the next you're treating me like a traitor. Is some guy we just met more important than the fact that we've been best friends practically forever? Huh?"

Sandy dropped her gaze and didn't answer.

"Friends are supposed to talk stuff over, not jump to crazy conclusions," I said. "What's the matter with you anyway? Is this what sixteen is going to do to you? I thought you knew me better." I marched past her across the street. Then I had to turn around and holler, "Are you coming?"

VIII

ecause of Sandy's tirade, we ended up on the later express and barely got back to Cementville on time. We didn't talk much on the way home. Sandy apologized at least five times, promising that I was more important than any guy. I knew she meant it—at least she meant it the moment she said it.

At that point, I didn't much care about what would happen when Sandy turned sixteen, or when I turned sixteen. I was more concerned about being late. Ginnie didn't often ask me to watch Dee. And here I was, letting some guy and sixteen make me break my promise.

"Sorry I'm late." I tossed my sweater on the sofa. "Where's Dee?"

"She's in her room." Ginnie came out of the bathroom and gave me a quick kiss. Her makeup hardly covered the yellowing remains of a nasty bruise on her cheekbone. I didn't say anything. We had an unwritten rule: no discussing Ed-inflicted injuries, period.

I was surprised to see papers strewn on the couch; Ginnie was a total neat freak. "What's this?" I picked up an envelope from the cushion that had Rita scribbled on it. "Who's Rita?"

"No one special. She's a friend." Ginnie took it from me and stuffed it into her purse.

"Are you seeing Ed tonight?"

"No." She pulled on a pair of retro Galaxy boots and slipped an imitation sheepskin vest over her sweater. "I've got a meeting. I shouldn't be home too late. Gran and Pops okay? Did you have fun?"

"It was all right. Gran and Pops are fine. There was a foray in their building, Johnny Pace was arrested. Supposedly, he had a transmitter in his room. The cops stopped us when we were leaving, checked our IDs. And Sandy and I had a fight."

"Johnny? Damn." She sighed. "No problem with the police, was there?"

"That's the first time I've ever been scanned. It freaked me out a little."

Ginnie threw her arms around me. "Oh, sweetie, I'm so sorry." She shook her head.

"You really need to teach me that breath-control thing. I thought they'd ED me for sure and then . . ."

"You're finally ready to learn." She beamed at me. "We'll start first thing in the morning." I followed her into her room, where she put some last minute touches on her outfit. "Anything else happen?" she asked.

"Yeah, one of the cops gave me a weird look when I told him my name."

"Really? That's just your imagination." I thought for a moment that I detected a note of concern in her voice, but she changed the subject. "So what happened with Sandy? You want to talk about it?" She checked the clock. "I've got a few minutes before I need to leave."

I did want to talk. But it would take more than a few minutes to sort out everything. "Oh, and I met this guy today, Sal Davis." I thought better of telling her *how* I met Sal.

"Sal Davis? That name sounds familiar." She tapped her lips. "Hmm . . . not coming to me . . . maybe later. Let me guess about Sandy. She thought this guy was cute, but he liked you instead."

It always amazed me how Ginnie knew exactly what was going on without even being told. "Yeah, and there's more, too, about Derek. But it can wait. I don't want you to be late."

"You sure?" She put her arm around my shoulder and gave me a squeeze.

I hugged her back. "I'm sure. I bet Sandy will call later tonight and we'll work it out. It's not like anything's going to change in the next few hours."

On the way back down the hall, Ginnie called out, "DeeDee, honey, I'm leaving. Mind your sister."

Dee came racing from her room and threw herself into Ginnie's arms. My little sister had more energy than ten genrons. "Can Nina make fried toes? Can we watch movies? When will you be home?"

"Yes, yes, and I don't know." Ginnie laughed, swinging Dee around in circles.

"Not too late, Mom, I want to show you a dance routine Corrine and I were just working on." Dee planted a big kiss on Ginnie's cheek and squirmed loose. "I'll pick out the vid, Neens." She dashed across the room to select her favorite from the AV list.

"I love you, DeeDee." Ginnie turned her attention to me. "And, Nina, remember . . . if anything—"

"Stop," I said. "Nothing is going to happen. Quit being silly. Now go, or you'll be late. I love you."

"I know, sweetie." She cupped my cheek in her hand and kissed me, then rubbed her lipstick print off. "I love you, too. We'll talk later."

"Be careful." I watched her silhouette disappear into the darkness.

***

Dee'd picked her favorite series, *Arriane Lightfoot, Moon Academy*. It was a comedy about a girl at boarding school on the moon. I slipped the chip into our FAV. When we moved to Cementville so Ginnie could be near Ed, he'd actually bought us a brand-new Family Audio/Video. I figured it was because he felt bad that he'd broken Ginnie's arm. She said it was so he could watch Athletics whenever he came over.

That wasn't all he watched. I'd accidentally clicked on playback once after he'd left. It was disgusting—worse than anything they'd shown us in Sex Ed. Just the thought of those images made me want to run and hide. I was never going to have sex if it was anything like those movies: men forcing themselves on girls, some who were much younger than sixteen. I never told Ginnie what I'd seen. Partly because I was too embarrassed, but mostly I was afraid that she watched that stuff with him. I didn't want to think about that, or Ed, so I focused on what needed doing in the present.

"You hungry, Dee?"

"Yeah," she said, without looking away from the screen. "Don't forget the fried toes."

In the kitchen, I punched a few buttons on the cook center. Ten minutes later Dee and I were snarfing down seitan burgers with the works and tofu fries, all caught up in Arriane's adventures. Sometimes I really liked watching kid shows. It was like a vacation from real life.

We were on episode two, Arriane was organizing a talent show for her school, when my PAV beeped.

"Keep watching. It's probably just Sandy. I'll be right back." I went into the kitchen with my plate of food. "Hey." It wasn't Sandy, it was Derek.

"Nina, whatcha doing?"

"Watching *Moon Academy* with Dee. What's up?" It wasn't at all like him to call and chat.

"I, uh, you know . . . it was fun today, the zoo and all." He cleared his throat. "You and me and—"

"Yeah." I cut him off before he could go any further. "It's always fun at the zoo with you guys and Sandy. What'd you do after we left? Did you all go to Sal's and check out the transports?"

"No." He sounded disappointed. "Sal said his brother might get mad if he brought over a bunch of people without telling him first. Maybe this Saturday. Are you coming into town? I told him you really like trannies, too. Man, I hope someday I can afford a Sonic or a Janji."

I laughed out loud. Once Derek got started on personal transits, he could talk for hours. "Sonics are okay, but I really want a Lacodian mini, they're so cute."

"Girly trannie."

"Hey, I've gotta get back to Dee. Ginnie's gone and we're doing sister stuff. See ya."

I rejoined Dee.

"I left you some fries," she said. "I've gotta watch my figure."

"Figure?" I laughed. "The only figure you have is like this." I drew a straight up-and-down line in the air.

"Do not!"

"Do, too." I tossed a throw pillow from the couch at her. She caught it and threw it back at me.

In no time we were wrestling around on the floor like a couple of kids. It felt good to play. Much better than angsting over what Derek was thinking. I didn't want to deal with him trying to be romantic, or interested in me.

We were up to episode four, where Arriane confronts a bully at summer camp, when my PAV beeped again.

I hopped over the pillows we'd thrown on the floor. "Hey there." I was sure it was Sandy.

"Nina Oberon?" a female voice asked.

"Yes." I didn't recognize the voice, so I grabbed my PAV receiver from the table to see who was calling.

"This is Officer Jelneck, Cementville police."

IX

I clicked on the tiny video screen, I could see red hair sticking out from under her black-and-white-checked hatband. Her lips were pressed into a hard line.

My first thought was that it had to do with the foray. But the police in Gran's building had let us go. Sal. Maybe he really was homeless—maybe I was in trouble for helping him out. "Yes, ma'am?" I couldn't keep my voice from trembling.

"I'm almost to your house. I need to talk with you."

Now I was shaking all over. "Have I done something wrong?"

Her tone changed from terse to sympathetic. "No."

And then it hit me—bad news. Ginnie. "What's happened?"

No sooner had the words left my mouth than there was a buzz at the door. I let Officer Jelneck in.

She told me about the attack. How Ginnie had been stabbed and left for dead in an alley. Like sleet bouncing off the sidewalk, her words weren't connecting to my brain. It couldn't be. Ginnie was always all right.

"We must get you two to the hospital," she insisted. "There's no time to waste."

"Nina? What's going on?" Dee came up behind me.

Office Jelneck started to speak, but I held up my hand. Putting my arm around Dee, I said, "Mom needs us. Get your jacket."

Dee's lower lip started to quiver. I pulled her close. "It's going to be fine, DeeDee. Go get your jacket, okay?"

She raced down the hall.

I looked at the policewoman. "She'll know what's happened soon enough."

Officer Jelneck transported us to Cementville Hospital, the largest, state-of-the-art hospital in the Midwest. We were whisked to the Trauma Wing in an area marked "Restricted." There were armed guards stationed at the entrance doors. Through a window I could see Ginnie immobile, inside a machine of some kind.

"What's that?" I asked the guard who was escorting us.

"Infinity machine." His voice, his whole manner, was as emotionless as a bot. He could've been one, except I'd seen him take a drink of water before he brought us here.

An Infinity machine. Ginnie was just a tier-two cashier. Why would they put her in an Infinity machine? They were only used in special cases and only for top-tier people. I would've asked the guard, but he was busy talking into his PAV.

I didn't know how the Infinity machine circumvented death, but it did, at least for a little while. There were only twelve such machines in the world. Situated near large metro areas, they were under strict government regulations and security. There were armed guards everywhere on the floor, not only at the entrance. Ginnie'd always said this technology was dangerous, especially in the wrong hands, and should be outlawed. I was glad it hadn't been.

I peeked back in the window. Monitor lights strobed above

Ginnie and tubes and wires snaked everywhere. Blinking hard, I turned away. Through my tears, I saw a man getting into the elport, talking with a nurse. She exited right before the door slid shut, and hurried past me into Ginnie's room. I stood staring at the closed elport, then glanced back at Ginnie.

Ed.

I didn't want him anywhere near her, not now, not ever again. After all the times he'd beat her . . . what if he'd had something to do with this attack? He was capable of murder, I was sure of it. Cold hate seeped into my veins.

A doctor came by to talk to me and Dee, and I turned my attention away from the elport. Her soft eyes and no-nonsense manner reminded me of Gran. She assured me that Ginnie wasn't in any pain and then explained the rules about the Infinity machine.

Her voice was gentle, but the words were harsh. "You can talk with your mother for ten minutes; that's five minutes per family member. You can touch her face and head, but be very careful not to touch any of the equipment. When nine minutes is up, a buzzer will sound and I'll come in; a minute later the machine will be turned off."

I pointed to the room. "Why is she here? We're not top tier."

The doctor shook her head. "The government doesn't tell me their reasons."

It didn't matter. At least Ginnie was still alive and we could see her. I hugged my arm tight around Dee and we entered the room. My stomach knotted—it felt as if I'd entered my own execution chamber.

Ginnie's bandaged head stuck out of the aluminoid cylinder

that encased her body. A nurse stood nearby, adjusting dials on a control panel.

"Mom," I whispered, edging closer to the Infinity. "Can you hear me?"

"Yes." She turned her head slightly in my direction. Her lips weren't moving, her eyes were sightless. The voice was hollow and metallic, not at all her—a reproduction from her thoughts. It was a sound I was sure I would never forget. "Guess I won't be home early, will I?" Her sense of humor was still there, but it wasn't funny.

"Mom." Dee's voice quavered and tears were pouring down her cheeks. "You can't die!" She wrenched away from me and ran to Ginnie. She tried to touch our mother, but was too short to reach. The nurse pulled a small stool out from under the machine and Dee scrambled up on it. She patted Ginnie's face and kissed her cheek again and again, crying the whole time.

"Oh, DeeDee, sweetheart, Nina will take care of you."

"Mom!" Dee stroked the bandages frantically. "You can't leave. I love you. You can't die."

"DeeDee," the tinny voice said, "you have to be strong. I raised you girls to be strong. You and Nina will have to take care of each other now. Understand?"

Dee nodded, gulping back her tears.

Ginnie sighed deeply. It rattled through the cylinder, and I wondered how the doctor knew for sure that she wasn't hurting.

"DeeDee, honey, go outside for a minute, I need to talk to Nina alone."

The nurse led a sobbing Dee out of the room. When the door closed behind them, Ginnie asked, "Are they gone?"

I glanced around. "Yes."

"Come close."

I scooted up to her head. "I'm right here, Mom." Since I'd turned twelve, I'd always called her Ginnie. It was not cool to call your parents Mom or Dad. Now I wished that was all I'd ever called her. Caressing her face, I moved aside the hairs that clung to her forehead.

"Sing to me, sweetie. That lullaby I used to sing to you."

"What?"

"Please. There isn't much time."

I began singing "Highland Fairy Lullaby," a song I knew so well. "'I left my baby lying here, lying here, lying here . . .'"

Ginnie began to talk softly under my singing. "If they're listening, they won't be able to make out what I'm telling you. Keep singing."

I didn't understand what she meant, but I kept on, straining to hear her every word. "'I left my baby lying here, to go and gather blaeberries.'"

"There's no time to preface this, Nina. Your father is still alive. I'm not sure where he is exactly, but I think he may be in Chicago."

I fell silent. My father? The man Ginnie'd always said she loved more than anything except me and Dee was alive. "How long—?"

"Please keep singing." The urgency in her voice was unmistakable, even through the machine.

"I'm sorry, Mom." My voice was shaking, but I went on. "'Hovan, Hovan Gorry og O, Gorry og O, Gorry og O . . .'"

Ginnie said, "There's no time for explanation. Listen to me. You must find him, and give him the book I keep in my bedside table. You know the one."

I did know. She only kept one book there—Dee's baby book. "'Hovan, Hovan Gorry og O, I've lost my darling baby, O!'"

"It's so important. It's got all the answers."

She wasn't making any sense. My father had died the night I was born. Maybe the Infinity machine was translating her thoughts wrong. Or, maybe she was hallucinating. I'd heard that people sometimes do that when they're dying.

"'I found the wee brown otter's track, otter's track, otter's track...'"

"The last time I saw him was a few months before Dee was born," she said. "Nina. Pay attention. I'm not crazy. Please."

Attention. Yes. There wasn't time for the emotions that were welling up inside of me. Later I could think about my father—my father who had been alive all my life, but hadn't had anything to do with me. "'I found the wee brown otter's track, but ne're a trace o' my baby, O!'"

The vocalization machine made a weird noise. It sounded like crying. I glanced up and a nurse was standing in the doorway. I wondered how long she'd been there. When she saw me looking at her, she slipped out of the room. She'd been listening to us, of that I was sure.

The weird sound happened again. I continued the lullaby. "'Hovan, Hovan Gorry og O, Gorry og O, Gorry og O...'"

Ginnie said, "You must get the book to your father, to Alan. You must keep Ed away from Dee. Don't let him near her. Promise me, Nina." It was like her voice was a hand, grabbing me, demanding my assurance.

The buzzer sounded. I stopped singing. Dee rushed back in, the nurse and doctor right behind her.

"I promise," I whispered.

"Just know that I love you two more than anything in this universe or any other. You have always been the reason for everything I've ever done. You've been my whole life. Keep each other safe."

I wanted to cry, but I couldn't. If I let the tears loose, they would never stop.

"I'm so sorry." The doctor placed her hand on my shoulder.

I pressed my cheek against Ginnie's and whispered, "Mom, I love you."

"Peace, dear one," she said, "at last."

The nurse motioned me away from the machine. I let my fingers linger on Ginnie's face as long as I could. Wrapping Dee in my arms, I willed myself to be strong for her.

The doctor pressed a button and my mother was dead.

X

When we walked outside the Infinity machine room, Officer Jelneck was down the hall with a man and woman. She said something to them and gestured toward me and Dee.

The doctor leaned over to me and whispered, "B.O.S.S. agents. Be careful."

My back stiffened as I watched them come to us.

"These are the daughters," Officer Jelneck said. "She's fifteen and the little one is eleven."

"I'm Agent Meadows," the man said. "This is Agent Crupp. You'll be coming with us."

This has to be some awful dream, I thought. *My mother's dead, my father's alive, and here are two B.O.S.S. agents who are taking me and Dee who knows where.* What little grip I still had on my emotions was slipping fast away.

"Now." The woman spun on her heel and walked away.

"What about my mother?" I said. "I need to call my grandparents."

"Your grandparents have been notified," Meadows said. "Due to regulations regarding the use of the Infinity machine, the body belongs to the government and will be disposed of in the usual manner." He attempted to shoo Dee and me along after Crupp.

I glanced at the doctor. "Don't let them hurt her, please." I knew it was just a body, but it was still my mother.

"I'll do what I can." Her shoulders sagged. "You'd better go."

We left the same way we'd come in. Except this time we were escorted by two B.O.S.S. agents. Neither of whom said one word to us, not even a "sorry about your mother." I kept myself busy comforting Dee. That way I didn't have attention to give to the clawing terror at the base of my neck.

They put us in the back of a multitrans with blackened windows. No one could see in, but we couldn't see out either.

"Where are we going?" Dee asked between sobs. "Are they taking us to Gran and Pops?"

"I don't know." I hugged her close. Before I'd had time to imagine all the possible places we might end up, the trannie stopped. When the door opened, we were in front of our modular.

Agent Meadows reached into his pocket. "Here's the warrant." He shoved an official-looking piece of paper at me.

"Unlock the door," Agent Crupp said.

"Warrant?" I said. "My mother didn't do anything. Someone killed her, not the other way around."

Agent Crupp tapped her stilettoed foot on the sidewalk.

I did as I was told.

Inside was exactly as we'd left it. *Moon Academy* was playing on the AV, the remains of dinner in front of it, and the pillows were scattered about where Dee and I had been playing.

"I'll get that stuff out—"

"Don't touch anything," Meadows said.

"You two. There." Agent Crupp pointed to the sofa.

We sat.

First they went through every vid chip we had. The man easily broke open the locked box where Ed kept his private ones. Agent Crupp was scanning them when she snorted. "Here's one called *Make Those Sex-teens Scream*. Real educational, that one."

I looked away, my cheeks burning.

After the vids, they inspected the few real books we had.

"Take these." Agent Crupp pushed *1984* and *Mars Rising* in the man's hand. "Not suitable reading for anyone." She narrowed her eyes at me. "Smut and sedition. Your mother was a real piece of work." I clenched the edge of the couch. Not daring to speak. "Come on." She motioned us to follow her.

We watched while they searched our room, then Ginnie's. Meadows dumped the contents of her bedside table drawer onto the bed. Dee's baby book lay on top of the pile.

My heart pounded and a chill ran through me. The book.

Picking it up, Meadows said, "What's this?"

My breath caught in my throat as he passed it to Agent Crupp. She flipped through the pages. "A mother's memory book of her kid. Nothing important." Tossing it aside, she and Meadows continued their search.

When they were done, they herded us back into the living room. Agent Crupp said, "If you girls are smart, you'll forget whatever stupid ideas your mother fed you about the government. It's radicals like her that end up bleeding to death in the gutter." She shut the front door behind her, leaving us alone amid the mess.

The two of us collapsed to the floor, crying. "I hate you!" Dee screamed at the shut door.

I caught her up in my arms, covering her mouth. "Don't. Just don't." I didn't know what those agents were capable of, or what they could hear. I wasn't going to risk getting them angry.

After what seemed like hours, I managed to pull myself together enough to call Gran.

"We're on the express. Should be in Cementville in about fifteen minutes," Gran said. "Where are you?"

"At home."

"You and Dee make some tea for us. You need to be busy right now. Don't think too much. We'll be there as soon as we can. We love you, Nina."

I clicked off my PAV. "Gran says they need tea. Let's get some brewing." I stood. Holding out my hands to my little sister, I pulled her up and hugged her. "We'll get through this, DeeDee. That's what sisters do. They get through things together."

I put Dee to work, hoping Gran was right, that a focus on a specific task would help. "Use the kettle. Gran likes tea made the old-fashioned way. I'll be right back. I need to get something."

Hurrying to Ginnie's room, I snatched up the baby book and opened it. There was a paper tucked in the front pocket. It was a list in Ginnie's handwriting: (1) Rita, with a check mark beside it. (2) FeLS contract—Gran, with a check mark beside it, too. I flipped through the rest of the pages. It looked normal. Ginnie had made notes about Dee by the sides of pictures and mementos. I wanted to study it more closely, but the teakettle whistled and Dee called me.

I secured the book in the bottom of my dresser. It would have to wait until later.

***

Low-tier murder victims didn't warrant big investigations—after a few days, we still hadn't heard if they'd found Ginnie's killer, and I was sure they weren't going to be looking very hard. I'd called Officer Jelneck a couple of times, wanting to tell her my suspicions about Ed, and how I was pretty sure he'd been at the hospital. I left messages, but she'd never called me back.

The landlord gave us until the end of the month—six whole days—to get out of the modular. We only took three.

The mod was so small that the four of us—Gran, Pops, Dee, and me—filled it to the bursting point, and there was so much to do, I didn't have an opportunity to be alone with the baby book or think about my father. I had no idea what kind of reaction I would get from him if I did find him. I wasn't even sure what kind of reaction I wanted to get, or what my response would be. I still couldn't believe he was alive—after all this time . . . I tried not to think too much about that, or why my mother felt the need to hide this from me, and just focus on getting through the next few days.

Gran and I busied ourselves with sorting, tossing, and packing up my life as I'd known it. We started packing up the living room when there was a knock at the door. It was two men. One of them handed me a card that said Johnson's Delivery.

"I'm here to pick up the FAV. Man said you'd know it belonged

66

to him." The guy stuck his head in the door. "That's it, there." He pushed past me. "Said there was a box of vids, too."

A dry laugh escaped me. "Vids? Not here." It was little satisfaction, but the morning after Ginnie died, I'd dumped Ed's disgusting chips into the trash when I was cleaning up the mess the B.O.S.S. agents had left us.

The guy shrugged. "Oh well, he shoulda come and got this stuff hisself." It took the two of them about three minutes to get the FAV disconnected and leave.

"Ed's?" Gran said.

I nodded, too angry to trust myself to speak.

"Well, he must have heard the news if he's picking up the FAV," she said. "I'm surprised he hasn't called or come by to see about Dee."

"I'm not." I could hear Ginnie's voice through the machine telling me to keep Dee away from Ed. My hands clenched. "Besides, Ginnie didn't want Ed to have anything to do with Dee."

"He was a horrible man. Horrible. I never understood why Ginnie stayed with him." Gran clucked her tongue. "Probably best if he doesn't come around. Although he does have rights."

I knew why Ginnie wanted me to keep Dee away from Ed. Even though he'd always treated her well when he was around, there was no telling what would happen now. Men were known to use their illegitimate daughters as Cinderella girls, servants—and other things—for their legit families.

I wanted to tell Gran what Ginnie'd said about Ed, about my father. But I didn't want to involve Dee or Pops. Dee would get upset about Ed, and Pops would just get upset. I loved him to pieces, but he could go off the deep end about most anything.

And with all of his health problems, telling him that his only son was still alive might be too much of a shock.

I almost told Gran then, but Pops and Dee were in the kitchen. The walls of the mod were so thin they would've heard everything. I couldn't risk scaring Dee with the thought of being a Cinderella girl.

Sandy popped through the door. "Can I help?"

"Why don't you girls go finish up in Nina's room," Gran said. "We're nearly ready to go."

Sandy plopped onto my bed. It, along with all the furniture, belonged with the modular. "I can't believe you're moving," she said. "What am I going to do without you?"

"I know." I blinked back an unexpected tear. "I'll only be an express ride away, though. And Gran and Pops's is close to the station."

"I guess." She leaned on the sheets and comforter stacked on the bed. "How are you all going to fit in their apartment? It's tiny. And isn't it just for retired people?"

"The building owners agreed to let us live there and are moving us into a bigger place." I took the bedding from under Sandy's elbow and stuffed it in a box marked Nina. In the bottom, under all my clothes and my meager stash of treasured art supplies, was Dee's baby book. I would search it as soon as things got unpacked at our new home.

"So where will you go to school?" Sandy said. "I can't imagine going to a Chicago school. They go all the way up to tier ten. Can you imagine? Top-tiers, right next to girls like us! We don't even have anyone above five. If I could be around all those tier-ten guys . . ." Her voice trailed off. I glanced over at her; she was lying on the bed staring up at the ceiling with a smile on her face.

"Snap out of it," I said. "The apartment building is in the same district where I lived before. So I'll be at Daley along with Mike and Derek. And, yes, there will be all tiers—all the way up to ten. Like that's going to make a difference."

"It will, too, make a difference," she said. "Besides, you'll have your friends and I won't have anyone."

"Those guys aren't you, Sandy." I sat down next to her. "Promise you'll come see me?"

"Of course I will."

She'd just launched into all the things we could do when Gran interrupted. "Nina, Mr. Eskew's here, ready to load up the trannie. It's time."

Sandy's stepfather had offered (at Mrs. Eskew's prodding I was sure) to help us move our things. There wasn't much to load. Fifteen minutes later, Sandy and I were standing at the curb with Gran and Dee, waiting for our ride to the express station. Pops had gone ahead with Mr. Eskew.

When the hire trannie rounded the corner, I grabbed Sandy and held her tight. Sandy was crying, but I didn't dare. Dee was watching us, and if I broke down, she would, too. I had to be strong. I shoved away the thought that maybe someone should be strong for me. That wasn't going to happen.

I hung my head out the window, waving until Sandy was a dot in the distance. On the trip in, I barely listened to Gran and Dee's chatter. I wanted silence . . . quiet . . . and the luxury of being able to cry. But none of that was possible. There was too much to do.

***

When we got to the apartment, Mr. Eskew and Pops were already there. Earlier the building maintenance guys had packed up all of Gran and Pops's things and moved them into the larger place. Dumped them, was more like it. The apartment looked more like a storage unit than a home.

I helped Sandy's dad get the trannie unloaded. I never liked him much, especially not the way he looked at Sandy, but I still thanked him for the help. Watching him drive away, the full force of the situation hit me. Ginnie was gone. My life would never be the same again.

***

After a dinner of nut butter sandwiches and soy milk—Gran hadn't been shopping and the cook center hadn't been programmed yet—Gran put us all to work setting the apartment in order. I was unpacking one of their boxes marked Living Room when I came across a handful of books.

I turned one over and over in my hand. "B.O.S.S. took all our books," I said. "I still don't understand why they went through all of our stuff. Ginnie wasn't the criminal, she was the victim. Do they always do stuff like that?"

"They do whatever they want," Gran said.

"Couldn't have stopped 'em if you'd tried," Pops said. "Nothing to find, though, was there? As if poor Ginnie had anything to hide."

Gran didn't respond, but I knew something was up from her expression, and I'd have given anything to know what she was thinking. Sometimes, when we'd all visited in the past, she and Ginnie would go into the kitchen and talk alone. They didn't think I'd noticed that whenever I walked in on them, they'd change the subject. I used to think they were talking about things that they didn't want a little kid to hear, but now I wondered if it was something completely different. Maybe even something that could get someone killed.

"Come on, Deedles." Pops grabbed Dee's hand. "Let's get busy on your room."

"But I'm going to sleep with Nina." The rims of Dee's eyes reddened.

Before she could start crying, I said, "Of course you are, but you might want to have a place to put some of the things you don't need all the time."

Pops winked over her shoulder at me. "She's right, Deedles. It'll almost be like you've got two rooms. That's better than me. I'm stuck with her"—he jerked his thumb at Gran—"for the rest of my life."

"Which won't be very much longer if you keep that up, old man." Gran wagged her finger at him. "Now the two of you git!"

When they were out of earshot, I decided to risk it. "Gran, did Ginnie have a friend named Rita?"

Gran peered over her glasses. "Hmm, I'm not sure. Why do you ask?"

"When I was packing, I found a piece of paper with her name on it. I never met anyone she knew named Rita."

Gran pulled on her lower lip for a minute. Finally, she said, "The only Rita I recall was a high school friend of Ginnie's. She was a couple of years older than your mom and dad were. I think she was related to . . ." She stopped to pick a piece of lint from her sleeve. "Nope, can't remember the name. Seems like she was another of Ginnie and Alan's friends' sister. As I recall, she was in one of the early groups of girls chosen when the FeLS program started some thirty-odd years ago. Strangest thing, if it's the same girl I'm thinking of, she disappeared on the way out to O'Hare to catch the space station shuttle for FeLS training. Never seen or heard from again." Gran shook her head. "Some thought it was her plan all along to get out of going, but I think she was kidnapped, plain and simple. She wasn't the only one of your father's acquaintances to drop out of sight over the next several years."

Ginnie never told me anything like that—friends disappearing. I was sure Gran knew more stories about my father and Ginnie that I'd never heard. I stopped myself from telling her about the book and my father being alive. I needed to look at Dee's baby book more closely first and make sure this was real. No sense in getting Gran's hopes up if all of this was the result of some medically caused hallucination.

"There's something else, Gran. Your name was on that same piece of paper, along with a note about my FeLS contract."

"Ah yes, Ginnie bought it out, dear, and sent it to me for safekeeping. She was worried that Ed might get his hands on it. He has quotas to make, and I'm not sure she trusted that he would leave you alone if he was short Chosens."

"Or if he was mad at her," I muttered.

Gran gave me a puzzled look. "What do you mean?"

"Last summer, Ed told Dee that he was going to move us to the tier-five flats on the west side of Cementville. She was so excited. We all were. Then one night Ginnie came home with bruises all over her arms. Next day, Ed told Dee that because of her mother we'd be staying right where we belonged, in low-tier mods. She was crushed."

Gran scowled. "There's something seriously wrong with that man. Who would do such a thing? And to his own daughter. I hope he doesn't come around here wanting to see her. Although, he very well might. He's got his rights." Her scowl turned to a frown.

My stomach knotted. "What if he wanted Dee as a Cinderella girl?"

"Ginnie made sure that if anything happened to her, your grandfather and I would become your legal guardians. He can't touch Dee." She gave my arm a squeeze. "No sense in borrowing tomorrow's troubles, dear. Let's focus on getting this house in order." She bent down and took a few knickknacks out of the box I'd been unpacking. "Put these over there."

I arranged things under Gran's direction and the knot in my stomach loosened a bit. I didn't trust Ed, but with Gran and Pops as Dee's legal guardians, he wouldn't be able to take her away. At least not without a fight.

But still, I was 99 percent sure that it had been Ed at the hospital. Which made me think he knew what had happened to Ginnie before it hit the news. I wondered if I would ever know what really happened to her. Anger surged through me. I wanted whoever killed her caught.

Gran's PAV beeped. "Oh, that's Harriet. I'd better make sure she's all right. She's not been well since they took Johnny away. You tell your sister it's time for you both to get ready for bed."

***

Lying on my new bed, an inflato-mat Gran had borrowed from Harriet, I stared out the window. Dee was across the room, asleep on Pops's old army cot. The rhythm of her breathing was occasionally interrupted by a catch—she'd been crying herself to sleep every night, still. The only crying I'd done was after the B.O.S.S. agents left. Since then, I'd willed every tear to stay inside me. Dee needed me to be strong. And so I was.

Squeezed between the buildings across the way, the night sky provided a backdrop for a pale quarter moon. I wondered if somewhere in Chicago my father, Alan Oberon, was looking at that same moon.

All these years he'd been alive, but he'd never tried to see me or contact me. How could he do that? Even harder to comprehend was the reality that Ginnie had known the truth, but let me believe a lie. She always said that he had been her one true love. I couldn't imagine he didn't still love her, too. Was it because of me that he wasn't there? Did he not want me? I had so many questions and no answers.

I knew I had to find him and give him that book. Not for him, not for me, but for Ginnie.

I tossed from one side to the other, willing sleep to come. Just as I'd dozed off, Dee's PAV beeped. I jumped out of bed and grabbed her receiver before she woke up.

"Hello?" I whispered.

A click and then silence.

Ed.

XI

Next morning I got up at the same time as Gran. She was in the middle of the kitchen, surrounded by moving boxes, her back to me.

I'd made up my mind to tell her what I knew. But she looked so frail and vulnerable, my knees trembled and my heart began fluttering. Before I could give in to my doubts, I blurted out, "Ginnie told me my father is still alive."

"Really?" She picked a coffee cup out of the box nearest her, unwrapped it, and rinsed it off in the sink. She usually made her own coffee in an ancient electric pot, but that morning she used the cook center. "I wonder why she would say a thing like that?"

Hardly the reaction I'd expected after telling her that her only son, my father, was alive—instead of being dead for nearly sixteen years.

"I believed her. She was dying. Why would she lie to me?"

Gran filled up her cup and pushed a button on the chiller. White liquid swirled under the surface of the coffee.

"She said that he was alive and probably right here in Chicago." I looked hopefully at Gran. Maybe she knew already. Maybe she'd been keeping this same secret. But why?

"Nina, dear." She took a sip of her coffee. "He drowned on the way home from the hospital the night you were born. A transport forced him off the bridge by Wacker and Michigan. His body was never found."

The same story I'd heard a thousand times. No variation, no change. Except Ginnie had said different.

Gran continued: "She was most certainly under the influence of that Infinity contraption. I don't know much about it, and still can't believe they used it on anyone besides a top-tier. Even then"—she looked off in the distance, her brow furrowed—"it's rarely used. Just in extreme cases where there are permissions to be given or a will to be authenticated or something. Unless they were waiting for some low-tier to come in practically dead so they could run an experiment." She took another sip of coffee, making a face like it tasted bad.

"Gran. She said he was alive."

"Nina, they were so very much in love. Sometimes, when people are dying, they seem to see their loved ones who have gone before them. I'm sure she believed what she was saying was true. He probably seemed alive to her at the moment."

"Eh?" Pops queried from the doorway, where he had hobbled on his crutch. "Who believed what? Who's alive? Besides me."

"Nothing, old man." Gran scowled at the empty space that should have been his prosthesis. "How many times do I have to tell you to put your leg on before you get up? Your thumping around on that crutch is bound to make us popular with the new neighbors downstairs." Even as she complained, she was unpacking another cup.

"Ginnie said that my father's still alive." I ignored Gran's disapproving glance. I didn't believe her explanations—and I needed someone to validate me. I only hoped Pops was stronger than he appeared. Ginnie'd had a good reason for keeping my father's life a secret. And I was determined to discover what that reason was.

Gran harrumphed and went back to unpacking the box of dishes.

"Alan alive? Wouldn't surprise me one little bit, Little Bit." Pops chuckled to himself. He took a sip of the coffee Gran handed him and attempted to pat her on the fanny with his crutch as she walked by. Except he lost his balance and nearly fell over. I suppressed a snort.

She turned back around and Pops, smiling innocently, held his cup in the air. "Best java in the world."

"It's cook center coffee, not mine," she retorted, but a smile danced at the corners of her mouth. Then she frowned. "Now, don't you be telling Nina that Alan's still alive." Her voice thinned. "You know as well as I do that he's gone."

Pops sat his cup and himself down. "I know what they told us, Edith. And I also know that he had everything to live for—Nina, for example." He patted my hand. "And I know that he could swim." Pops's tone became strident. "I don't believe anything the government says. It's all lies." His eyes flashed. "Just look at me." He slapped his stump for emphasis. "They took care of me good, just like they promised, didn't they?"

"The ravings of an old lunatic." Gran ran her hand across her forehead. "They should've replaced your brain while they were at it." She started rummaging through the boxes. "Since the cook center's not set up for food yet, I'll make us a real breakfast."

"Flapjacks? Syrup and butter on top?" Pops sounded like a little kid asking for cake.

"Coming up." She dug around for the ingredients, stacking them on the counter one by one. "I've got everything except baking powder. Here, dear." She handed me her card. "Run to the store and get a box. Make it quick, I can't start until get you back."

I grabbed my sweater from the hook by the door and ran out. The elport took forever, but soon I was on the ground floor. I rushed out of the lobby into the crisp fall morning.

I hurried the two blocks to the nearest Foodland. At the closest self-service kiosk I tapped in baking powder. I slid Gran's card through the scanner, and a second later, the register dinged. I removed the box from the delivery chute, not bothering to bag it. The kiosk voice said, "*Please confirm receipt of all your items. Remove your card, and thank you for shopping at Foodland.*"

"You, too." I was glad the store was empty, so no one heard me conversing with robo machines. I was almost to the "out" door when I noticed Sal coming through the "in" door.

"Nina," he called out. "Wait up."

I hadn't seen him since the day at the zoo . . . the day Ginnie'd been killed. It was hard to believe that was only five days ago. It felt like forever. He'd called, but I'd ignored his calls. I didn't want to talk to him then, either, but still I stopped. Sometimes I was too nice for my own good.

"I tried calling." He rounded the counter. "Mike told me about your mother."

"He did?" I made a mental note to yell at Mike the next time I saw him.

"Yeah, I was checking to make sure I had your number right and he told me about the, uh . . ."

"Murder?" I glared at him. "You can say it. It's what happened. Somebody murdered my mother, okay?"

He was studying my face, trying to size up my emotional state, I supposed. "I'm really sorry. I know how hard it is."

"You don't know anything about me." I didn't want sympathy from him, and I didn't want him prying into my life. "I'm in a hurry, okay?" I started out the door, but he reached for my arm.

"What?" I yelled, jerking away from him. The lone store attendant peered through the side of her therma-glass cubicle. I gave her a halfhearted wave. Last thing I wanted was for her to call the cops. She frowned before going back to her AV game.

"What do you want?" I hissed.

"To get to know you a little better. Okay?"

"I've gotta run. Gran's waiting."

"Can we talk later?"

"Fine, whatever." No way would I answer that call.

XII

I'd finally gotten all Gran's recipe chips loaded into the cook center and was busy cleaning the containers and filling them with ingredients.

Ginnie hadn't been great in the kitchen. Lots of times she brought food home from the cafeteria where she worked. I'd have given anything to be eating some of that institutional garbage right then, to be laughing with her at the counter.

Ginnie'd never told me the real reason she quit her tier-five job in Chicago to take that tier-two in Cementville. She said it was to be closer to Ed, but I'd always thought there had to be another reason. I guess I'll never know the answer.

It had been so hard moving from our nice apartment in the Wrightwood Arms to that horrid modular. Living next door to Sandy was the only thing that wasn't awful about Cementville. I'd learned to deal with cheap clothes and school lunches and snubs from higher-tiers. Ginnie'd managed to find the credits to get me into art classes, thankfully. I don't know what I would have done without those. Usually only tier-fives or higher took art, so they could get a Creatives' designation. Ginnie wanted me to have that opportunity, too. But when the kids in the class found out my mom was a tier-two cashier, most of them quit talking to me. I didn't let it get to me too much—when we were tier-five, I never talked to tier-twos. Besides, I get so caught up in my drawings that I'd have probably ignored Van Stacy if he'd walked in the room.

Even thinking about that move made me feel angry, and then guilty . . . how could I be angry at Ginnie now? Then Dee came in and hung over the back of a chair, her toes skimming the floor. "You think Maddie and Justin still go to Dickens?"

"Sure. I bet most of your friends will be at your old school. We've only been gone four years." I hoped I was right. She needed something to make her feel better. She needed friends.

"Neens . . . I miss Mom." She sobbed quietly next to me.

I scooped her up, knocking over the container of flour with my elbow, hugging her as tight as I could, holding back my own tears. Even though she was eleven, she felt so small, so vulnerable. Eventually, she stopped crying.

"I'm sorry." She sniffed and swallowed hard "You miss her, too, don't you?"

"Yes, I do."

"What did they do with her body? Is it out in space with all the burial pods?" She wiped her eyes with the back of her hand and looked at me expectantly.

I didn't know what had happened—*"We'll dispose of the body in the usual manner . . ."*—I had to say something comforting. "Yes, it is. They sent her body out that very morning. She's up among the stars now."

"Gran says she's in heaven." Dee looked at me. "You don't believe in heaven, do you?"

"If Gran says so, then it has to be true, Deeds. Gran does not lie." Not like me.

Religion was one thing I'd never really thought much about. We'd studied the Religion Wars of the past and I'd decided then that it was not for me. It helped that Ginnie'd felt the same way. Religion seemed to me like one group of people telling another group that their color of red was the best. And that everyone had to believe that, or else.

The End-of-Wars treaty required that churches not attempt to impose their beliefs on anyone. The Governing Council had taken that a step further and made it illegal to preach religious beliefs in any form of Media. They claimed such preaching could be used to sow discontent and incite rioting. After everything I'd read about the Religion Wars, it was easy to understand how people would accept the GC's edict.

Without Media support and broadcasts of religious programming, most churches ended up closing. Gran and Pops occasionally went to one of the only ones left in Chicago. Gran told me once that they could close all the churches in the universe, but they couldn't close a body's heart to God. I hadn't done a lot of thinking about God in my life, either.

Dee startled me back from my thoughts. "I'm glad Mom's in the stars," she said. "Gran says we'll all be together in heaven someday."

"Then I'm sure we will." No sooner were the words out of my mouth than my longing for Ginnie ripped through me like a blade. She wouldn't be there when I earned my Creatives. It wouldn't be her hand holding mine when the needle pierced the XVI into my wrist. We'd never again snuggle together on the couch, after Dee was asleep, watching old movies, munching popcorn and sipping Sparkles. She'd never make it all better when I couldn't figure out how to.

And now that I needed answers about my father, the book, and just how I was supposed to deal with turning sixteen . . . I could feel the tears welling up. I had to focus on something else. My eyes lit on the flour I'd spilled everywhere. "Look at this mess! Will you help me clean it up?"

"Sure." Dee pulled the vac hose from the wall and swept up what had landed on the floor. "Think Gran will let us make lunch?"

"You go ask. I'll finish up."

"Oh, Neens," Dee called out from the hallway. "My dad called me this morning. Just to make sure I was okay."

My knees buckled and I had to grab the countertop to keep from falling. I knew he'd call again. He was, after all, Dee's father. Ginnie's words rang in my ears: *Don't let Ed near Dee.* I'd promised. The comfort I'd felt at Gran's telling me about her and Pops's legal guardianship of me and Dee vanished. I didn't trust Ed. Not one tiny bit.

***

Over lunch, I questioned Dee about the call. "So, Deeds, what did Ed say?" I tried to appear nonchalant, but nearly choked on a spoonful of soup while waiting for her answer.

"Ed?" Gran exchanged a look with Pops, then turned her attention to Dee. "When did you talk to Ed?"

"What's the big deal? He called this morning to ask if I was all right." Dee took a bite of her sandwich.

"And?" Trying to get information out of her if she wasn't in a talkative mood could be tougher than avoiding verts downtown.

"I said I was fine." She continued munching.

"Did he say anything else?"

"Nuh-uh, just that he was sorry he hadn't called before but he was gone somewhere on business."

I didn't believe that for a minute. He'd been at the hospital that night. He probably knew more than anyone else about what had happened.

"Pops?" Dee said. "We're going to Grant Park for the Ethno-festival like last year, aren't we?"

"Yes indeedy, Deedles." Pops grinned. "Remember last year when those clowns tried to get me on that trapeze?" He feigned falling backward, flailing his arms about. Dee giggled and they put their heads together, planning what they wanted to see at this year's festival.

While it felt good to see Dee smiling, my suspicions about Ed were growing stronger. Since Ginnie set up the custody, she shouldn't have had to warn me against him. But she did. She didn't think that Dee was safe. I had to keep my guard up. No way was Ed going to take Dee away from me.

***

Dee, Pops, and Gran headed out to the festival, but I'd decided ahead of time to stay home, supposedly to get my room together, but really I needed time to search the baby book in private. It was the first time I'd been completely alone since Ginnie's death. Knowing Ed had called Dee, I felt even more of an urgency to find my father and get in contact with him. Surely he would help me keep her safe. Even if Dee wasn't his daughter, she was my sister and Ginnie's daughter. That had to count for something.

My PAV beeped. It was Mike.

"Hey, whatcha doing? Wanna go downtown?"

"Not really. I'm busy unpacking."

"Okay. We might stop by later anyway."

"Please don't," I said. "I really need to get this done. Besides, I don't feel like hanging out. I kinda want to be alone."

"Oh, okay. Yeah. Sure. See you later then Nina. Bye." Mike clicked off.

That taken care of, I retrieved the book from my dresser (which was nothing more than a packing box turned sideways). I took it and a little notebook to the living room and plopped into Pops's chair. It smelled like him—ginger and aftershave. He loved candied ginger, said he picked up the habit from one of my father's high school friends. I made a note to ask him about that—I needed any information I could get about my father now. Snuggling into the folds of the chair, I opened up "Baby Days."

The first page was covered with pastel pink flowers, pale green leaves, and a blue sky filled with fluffy clouds. There were kittens and puppies among the flowers. The whole thing shouted "cute little baby stuff." The facing page was a form filled out in Ginnie's neat cursive.

Name: Delisa Jane Oberon

Born: April 21, 2139

Mother: Virginia Dale Oberon

Father: _____

I wrote all that down, making a particular note that Ed's name was missing. He was married to someone else. Besides, this wasn't her birth certificate. Maybe Ginnie hadn't wanted a reminder of Ed in the book.

There were hand-drawn curlicues and flowers all around the page. Ginnie'd been a real doodler, just like me. She and I would even draw pictures together sometimes. She'd stick them up on the cook center in the modular, next to my art class drawings. The door buzzer went off. I nearly jumped out of my skin.

Running to the viewer, I squinted into it. "Hello?"

"Let us in." Mike's face was plastered up to the screen—his nose a big blob. "We're here to cheer you up."

Crap. Why did none of my friends ever listen to me? I'd really wanted to be alone. I couldn't be angry at him, though, he meant well. I pressed the entry pad. "Get up here."

Racing into my room, I hid the book and got to the door right as they knocked. Mike and Derek tried to push past each other, like some comedy team. Derek tumbled in first.

"Look who we found on the way over." Mike pulled Sal out from behind the door.

"Hi," he said quietly.

I barely nodded. Sal was the last person I'd expected, or wanted, to see. The minor heart palpitation I felt could not possibly have been caused by the twinkle in his brown eyes as he half suppressed a full-out grin.

He pointed behind me. "Looks like you dropped something."

I glanced over my shoulder, and there on the floor was the pad with my notes—faceup and wide open.

XIII

contemplated diving for the notepad but thought better than to make a big deal out of it. Before I could do anything, Sal crossed the floor and picked it up.

In two strides I was beside him. "Hey . . ." I snatched the notepad away.

"Sorry." He raised his eyebrows.

"Touch . . . eee," Derek said. "What's in there, government secrets? Lemme see . . ."

"It's private." I stuffed the pad into my back pocket.

"Wow!" Mike called out from the kitchen. "This is lots bigger than their other place. Where is everyone? Hey, Pops, it's Mike!" He strolled back into the living room with an apple in his hand.

"They're at Grant Park," I said. "And yes, Mike, why don't you just make yourself at home?"

"I did." He took a bite of the apple and grinned at me.

Some things never changed.

He and Derek prowled around the living room while Sal studied the contents of the bookcase.

It was impossible not to notice how cute he was. I purposely turned away. I was not going to go all sex-teen like Sandy, ogling every good-looking guy she saw. It was only to see what he was doing that made me peek over my shoulder, taking in his profile.

"Is this your dad?" He pointed to a photo on the shelf. "You look like him." He picked up the picture and held it out, looking from it to me. "Hey, Derek, don't you think Nina looks like him? His name was Alan, right?"

"Yup, Alan Oberon."

Derek and Mike joined Sal, glancing from the photo to me.

"She does, I guess." Mike shrugged.

"Yeah, lots," Derek said. He, Mike, and Sal all peered at my face.

"Are you guys done inspecting me?" I rubbed my neck to hide the blush that was rising up under Sal's gaze. He put the picture back.

"Where's your room, Neenie?" Mike said. "You get one all to yourself?"

Mike's questions stopped any further comparison of me to Alan, and they all stopped staring at my eyes, my nose. I wondered, did Sal think they were okay, maybe even pretty? I raised my eyes to look at him, and a warm feeling enveloped my shoulders for half a nanosecond. ..

Ugh! How typically sixteen could I get? Turning around, I stomped down the hall, totally aggravated with myself. What did it matter if he thought anything about me? I refused to be like Sandy, or practically every other almost-sixteen-year-old girl. I didn't primp in front of a mirror or practice *XVI Ways* tips on getting boys to notice you. I was not going to let some random guy complicate my life, period.

I opened the door to my room and cringed. It was a mess, filled to capacity with the two beds, several boxes, and my fake dresser. I'd never worried about Mike and Derek seeing my stuff. It wasn't the tier thing. Even though Mike was tier one and Derek, well, he was tier five, we were all friends. Tiers didn't matter to us. But what would Sal think? He'd been dressed homeless when I'd first met him, but later, when we saw him at the zoo, he was wearing clothes that were definitely not Sale or Megaworld. They were at least as good as, if not better than, what Derek wore. I noticed the corner of the baby book jutting out from under my clothes. Sidling over, I nudged it back into hiding with my heel.

"Dee's staying in here, too, for right now. She's still really upset about Ginnie and it's hard for her to get to sleep. Eventually she'll move into her own room across the hall."

"How are you?" Sal's look was penetrating and the sympathy in his eyes was so obvious, A lump caught in my throat and I didn't dare say a word; I would've lost it. He picked up a picture of Ginnie that was by Dee's bed. "Is this your mom? She's beautiful."

I wanted to rip her picture out of his hands and scream at him to keep his hands off my mother's picture. "Yes, that's her, and I'm fine." I reached for the frame, and grabbed Sal's hand by accident. Our eyes met, and like a couple of kids playing staredown, neither of us was willing to break the gaze. What started as a confrontation, however, morphed into a place I'd never been before. I wanted to look away, but something inside of me didn't want to stop what was happening. Mike popped in.

"Holding hands?" He gave me a sly grin. "Gettin' all lovey-dovey—"

"Ugh, no." I dropped Sal's hand like it was a river rat and seized the photo.

Derek frowned at me. I pressed the picture to my chest, wishing Ginnie's wisdom about boys would flow out of it and into me. We'd never talked about guys. I'd always said I wasn't ready to when she'd tried to bring it up. I hugged the picture closer.

"I almost forgot." Mike pulled a Wolf Bar out of his pocket. "You guys want some? It's the seventy-two percent kind."

"Where'd you get credits to buy that?" Derek asked.

"Mom snuck some to me after Dad got paid for one of those experiments he does."

Figured, I thought. His dad would never be that nice to him. He used to smack Mike around but eventually quit when Mike got bigger than him.

We divvied up the chocolate and for a few minutes the only sound in the room was *mmmm*.

"Let's go to Jackson's and check out new releases," Derek said.

"I'll be right there." I motioned them out of the room. The baby book would have to wait. "Mom," I whispered to her photo, "I miss you so much." I kissed her smiling face and set the picture back in its place, swallowing the tears that were aching to come out. Finally, I found the spot inside, the one empty of emotions, and then I was ready to join my friends.

***

After we crossed the river, Derek and Mike immersed themselves in the verts. I should've, too, because the alternative was talking with Sal.

"Mike told me that your dad died a long time ago," he said. "You never knew him?"

"No." I hoped monosyllabic answers would stop any

conversation. But I hadn't factored in his tenacity, or the ridiculous urge I felt to hear to his voice.

"Gran and Pops are his parents or your mom's?"

"His."

"Mike told me about Pops's leg. What happened to him?"

That question was going to take at least a couple of sentences to answer. I would be brief. "He was an engineer working on the Beyond Atmosphere space launch elevator at the Cape. During testing, there was an explosion; two guys got killed. Pops lost his leg. One of his friends lost both legs and an eye."

"That's awful." I felt Sal shudder. I hadn't realized we'd drifted that close to each other. I always tended to list toward whomever I was walking with; Ginnie did, too. I moved to the right, putting plenty of space between us. If Sal noticed, he didn't say.

"What about bionic replacements? Those are pretty standard, aren't they?"

"Pops was lucky to get what he's got. The government wasn't going to do anything at all for him or the other guy. There was enough blog rage that Media picked it up and turned the incident into a major news event. That put the pressure on. As far as I'm concerned, it's the only time Media ever did anything worthwhile." I sounded like Ginnie; that was exactly the sort of thing she would've said.

"They wouldn't do anything like that now," Sal said. "Instead they'd shut down the blogs, and probably the bloggers, too." He gave me a sideways glance, almost as if he wanted to make sure I understood the danger and the enormity of his statement.

I did. The first thing that crossed my mind was surveillance, causing me to automatically look skyward.

"Don't worry," he said. "Too many verts for them to make out what we're talking about."

Even though the sun was shining, goose bumps popped up on my arms. Wrapping my sweater tight about me, I stayed silent, not willing to be pulled into any arguments about the government. Certainly not with some guy who dressed like he was homeless and turned up in places he shouldn't be—like my apartment— with people he shouldn't be with—as in, my friends.

Still, part of me was curious about Sal Davis and the things he might have to say. Things that reminded me of Ginnie . . . and ran dangerously close to NonCon and Resistance talk. I should have left him there, and gone to catch up with Mike and Derek. But I wanted to hear what he had to say, even if it scared me.

"I know all about the government and Media and what they do." The bitterness in Sal's voice surprised me. "My dad was a reporter for the *Global Times*. The Governing Council insisted he be the one to do an in-depth report on a suspected Resistance movement in the Outer Hebrides. Mom went with him because she'd never been to the Greater United Isles. The leviton taking them from the main island to the Hebrides crashed into the sea. Their bodies were never recovered, so the government refused to pay survivor benefits until the obligatory eight-year waiting period ends. Of course, by the time that happens, I'll be too old to collect benefits." He let out a hollow laugh. "The *Times* gave John and me a small pension to make themselves look good." He shoved his hands in his pockets. "Almost makes you want to do something about it . . ."

Behind his hard gaze, I glimpsed a huge sadness. At least the Infinity machine had given me a chance to say good-bye to

Ginnie. I instinctively reached for his arm. "I'm sorry."

He stopped walking, stared first at my hand and then at me. Maybe, like me, he didn't deal well with sympathy. I drew back my hand, and ventured a tiny smile. When he smiled back, a rush of warmth, like hot chocolate in December, ran through me. I wasn't used to this—I needed something familiar, and fast. Where were Derek and Mike? I spotted them outside an electronics store down the street listening to an old music player, and hurried over with Sal following behind me.

"Hey guys, listen to this," Mike said. "It's great!"

I recognized the tune. "Hey, I know this song. You play this, don't you, Derek?"

"Yup, it's Van Morrison. Pretty cool, huh?" He turned to Sal. "My older brother, Riley, has a bunch of his tunes. He studies early music at the University, specializing in mid-1900s. I'm gonna do the same thing when I graduate. I applied for a scholarship, too. Though they accept tier four and up, so I would get in anyway."

"Smart-ass." Mike grinned at Derek. "You know you're getting that scholarship anyway. Hey, anyone hungry?" Mike asked. "These credits Mom gave me are dying to turn into food."

"Are you kidding? Even if I'd just stuffed myself on Unity Feast Day, I'd say yes," Derek said. "I can't remember the last time you bought."

"TJ's?" I suggested. It felt nice—normal even—being around friends.

Sal glanced up at a nearby time/temp sign, then directed a look at me. There was something about him that made my knees turn to jelly. "Sounds great, but I can't. A couple of wrecks came in late yesterday, so I've gotta work today. See you guys at school."

I watched his reflection in the store window as he crossed the street. He moved effortlessly, like a cat. He glanced up the street, his hair obscuring his face, but when he turned the other way, his jaw was clenched and he was frowning. I felt bad that our conversation had turned to his parents' death, but I had wanted him to leave, hadn't I? A yearning to follow him and say something, anything, to help surged through me. I crossed my arms, grabbing my shoulders, and holding that feeling inside.

***

Sal hadn't been gone more than five minutes when it happened. This time there was no silence, and no trannies crashed. Just a broadcast:

"The Governing Council, in its bid to keep the tier system in place, has instituted programs like Female Liaison Specialist and Human Bio-testers. What they don't tell you is what really happens to the tier-ones who are testers and where the girls who are inducted into FeLS end—"

As abruptly as it started, it stopped. People, who had instinctively clustered together when the transmission started, shook off the anxiety caused by their close proximity and proceeded along their way. The air fairly crackled with tension. Several people cast furtive glances over their shoulders, and no one made eye contact with anyone else—as if fearing their private thoughts would be discovered.

"NonCons. Wow! And that was the Eliminator." Admiration coated Derek's words like chocolate. "I think—"

"Derek—not now." I gripped his arm, pointing upward. It was certain that the audio surveillance cops would be monitoring downtown following that broadcast. It was definitely not a good time for Derek to voice any pro-Resistance views, which I hadn't been aware he'd had. We were lucky the Governing Council hadn't perfected thought surveillance. Although there were rumors about B.O.S.S. testing prototypes in New York and Los Angeles.

I'd heard about the Eliminator, but I never actually heard one of his broadcasts. I didn't know much about him, just what I'd heard from Media reports. He was the main NonCon leader of the Resistance, and Ginnie'd thought of him as a hero, though she could never say as much out loud.

"I wonder if Sal heard it?" Derek said.

I thought of Sal's sudden departure. Unbidden, my brain drew a line from the homeless guy sneaking down the alley after the vert interruption the day Ginnie'd been killed. I shook it off. It was coincidence, that was all.

***

At TJ's, I knew everyone's mind was on the NonCon broadcast, but no one dared talk about it. We ordered food, and the guys chattered on about verts and trannies. I just ignored them.

Supposedly there was so little to worry about in the world— at least according to the Governing Council. No hunger, no unemployment, a roof over everyone's head . . . at least for anyone who wanted one. So why was my whole life was lived on constant high-anxiety alert?

For years, I'd tried to ignore the way Ginnie was abused, kept out of Ed's way, and dreaded turning sixteen, and everything that entailed. I knew that I'd never get those images from Ed's porn vids out of my head. Now I had to keep Dee safe, find my father . . . and I had to do it all without my mom. It was almost too much.

Maybe I was too sensitive to things. Most girls my age worried about unimportant stuff—what to wear, hanging out with the right tier, using the right slang, and guys. They didn't think turning sixteen was something to worry about—not the way I did. Of course, everyone had their dread about the tattoos, although most girls I knew wouldn't admit it. They said they were afraid of needles or that it would hurt. But they never said that they didn't feel ready to have sex, or that it scared them to be so vulnerable to the advances from guys. Maybe they weren't afraid, but it terrified me.

Then there was the whole FeLS application and the Choosing. At least with Ginnie having bought out my contract, I could cross that off my worry list. Still, Sandy was stressing to the edge of the universe about getting chosen. Her best chance to get out of low tiers was FeLS. I had art and my Creatives, but Sandy wasn't smart enough to get a scholarship and she certainly wasn't interested in anything creative. There was the possibility that she'd meet some higher-tier guy, but every low-tier girl hoped for that. It didn't mean it ever happened. Maybe I should be a better friend and call Ed—but how could I bring him into our lives when it was everything I could do to keep him away from Dee? Who knew what he'd want in return for a favor? I shuddered.

I'd resigned myself to either staying a low-tier, or maybe getting a scholarship. My grades were good, and with the Creative designation, I'd have a chance to get into the Art Institute. Creatives who came from lower tiers were usually serious about their art, whether it was music, painting, acting, or writing, and the GC left them alone, unless their work crossed some aribitrary line and became über-political. Those Creatives just disappeared. No one ever talked about what happened to them. I had no plans of being political, ever.

I was depressing myself by overthinking when Derek snapped me out of it. "You know, Sal's cool. He likes music and his brother has all those great trannies. How'd you meet him anyway?"

"Actually . . ." Should I tell them how? So far only Sandy knew about the incident in the park. What could it hurt? They were my friends, too. And with all the noise in TJ's I wasn't too concerned that AS cops would pick up on a conversation that was some girl talking about some guy.

"Some 'letes in Lincoln Park were beating up on him. I, uh, told them to take off."

"'Letes." Derek made a face, shaking his head and shoulders.

"Shut up, man," Mike hissed and nodded in the direction of a table full of guys wearing Chicago University letter jackets.

Derek shrugged. "Huh, so that's how come Sal was all cut up and bruised."

"Yeah," I said. "They really did a number on him. Anyway, I kinda helped him. Made sure he was okay. You know . . ." They both nodded. "He was dressed homeless, and I still don't understand why he was dressed that way. What's up with that?"

"Girls," Mike said, shaking his head. "Skivs! The guy's lying there half dead and you're worried about what he's wearing?"

"Could be he's into stuff he doesn't want anyone to know about. Black-market parts? Big business there, soupin' up trannies. Maybe that's why he hasn't had us over to his brother's shop yet?" Derek's eyes crinkled mischievously. "Or maybe he was playing around—like when you change your hair color or wear different clothes."

"I don't change my hair color," I retorted, "and I wear the same clothes all the time."

"I know." He pinched his nose and made a face. "P-U."

"Oh, what are you, five years old, Derek?" I gave him a little shove. He was sitting on the edge of the booth and he slid off, landing on his butt.

Mike howled; I laughed. The waitress scowled.

Derek stood up. Grinning, he brushed off the seat of his pants and sat back down. "Don't know your own strength, eh? As far as Sal goes, why not just ask him?"

"Yeah. I'll do that. But I think I'll leave out the part that you think he and his brother are big-time gangsters." I didn't bother telling Derek I already had asked Sal about it, not to mention that Sal's answer had been cryptic to say the least. "I wish Sandy were here. I miss her. I can't wait to be back in school again and see everyone."

"Well, we mith you, too," Mike mumbled through the fries in his mouth.

"Uh-huh." Derek looked at me with the same dreamy eyes as before. I fingered the horse charm around my neck.

Once again, the memory of what Ginnie and I had been going to talk about that night surfaced. I'd eventually figure out how to deal with Derek. But I didn't have a clue how to deal with missing Ginnie.

XIV

On Monday morning, Dee and I stepped off the number 33 transit at the corner of Dickens and Clark and into our old neighborhood. I doubted she remembered it the way I did, since she'd just turned six when we moved.

We passed the ancient brownstone walk-ups and trendy little boutiques. Mike and Derek were waiting for us at the next corner. The four of us swished our way through the leaves toward Dee's school. Halfway down the block we ran into her friend Maddie. They were so thrilled to see each other I had to tell Dee twice to wait for me by the trans stop after school. Seeing her PAV receiver clipped to her bag reminded me of Ed. I grabbed her arm. "Dee, be careful and don't go anywhere with anyone else. Promise?"

"Skivs! What kind of idiot do you think I am? See ya!" She yanked her arm away and ran off with Maddie, instantly swallowed up in the crowd of elementary school kids surging toward Dickens.

Several blocks later, I was standing in front of Daley High, nerves jangling. Even though it had been four years since I'd seen them, I recognized a couple of girls. They remembered me, too, and said hi, and I calmed down some.

"Nina, meet us back here at lunch," Mike said. "We'll go to Mickey's."

Inside, we went our separate ways. I checked my receiver for my schedule; I'd downloaded it the night before. My first two classes were predictable and boring, then I got to homeroom. No sooner had the teacher pointed me to an empty desk than a petite Asian girl, with straight black hair that hung halfway down her back, danced into the room singing "One-way Flight to Venus" at the top of her lungs.

"Wei Jenkins," the teacher commanded, "sit down and be quiet."

She saluted him. "Yes, sir, Mr. Haldewick." Marching to the desk across from mine, she flashed me a smile and plopped down.

Mr. Haldewick rolled his eyes and sighed. He sat down, too, and shuffled through some papers.

"I see we have a new student." Peering over antique glasses that pinched his nose into a point (they had to be for show; no one wore glasses anymore, unless they were tier one and couldn't afford the correction surgery), he pointed me out. "You there." He motioned to me. "Come up front and introduce yourself."

I'd been dreading this. None of the other teachers I'd had so far bothered with this part. Everyone stared as I made my way down the aisle. I recognized three kids, but that was cold comfort. My mouth felt like I'd been on the Martian desert for a year, and I was sure my lips were stuck fast to my teeth.

I looked out over the class, managing a tiny wave. "I'm Nina Oberon." Good, at least my lips were moving. With great effort I eked out, "I used to go to Granite Middle School. I just moved back to Chicago."

Somehow, in spite of my jelly legs, I managed to get back to my desk and sit down without collapsing into a little pile of body parts. I wondered if I'd ever be able to swallow again.

"Oberon?" Wei leaned across the aisle. "Are you—"

"Miss Jenkins!" Haldewick's salutation snapped us both to attention. "Quiet is the word. One more peep out of you and it's off to Mrs. Marchant's office."

She gave him a thumbs-up. He didn't look amused.

During the lecture on the Socialization of the Mars Colony in the Twenty-second Century (of all the luck, I got Health and Soch for homeroom), I noticed a tattoo on Wei's wrist, right where the XVI was supposed to be. *She's probably fifteen*, I thought. It was illegal to cover your XVI; it had to be a wash-off. Otherwise she'd be . . . well, I wasn't sure what would happen to her. I hadn't heard of anyone messing with their XVIs. Not since the incidents that made the underground blogs . . . One girl tried to burn hers off, and more than one girl bled to death after trying to slice it off with a razor blade. The Media reported the incidents as suicides; maybe they were.

Wei saw me staring and tapped her wrist with her rapido. Then I saw the XVI—right in the center, completely untouched by the intricate tattoo surrounding it. She winked at me.

I wanted to talk to her. There was something about her, the way she held herself, her attitude. And I had to know about her XVI. Maybe she was a Creative. I'd heard about Creatives inking around their tattoos; some of the higher-tiers in my art classes had talked about some places you could get it done, but I'd never seen anyone actually do it. Maybe after I got my designation . . . no, I'd never be able to afford a tat. That was just for upper-tiers.

The bell rang, and we all filed out of the classroom. I saw Sal hurry over to Wei as I got a drink at the fountain, but neither of them even glanced at me. I watched them leave together down the hall. I told myself the empty feeling in my stomach was hunger.

***

Mike, Derek, and I had lunch at Mickey's Diner, a little café right next to the school. It was packed with students of all tiers. The only adults in sight were Mickey and his wife. Mickey's took cafeteria credits and everyone would much rather stuff themselves with tempeh burgers and tofu fries than the watered-down, reconstituted TVP glop the school passed off as food.

We squeezed into a booth by the window just as its occupants were leaving.

"So this girl in my homeroom, Wei—"

"*She's* in your homeroom?" Derek said.

"You're in for a wild year," Mike added.

"Her tattoo," I said. "How'd she get away with that?"

"The thistles aren't touching the XVI," Derek said.

"Thistles?"

"Yeah, after some archaic symbol is what I heard. She got it last spring. Some parents made a big deal about it, so government inspectors showed up. Since it didn't interfere with a wrist scan, they couldn't do anything. Besides, she's a Creative, they can do almost anything. I think it's cool."

Mike gulped down the last of his food. "She's upper tier—ten, I think." He reached across the table. "Can I have the rest of your burger?"

"Sure." Hoping to come across as nonchalant, I asked, "Is she Sal's girlfriend?"

"I dunno." Mike shrugged and chomped into the remaining burger.

"He showed up after class and they left together."

Derek narrowed his eyes ever so slightly. "So what if she is?"

He was watching for some reaction from me. "No big deal. I just wondered."

At that very moment Sal and Wei walked by the window. She noticed me and smiled—she had a really nice smile and I couldn't help but return it. She said something to Sal as they passed. He looked over his shoulder at me and then turned back to Wei. As they walked away, I noticed they weren't holding hands, not that it would've mattered if they had been.

XV

The rest of the afternoon at school was uneventful. I saw a few more people I remembered from middle school, but I didn't see Wei or Sal again. The rush of relief I felt when I saw Dee waiting on the corner surprised me. I hadn't realized how worried I was about Ed until then. She was so excited about her first day at school that she chattered the entire way home and I couldn't get a word in edgewise.

After dinner Dee was arranging her text chips on the table when Pops asked, "Want some help with that?"

"Sure." Dee scooted her chair close to his and pulled an AV viewer out of her backpack.

"What kind of homework do you have?" I asked.

"Regional History and . . ." She wrinkled her nose. "Math."

"Pops is great with math. That's why he's an engineer." I planted a kiss on his cheek.

"Newfangled way of doing it on this tiny little screen." He retrieved his glasses from his pocket. "Think I can get close enough?" He touched his nose to the viewer and Dee laughed.

Hearing her laugh made my heart sing. I finished clearing off the dining-room table and was heading to my room to see if I could take some time to examine Dee's baby book when I noticed Gran sitting on the sofa. She was dabbing at her eyes.

"You okay?"

"Here, dear." She patted the cushion beside her. "I found this old album while I was unpacking."

I recognized the worn red cover. "We used to look through this when I was little." I snuggled in beside her on the couch. "There's my father." I pointed to a photo of a little boy wearing a black-and-red costume with a big E in the middle of it and a cape flowing behind him. "How old was he here?"

"He was nine. That's his costume for Imagination Day. He wanted to destroy evil." Gran's eyes got all misty. "I should have known . . ."

"He was always the good guy, wasn't he?"

"Yes." Gran turned the page. "Here he is in high school, just about your age now, maybe a little older."

In that picture even I could see how much we looked alike. Brown hair, parted on the same side, wide eyes, and a straight nose. "What's he holding there?" I pointed to a medal in his hand.

"He'd just won a debate on Media influence and the erosion of free will. He was pro-citizen—his unfortunate rival was pro-Media."

I could hear Ginnie's voice in my head: *Don't ever believe what comes out of government sources. Find out the truth for yourself. Don't be a Media sheep—promise me.* I always promised. But still she taught me not to question things out loud in public—you never knew what would happen.

Gran brought me out of my thoughts. "See here?" She pointed to a photo. "Ginnie and Alan were perfect for each other."

The two of them, side by side. My father's arm was around my mother's waist. They were looking at each other instead of the camera.

The next page was him and another guy in front of a building under a huge awning. I'd seen this album so many times, but I still didn't know half of the people in it. "Gran, who's that?"

"Jonathan. He was Alan's best friend. The last time I saw him was at the memorial service fifteen years ago. He and his wife, Jasmine . . . No, that's not it . . ." Gran searched the ceiling, like the name might be hiding up there. "Oh yes." She smiled. "Jade. She's the one who got your grandfather hooked on candied ginger." Gran chuckled. "They were there with their baby, who was just a little older than you . . . cute, very cute. Dark hair and big brown eyes. I can't remember if it was a boy or a girl. You know, I never did see them again. I believe they eventually went overseas. At least that's what Ginnie said."

Funny, Ginnie had never mentioned them to me. "Did they keep in touch with Ginnie?"

"I think so, yes. At least until she started seeing Ed." Gran frowned. "After that, I don't know. I think she lost most all of the friends she and Alan had in high school. If it hadn't been for you, and then Dee, I doubt we would've seen her, either."

"You treat Dee like she's your real granddaughter," I said. "Even though Ed's her father."

"Of course we do," Gran said. "She didn't get to choose him, but we certainly got to choose having her in our lives. We would never have treated you two differently. You're both our granddaughters, blood or not."

I snuggled close to Gran. "I love you."

"I love you, too, dear." She laid her hands on the album. "Do you want to keep looking? I'm not boring you with all these old pictures, am I?"

"Oh no, Gran, these are great." Maybe there was more in the book, something that might give me a place to start in my search for my father. I looked back at the photo. I supposed Jonathan, Jade, and their baby were long gone.

I stared closer at the photo, and noticed something else in the background. I took the album from Gran and looked more closely. There was a sign on the building behind them. "Do you know where they are? It says 'Roost.'"

Gran adjusted her glasses, squinting at the picture. "Oh, that's Robin's Roost. They all practically lived there. What a grand hotel it was. It's where Alan and Ginnie had their wedding reception." Her eyes got that misty faraway look old people's do when they're drifting back in their memories.

"Robin's Roost? Where was it?"

"It was at Wells and Lincoln. But, the government closed it down after several forays confirmed it as a hotbed of NonCon activities."

"NonCons? Ginnie was outspoken about the government," I said. "But she wouldn't have been involved with NonCons, would she? She never would have put me and Dee in that kind of danger." I wasn't sure what my father was capable of doing.

"Oh, no, never. Alan didn't go for underground activism either. He was candid and publicly vocal with his views, which did eventually get him in a bit of trouble. But nothing underground."

"I wonder if the building is still there." I was curious about a place where Ginnie and my father had spent so much time together. Knowing Ginnie, there must have been something really special about it.

"Oh, it's still there. First it housed a Bureau of Safety and Security office. The location was too public for them." She sniffed. "Didn't want people to figure out what they actually do. Several groups tried to have it converted to housing for homeless, but the Governing Council refused. They boarded it up and there it sits, empty and useless."

"Really? But they always go on about not wasting space and how they provide for homeless. Maybe since it's old, the building's not safe."

"Humph. Hold this." Gran handed me the album and left the room. When she returned she was carrying a little black machine, no bigger than a box of tissues, which she plugged in and flicked a switch. I'd never seen anything quite like it. And I'd never seen Gran do much of anything with electronics. She rarely even got online on her PAV.

She sat down next to me. "This is my safety net." She tapped it with her finger. "The GC wouldn't approve that building as housing for homeless because it wasn't a rat-infested dump in a bad neighborhood." Her eyes were flashing and I was startled by the vehemence in her voice. "What the government does approve is substandard housing in dangerous neighborhoods, minimally nutritious food, and menial jobs that barely pay enough to cover the cost of everything. It's total crap!"

"Gran!" I couldn't believe she was saying this; what if there were surveillance satellites turned to us? She sounded like Ginnie going off on an antigovernment rant. "Think about . . ." I looked upward, hoping she'd pick up on my concern.

"Don't worry. This little box is taking care of any surveillance. Nina, dear, you mustn't believe everything—maybe not anything— the government says. For several generations the GC has been blatantly brainwashing society through Media messages. Look at your friend Sandy—see what sixteen propaganda has done to her? Why, two years ago she was as sweet and innocent as they come. Now she's on the verge of becoming a wild sex-teen. The GC wants to keep people in their place—GPS implants, XVIs . . ."

"But FeLS . . . isn't that a good thing? Sandy wants to get in to move up through the tiers." My own words sounded halfhearted.

"That's the kind of disinformation they teach you in school, isn't it?" She sighed. "It's not true. The government does nothing for the people, it only takes care of itself. Our whole system is designed to keep the GC in control. They run the Media, the Media runs us. It's been going on for so many years that no one even notices anymore." Gran closed the photo album and turned off the machine. "Alan noticed." She took my face in her hands. "You're so much like him." Her PAV receiver beeped and we both jumped. "It's Harriet, I'll be back in a bit." She looked over her shoulder at me as she was going out the door. "We'll talk more later."

I had never realized how alike Gran and Ginnie were. I picked up the album and flipped through the pages, stopping at the photo of my father and Jonathan. I knew the corner of Lincoln and Wells, but as hard as I tried, I couldn't visualize the buildings. I made up my mind—tomorrow I'd go find Robin's Roost. If it had meant so much to both of my parents, maybe there was some kind of feeling I could get from it. Perhaps an intuition, a hint or a nudge in the direction of my father. I knew I was being a little crazy, but without any concrete clues, I didn't have a choice but to explore every bit of information I found about him.

Pops hobbled in on his crutch. "What's this doing here?" He tapped the machine.

"Gran got it out. She said it was her safety net."

He threw back his head and snorted. "It's my old scrambler."

"Your what?"

"Scrambler. It scrambles *them*." He stuck his crutch in the air and circled it around. Then he leaned over and whispered, "Picked it up on a job and never gave it back." He patted it like a dog. "Done me a lot of good over the years. You women planning a galactic takeover?" He laughed at himself. Then his eyes started to get that faraway look I'd seen so many times before.

"Gran went to Harriet's," I said. "Should we leave this out?"

"Huh? What?" Pops came back to the present. He switched the scrambler on and said, "You'd better put it away in its hidey-hole, Little Bit. It goes in that cabinet above the chiller, behind the vent, you'll see it."

After I'd hidden the scrambler, I went to my room. Since Dee was finishing up her homework there, I slipped into her room to call Sandy. Sitting on the floor, surrounded by moving boxes, I poured out my new-school blues to her, leaving out any mention of Sal. She was still kind of touchy about that day at the zoo. And I certainly didn't mention Robin's Roost. Even though I loved Sandy, that was not the kind of thing I could talk to her about.

Later, as I was lying in bed, I mulled over everything Gran had said. My thoughts spun around like a blender. Homeless. I had thought the government was doing right by them: a place to live, food and jobs if they wanted them. I didn't realize the price, however. Their lives were not their own. FeLS. Ginnie'd wanted so badly for me to stay out of it. She'd managed to buy out my contract. How she'd gotten the credits, I didn't know. I wasn't sure I *wanted* to know. Tattoos. I slid my wrist under the covers. There was no way out. My birthday was soon. In a few weeks I'd be branded and legal. GPS implants. I wanted mine gone—at least there I had an option. I could get it removed when I turned sixteen. I didn't need the GC to keep me "safe" and track my every move. I crossed my arms over my chest, hugging myself tight.

Maybe I should give up, start reading *XVI Ways*, and figure out how to deal with the inevitable. A sliver of light from the hallway shone under the door and illuminated the room just enough for me to make out Ginnie's picture by Dee's bed.

Ginnie. She'd never been like Sandy's mom, who always pushed and encouraged Sandy to follow Media guidelines. Mrs. Eskew'd bought Sandy every how-to vid that *XVI Ways* put out. She even made Sandy practice flirting and flaunting herself in front of her leering stepdad. I'd never say it to Sandy, but her mother was an idiot.

Ginnie never pushed me—except to do art, and that wasn't exactly pushing. She'd been so against Media hype that she'd installed a disabler for the commercial feed on our FAV and would switch it off whenever she could. Once, she'd forgotten to turn it back on before Ed came over; as soon as he realized what she'd done, he was furious.

Lying there under the covers, I shivered. The ice-cold memory of his brutality gripped me. I could still hear him after he found the masking device in the controls: "Where did you get this?" When Ginnie refused to answer, he made her get out his box of vids. "You need a refresher course, babe," he'd said. Then he ordered me to take Dee next door to Sandy's. He never wanted his daughter to see what a horrible person her father was. Me, on the other hand, he didn't care about at all. I knew I'd come back, and Ginnie would be in bad shape. She could barely walk for a week. Her right eye was swollen shut for days. He told Dee her mother was clumsy and ran into a cabinet door.

I hated him.

I wanted to believe in a different kind of love, like Gran said Ginnie and my father'd had. But I didn't even know what that would look like. If it was all as bad as Ed's vids made it out to be, I had a hard time imagining the human race would've survived. Fingering the T on my charms necklace, I stuffed back tears, whispering into the darkness, "How am I supposed to know what the truth is?"

XVI

Next day in homeroom, Wei turned to me and said, "Sal told me about your mother. I'm really sorry. That is so awful. And then to have to move to a new school ..."

Her expression was so kind and the remark was so unexpected, I thought I was going to lose it and cry right there.

"I'm doing okay." I didn't look at her. Instead I fiddled with the text chips on my desk. "Actually, I'm fine." Lying about my feelings was becoming a lot easier.

"If you need to talk, I'm a good listener. Sal is, too." She reached across the aisle and pressed my arm. "And he knows how it feels."

"Why would I—"

Mr. Haldewick sashayed into the room tapping the floor with his pointer and shushed us all.

I knew Wei and Sal were friends, but I wondered just how well she knew him. Though she was right, Sal must have known how it felt—he was alone, too.

The bell rang, and Wei ducked out after class before I had a chance to say anything else to her.

***

I spent my last period running back through my plans to visit Robin's Roost instead of focusing on Media Throughout History. Maybe today I would find something that led to my father. Dee was going home with her friend Maddie this afternoon. Derek and Mike weren't expecting me either: Derek was rehearsing music with his brother and Mike had to go pick his dad up after a day of Bio-tester experiments at the government's medical research building. If anyone asked, I said I was going to the zoo, then home. I was ready.

Finally, school ended and I got on the number 33 heading south, and got off the trans at Lincoln and Wells. I stood on the corner, like I was waiting for the light to change, until the transit was out of sight, then turned around. There, looming right in front of me, was Robin's Roost.

I was stunned. I must have walked by this dilapidated wreck of a building a thousand times or more, but had never taken a second look. Let alone known what it once had been.

I don't know what I'd expected to find there, but Robin's Roost wasn't much. The green awning from the photo was long gone. Its pitted and broken framework clung to the grimy, tagged walls like dead vines. Most of the windows at ground level had been broken and boarded up. A ghost of a rectangle on the stone by the front doors was the only evidence of where a sign had been. Someone must have taken it for scrap metal, or maybe for a souvenir of happier times. I hoped it was the latter. An orange plasticene notice glued on one of the doors proclaimed THIS BUILDING CONDEMNED. Underneath, in smaller print, it said, DEMOLITION SLATED AND CONFIRMED, DECEMBER 10, 2150. My birthday—only a month away. If I'd found out about this place much later, it would've been gone. For once, luck was on my side.

A heavy chain and padlock ran through the door handles. I rubbed on the glass, trying to clean a spot so I could see inside, when a voice behind me said, "Something interesting in there?"

I whirled around, surprised; it was Sal.

"No." I felt heat creeping up my neck—what was it about Sal that had this effect on me? It was like I was two different people. I wanted nothing to do with him; but I also seemed to want him so much closer to me. It seemed to me that I was in a constant struggle to keep my wits about me. And when he stood so near to me, it was like I had no desire to struggle quite as hard as I should.

He cupped his hands to the door and peered in. "Dirty, probably stinks in there, too. So, Nina, what's the fascination with this building?" His eyes searched mine and the blush on my cheeks kept growing.

"I was curious, that's all." I didn't need to explain anything to him. What I did was none of his business.

"Really."

"I have an old picture of my dad and a friend standing in front of this building." I fiddled with my necklace, twisting the charms. "His and my mother's wedding reception was here—I thought I'd take a look." It was true. And he didn't need to know anything more than that. I tried turning the tables. "What're you doing here?"

He didn't answer. "C'mon, you want a Sparkle? I'm buying."

Why was it that he could get an answer out of me, but I could never get an answer out of him? I didn't want a Sparkle, but I did want away from Robin's Roost. "Sure . . . I guess."

We crossed the street, dodging through the crunch of transits and hire-trannies and stopped at a vendor wagon on the edge of the park. Sal tried to pay, but I swiped my card before he had a chance to. Drinks in hand, we walked down the path.

"That's where we met." He pointed to the mound where I'd been standing when I first saw him.

"Yes." Just thinking about it made me feel embarrassed for him. "I'm sure you'd rather not remember that day."

"Why not?"

"Well, you were, uh . . . getting beaten up."

"Yeah." His voice softened. "I wasn't thinking about that."

I was trying to imagine what he was thinking about, when an unexpected stampede of butterflies invaded my stomach. I took a long drink of the soda; it didn't help. When I lowered the can, Sal was smiling at me.

"What?" I swiped my chin with the back of my hand and checked the front of my sweater.

"You have dimples."

I didn't trust myself to speak. I started to take another sip, but when I raised my hand it was trembling and I was afraid I'd spill the drink all over myself. It was easy for me to rebuff Derek when he was being ridiculous, because I knew what ridiculous was with him. With Sal, I was completely out of my element. I felt both warm (which was nice) and tingly (which was scary) being close to him. It was almost as if my body wasn't attached to my brain. A thrill ran through me, and I wasn't sure if it was terror or excitement. I wanted to leave, but I didn't want to leave him. The silence and the confusion in my brain were killing me. Finally, I thought of something to say.

"I've been coming here since I was little. I call this my mountain."

His big brown eyes under those dark lashes were studying my face. I sounded like a ten-year-old, I thought. "Well . . . when I was little it seemed like a mountain."

Sal sat down on the grass; I did, too.

"Who did you come here with when you were little?"

I looked down at the grass. Concentrating on anything besides his eyes was good. "Ginnie. We'd bring a picnic basket and spread a blanket out here." I moved my hands across the grass, imagining the blue paisley throw in front of me and Ginnie's warm laugh when I flopped backward on it, squinting into the sun. "I haven't thought about that in forever."

A flood of memories washed over me and I was lost in being five again. I could almost taste the peanut-butter-and-grape-jelly sandwiches. They'd be laid out on the blanket along with soy milk, veggie chips, and brownies. Ginnie and I would play hide-and-seek—I always found her. Sometimes I'd be so tired afterward that she'd carry me home, nestled against her shoulder. I closed my eyes, remembering the way her hair tickled my nose and how she smelled like roses. She'd always loved roses.

"Hey, Nina, you okay?" Sal said softly, touching my elbow.

Something about the way he looked at me, the warm sun on my back, this place . . . My eyes welled up and my voice cracked. "I miss her so much." I couldn't stop the tears from spilling down my cheeks. This wasn't the plan, this wasn't at all what I'd had in mind, crying in front of Sal—a boy I hardly knew! Crying was weakness—I knew that. Ginnie never cried after Ed's brutal beatings. Not once. How could I let any guy, especially Sal, see me cry?

No way in the universe could I ever have anticipated his

reaction. He didn't look away, or urge me to stop. He reached over and touched my shoulder. I covered my face with my hands and cried until I couldn't cry anymore. When I felt like I had some measure of control, I dared to glance at him.

"You all right?" he asked.

I nodded, sniffed, and wiped my nose on my sleeve. He reached into his pocket and pulled out a napkin.

"Allow me to return the favor."

I took it and wiped my eyes. "Thanks. I feel pretty stupid . . . crying . . . you know."

"I do know, but it's okay." He produced another napkin since the first was now in damp shreds. "Here." He stuck it in my hand.

Suddenly, out of nowhere, I asked, "Is Wei your girlfriend?" I could've died. I don't know why I let that stupid question pop out of my mouth. It was definitely not my afternoon.

Sal started laughing. "Wei? My girlfriend?"

"Well, yes." I glowered at him, prickles running up my arms. I wondered if all our conversations on my mountain were going to end with him laughing at me, or making me angry.

He stopped laughing. "Sorry, it's just that I've known Wei since we were babies. She's like a sister. Our parents were friends and we grew up together. And, well, since we're asking . . ." He focused on the ground, pulling out small clumps of grass. "Is Derek your boyfriend?"

"Derek?" It was my turn to be amused. "No way. He and Mike and I have been best friends since kindergarten. Where did you get the idea that he was my boyfriend?"

"He talks about you all the time." His gaze was still on the grass. "Like you're, uh . . . special."

I shook my head. "I knew it. That horse charm meant more to him."

"Huh?"

"The day I met you Derek gave me this charm for my necklace." I showed it to him. Sal leaned in for a closer look. "He was acting so odd, so not the way Derek acts. I thought that maybe he was getting a crush on me, but I told him flat out, the last thing I wanted was a boyfriend."

"Oh . . ." Sal straightened up suddenly.

I realized what I'd just said. I didn't know how to explain, how to make him understand what I wanted without making a complete fool out of myself. The thing was, I didn't know what I wanted, not anymore. I felt so conflicted around him. I didn't want to be a sex-teen, but I didn't want to push Sal away either. Even before I had it, the XVI tattoo was ruling my life, and I didn't know how to stop it.

The butterflies in my stomach turned into sinking weights and I struggled to say the right thing. "Sal . . . I've never had a boyfriend. And the only people I've seen who have boyfriends make fools out of themselves, or hurt each other. Like Ginnie and Ed, her . . . her boyfriend." Sal looked puzzled, and I realized he didn't know anything about Ed. "Ugh, I'm not making sense. See, Media says you're supposed to act a certain way, and Health and Soch says that when guys and girls . . . and you expect this and that to happen and . . ." I was rambling, I wasn't making sense. Like Dee when she doesn't want to go to bed and keeps talking and talking and talking.

I fingered my charms necklace, again, and latched onto the T. I stopped babbling, took a deep breath, and looked Sal straight in those deep dark eyes. "I'm afraid to have a boyfriend. I don't know how to do that and not lose who I want to be. And I'm afraid of what it means to be close to a guy, a guy I might really like."

There it was: the truth.

He took my hand, and looked at it for what seemed like light-years. "Yeah, it is scary." He raised his eyes to meet mine. "But I don't think you can avoid it forever, Nina."

Then he leaned over and kissed me. Right on the mouth. My first kiss.

It was so tender, his lips were soft, and I felt like I was floating. Out of nowhere, I started crying again. He pulled me close to him and held me. I'd never felt so confused, happy, scared, and safe in my whole life. For the first time, the fears that had ruled my life faded to the background, and I felt calmer, lighter. I knew they'd come back, but at least I'd had a taste of freedom. I sank into it like it was a fluffy white cloud on a summer's day.

We sat there for a long time—wrapped around each other, not saying anything. Eventually, a park security officer doing rounds on her ped-tran slowed down and gave us a look. Sal stood up and helped me to my feet, and she glided away.

"I'd better go," I said.

He ended up walking me home. Neither of us said a word, but he held my hand. I was afraid if I spoke, some kind of spell would be broken.

When we got to my building, he brushed his lips across mine. "See you tomorrow."

XVII

The next morning was pretty normal, though I couldn't stop thinking about Sal's kiss, and how it would be to see him. I alternated between being über-happy and scared to death as to what I would say, what he would do. Most of his classes were in a different part of the building, so we didn't see each other until after school, and then it was only for a minute, and surrounded by everyone else.

"Hey, I've gotta run. John and I are working on a multitrans for some bigwig at Infinity Corp." Sal gave my hand a quick squeeze when no one was looking. I don't think either one of us knew how to act around our friends. "I'll call you later." He peeled off, and Derek and Mike waved good-bye to me as I headed down to pick up Dee.

I was glad he hadn't made a big fuss, at first. But what if that kiss didn't mean anything to him? He was upper tier—he could never like a low-tier, no flash girl like me. My insecurity took over, and caught me in a whirlwind of my defects, when Wei interrupted.

"Hi, Nina." She was wearing her usual smile and fell into step with me. "Whatcha doing?"

"Hey. I'm headed to Dickens to pick up my little sister."

"Oh, ultra! That's on my way, I'll walk with you. Let's go slow, though; I have to practice when I get home."

"What kind of practice?" I'd heard Sal tell Derek that Wei was some kind of martial arts expert.

"Piano." She wrinkled her nose. "I love it and I hate it. Some days it's just hard work. Do you play an instrument?"

"Uh, I'm not musically inclined." I was too embarrassed to admit we'd never had enough credits for music or dance lessons. No one under tier four did. I was lucky Ginnie was able to scrape together enough to pay for my art classes. I knew it had been a burden on her.

"But you're in art, though, right? I saw you going into Mr. Tobin's class. When do you get your designation? I qualified for mine last summer. That's' when I got this." She pointed to her XVI. "And then . . . I got this." She grinned, turning her hand back and forth so I could see the thistle tattoo that circled the XVI and then spread across the back of her hand.

"It's so beautiful." Even if I did get my Creative, I knew I'd never be able to afford a tattoo like that.

"When the XVI fades, I'll get more ink. No one will ever even know it was there. You know, you could design your own tattoo to hide the XVI. I bet you're a good artist. What kind of stuff do you do?"

"Mostly drawing with colored rapidos. I'm not that good." In Cementville I'd been at the top of my class. I hadn't been at Daley long enough to see much of what the other kids in my class were doing.

"You're probably lots better than you think," she said.

"Maybe. I'll show you sometime." I was more than a little

surprised that someone who was obviously as upper tier as Wei would take any interest in me at all, even if she was friends with Sal. It made me uncomfortable to talk about my art, so I changed the subject. "Do you have brothers or sisters?"

"Both. I have a sister, Angie, and a brother, Chris. He graduated college last year and got on as a techie at Orion Research. He's really smart."

We stopped at the corner, waiting for the light to change. Wei tilted her head and studied my face. "Your dad's Alan Oberon, right?"

I nearly fell off the curb. "How did you know that?" It's not like I'd told her anything about me. Did Sal? Why would she care, anyway? It's not like my father was anyone.

"After Sal told me about your mother, I told my mom and she asked what your name was. She said she knew him. Her and Dad and Sal's dad, too, were friends with your mom and dad."

My heart nearly stopped. They knew my father? "You're kidding." '

"Nope. Let's go this way." She turned onto Lincoln at Belden, and I followed.

I could hardly believe my luck—I hadn't even had a chance to think about finding my dad. Not since Sal's kiss. "Wait—what's your parents' names? Maybe Gran knows them."

"My dad's Jonathan Jenkins."

Jenkins. This was almost too good to be true. "There's this picture my Gran has. It's your dad standing with mine. They were standing in front of a place called Robin's Roost. I—I went by there the other day."

"Oh yeah, Dad's mentioned that hotel before." Wei stopped to look at clothes in the window of a top-tier boutique. "Hey, my parents want to meet you. "

My heart was pounding so hard I thought the whole city could hear it. They knew my father. I was going to meet someone, besides Gran and Pops, who actually *knew* my father. I wondered if they knew he was alive, if they would help me find him.

I glanced up the street and saw Dee with some of her friends.

"Hey, Dee . . . wait up," I hollered. Then I turned to Wei. "When can I meet your dad?"

"I'll ask and let you know tomorrow. I'd better get home and hit the piano. See ya." She headed up the street and I hurried to catch up with Dee, practically vibrating with excitement.

Wei's parents knew him. My brain was spinning with thoughts of Ginnie and my father. How different things might have been for all of us if only—

I caught myself. Ginnie'd said he was alive. If we'd been together as a family, I might have known Wei for years, since we were little. Would I—would we have been a top-tier, a tier ten, like her? I could hardly imagine it. My life would have been nothing like it was. But . . . then I wouldn't have had Dee, and I didn't like that thought, not at all.

Too wrapped up in my own thoughts, I stepped off the curb without a glance at traffic. A green transport whizzed around the corner, just missing me. "Stupid jerk!" The near miss brought me back to earth. The trannie had come out of nowhere—for a second, I thought it had actually swerved toward me. I hurried across and caught up with Dee.

XVIII

Gran and I moved Dee down the hall to her own room that evening. I snuggled under the covers, supposedly reading my Language & Literature homework, alone. In reality, my thoughts were hip-hopping around: Sal . . . my dad . . . the kiss . . . Ginnie . . . my dad . . . Sal . . .

My PAV beeped. Who would be calling me this late? I checked the receiver. Sandy.

We hadn't talked in days—not since before Sal's kiss. I had no intention of telling her about that, but it seemed like my life was now divided up into BK and AK (before kiss and after kiss). It was no wonder I couldn't concentrate. I clicked on the PAV. "What's up?"

"I meant to call you earlier, but this is the first chance I've had—school is murder. I have so much homework!"

Poor Sandy. I'd always helped her out with classes and homework. Without my tutoring, I imagined it was a lot harder for her than usual. I missed getting together with her after school at the modular. Dee would watch the FAV or do her homework while I helped Sandy figure out Government or Health and Sociology. Sandy wasn't dumb, she just had a hard time staying focused. And the closer she got to sixteen, the harder it was for her.

"So how's things with you? Hanging with all the upper-tiers yet?" she asked.

"Different." I wasn't going to complain. Gran and Pops were trying—but they were old, not like Ginnie at all. "Pops falls asleep early, sometimes even before dinner. Gran spends a lot of time with Harriet. Dee's all wrapped up in her friends. The guys are guys. I miss you."

"Aren't all your old friends at Daley?" She sounded lonely. Which made me a little homesick for her.

"Everyone has their own tier clique," I said. "So I mostly hang with Mike and Derek. There is this one girl, but . . ." Midsentence I changed my mind about telling her about Wei. "She's in my homeroom, that's all."

"What about Sal? Do you see him?"

"Sometimes. The guys hang out with him more." I wasn't lying—that was true. I didn't want to go into details, not yet anyway. I changed the subject. "You got a boyfriend yet?"

"There's this new guy, Lochlan. He's ultra!" Her melancholy tone switched to bubbly as she caught me up on all the boys in her class. Ones I didn't remember as being cute three weeks ago were now "so hot you'd melt," and everyone was paying attention to her. "Sixteen" was all over her conversation.

"Skivs!" she interrupted herself. "I almost forgot why I called. It's about Ed."

"What about him?" Just the thought of him made me angry.

"He was at school today. I just know he's going to be the Chooser. Do you think you could talk to him? Pleeeeeeease?"

"No." Dammit. I did not want to talk about Ed, think about Ed, or ever have a conversation with him again as long as I lived. Wasn't it enough that I had to think about him to make sure Dee was safe?

"Oh, come on. It's not like you have to see him or anything. I really, really, really need to get into FeLS. My mom is expecting me to get in. She's already planning where we'll move to when I start getting paid. It'll kill her if I'm not chosen."

"It will not kill her," I said. There was nothing keeping Mrs. Eskew from getting a job; then they'd have twice the credits they had now and could afford to move.

"Come on, Nina." Sandy didn't let up. "Ed would probably do it for you because of your—" She stopped herself, which was a good thing, considering how my temper was rising.

I felt the blood pounding into my temples "What, Sandy? Because of Ginnie? I don't think her death miraculously turned him into a nice guy."

"Well . . . I guess . . . I kinda thought . . ."

"You thought? After the way he treated her? You think he's sorry? You think it makes any difference to him that she's dead? He didn't have a problem beating the crap out of her himself. He was mean enough—he could have had something to do with her death. Did you ever think of that, Sandy?"

"Nina, calm down. I only meant that—"

"He never stopped by to see what happened, or how Dee was doing. All he did was send some stupid thugs over to pick up his precious FAV and his disgusting vids. He's made one lousy call to Dee—and all he said to her was he'd heard about Ginnie on the news. The *news!* I doubt it was even on the news. No tier-two murder makes Media headlines. He's a lying, cheating, filthy skiv."

"Nina, maybe he called Dee because he wanted to make sure she was all right. He asked me if you guys were happy living with your grandparents. He thought maybe they were too old to take care of Dee."

The hairs on the back of my neck stood up and I tried desperately to remember that Sandy was my best friend. Ed could try to contest Gran and Pops's guardianship, claiming they were unable to take proper care of Dee because they were old. I couldn't let that happen—I couldn't let Dee become his Cinderella girl. I didn't say anything, just tried to calm down so I didn't lash out at Sandy again.

After a long moment of silence, Sandy said, "It was a bad idea, Nina. I'm sorry."

My anger lessened, but I was more anxious than ever. "It's okay." I should have been used to Sandy by now. More often than not, her mouth spoke before she had a chance to think about what was she was saying. We'd stayed friends because I'd always understood that and never held what she said against her. I hoped I could get back to that place.

We talked a little while longer about nothing special, and finally Gran called for lights-out. I knew she meant it for Dee, but I took the opportunity to say good-bye. I didn't trust what else I might say.

I lay awake for the longest time. Ed. Dee said that he told her he was away on business when Ginnie was killed. I knew that was him I'd seen at the hospital. And that line about seeing the report on the Media was bunk. I hadn't seen any news stories about Ginnie's murder. She wasn't anybody important, except to me and Dee. A back-alley stabbing of some tier-two woman was hardly newsworthy. But Ed had sent those guys over to get the FAV, so clearly he knew what was going on. I suppose he might have called her work and found out, or found out through his job.

I had to keep him away from Dee. He didn't want to be a father to her—he didn't want to be a father to his actual family. She'd end up as his family's Cinderella girl and there wouldn't be anything I could do about it.

I tossed and turned for hours. Finally, exhausted, I fell into a fitful sleep filled with strange dreams. Ginnie was in them, and Ed, too. He had Dee, and Ginnie was chasing him in a red trannie. I was riding Pepper and caught up to him at the edge of the river. I grabbed Dee just as he was getting ready to throw her into the water. Ginnie slammed into him with the transport and jumped out as he disappeared under the water. "Good work," she said to me.

I woke up to what I thought was Ginnie's voice through the Infinity machine. It was only Gran's alarm saying, "*Edith, it is six-oh-five. Do you wish to snooze?*"

I heard her shuffle down the hallway to the bathroom. "Oh, shut up," she grumbled. I knew exactly how she felt. Pulling the covers over my head, I tried to shake off the dread that was growing inside me.

While Dee was in her room getting ready for school, I told Gran and Pops what Sandy had said about Ed.

"The stinking weasel." Pops snorted. "First calling Dee, and now this. Who does he think he is asking whether or not we're healthy?"

Gran poured him some coffee and set the pot down like it weighed a ton.

He took a sip. "Healthy as a damn horse!" He slapped his chest, which set off a coughing fit.

I had to look away in order to keep from laughing, or crying. He wasn't healthy at all. I wasn't sure about Gran.

"It's not so strange," Gran said, putting toast and orange juice in front of me. "Sometimes people get to feeling guilty when someone dies."

"What would Ed have to feel guilty about?" I said bitterly. Beating my mother? "He never wanted to take care of Dee when Ginnie was alive. I don't understand his sudden interest in her now, unless he wants her for a Cinderella girl."

"That'll never happen. Not while I'm alive." Pops set his cup down so hard, coffee sloshed over the side.

Gran rolled her eyes at him. "He didn't spent time with her before?" she asked me.

"Not much. I mean, he'd say that he loved her and all, because she's his daughter. But he never came over just to hang out, like a real dad would have."

"I'm sure Ginnie was protecting you both," Pops chimed in.

"Protecting them from what?" Gran asked carefully. She gave him her version of the evil eye.

"You know . . . FeLS and this whole Cinderella business . . ." He cleared his throat. "Things aren't always what they seem."

"What do you mean, Pops?" I asked.

Pops took a drink of his coffee. "Whew! Good and strong today, Edith." I waited while he took another sip. "Now, Little Bit . . ." He looked across the table at me. "When I say things aren't what they seem, what I mean is . . . well . . ." He stopped and looked at Gran, who had one eyebrow cocked and was staring him down. "Well," he went on, "I mean that . . ." He paused and looked at her again.

"Well, old man?" Danger dripped from her words.

Pops glared back at her. The air between them was thick with secrets.

"It's okay, Pops. I think I know what you mean."

"Really?" He set his cup down and rubbed the back of his neck, avoiding Gran's eyes.

"It's just one of those things people say—right?"

Pops nodded and Gran gave him a look I couldn't read before she turned back to the cook center to finish scrambling up the tofu. I sipped my orange juice quietly, watching them both.

***

Mike, Derek, and I walked Dee to school like normal, but Ed was still foremost in my thoughts. I needed help—this was not something I could do alone. They had to know something was up, since I dragged them along with me to Dee's school. As far as I was concerned, they could get used to it, because I was planning on walking Dee from the transit stop to school every day for the rest of my life.

As soon as Dee and her friends turned down the street to school, I told Mike and Derek about how I'd promised Ginnie I'd keep Dee away from Ed, my conversation with Gran, and Ed's phone call to Dee.

"I'd say Gran's right," Derek said. "He probably feels guilty for being such a jerk."

"Who's a jerk?" Sal walked up behind us.

"Ed," Mike said.

"Who's Ed?"

"He's Dee's father." I filled him in on what I'd told the others. "I'm worried that he wants her for a Cinderella girl."

There had been two Cinderellas in my school in Cementville. They were never on time, always looked tired, and left right after the final bell. I don't think I saw them talk to anyone. Not that anyone, even tier-ones, wanted to associate with Cinderellas. No way was I going to let that happen to Dee.

"Don't you think he just—" Sal began.

"Listen." Derek jumped in like he used to when we were little and I needed protecting from some bigger kid who was picking on me. "You don't know the whole story. Ed's worse than a dog with Dark Side fever."

Sal's forehead wrinkled. "Nina?"

"I'll—Derek's right. Ed's no good."

"Maybe he thinks Ginnie had a bunch of credits stashed somewhere and he wants them," Derek said.

"Maybe he's a government spy and Ginnie was really a NonCon?" Mike said, laughing. He couldn't have had any idea of the effect his words had on me. It wasn't like I hadn't thought that myself sometimes, especially lately. Ginnie certainly wasn't shy about her views. And Ed was a Chooser—that was a government job. My heart beat faster.

"Maybe you guys have been watching too many detective AVs," Sal said. "Dee's his daughter and he's just looking out for her."

"Seriously, Sal." Mike shook his head. "You don't know what you're talking about. Nina'll tell you—that Ed skiv makes my dad look like a hero."

A sharp gust of wind crashed into me and I heard Pops's words again. Things aren't always what they seem. I was afraid he was right.

XIX

Wei caught up with me in the hall after the last bell. "Nina! Where are you going?"

"I was looking for Sal." I had a little bit of time before I had to meet Dee.

"He might have left after fourth period. I didn't see him on the way to my last class. I usually do."

"Oh." Apparently my disappointment showed.

She studied me through her choppy black bangs. "You like him, don't you?"

"He's nice." That sounded lame even to me. But at least I wasn't being all sex-teen and gushing about him.

She smiled. "Yeah, he is. Come on, I'll walk with you."

Outside in the late fall sun stood Mike and Derek, and Sal, too. My heart made a little leap when I saw him and I couldn't hide the smile that played around my lips.

"Thought the teacher kept you after school," Derek teased me. "You been bad?"

"Shut up." I poked a finger into his ribs.

He jumped backward. "Hey now . . . watch it."

"Yeah," Mike said, "you might bruise his tender widdle body."

Derek shoved Mike and Mike shoved back. Wei and I just rolled our eyes at that kind of mock fighting guys start doing when they're little kids and never seem to stop. When Mr. Haldewick appeared on the top step, tapping his ever-present pointer and frowning at them, they quit.

Sal took my arm and steered me away from everyone's chatter. "Let's go to the park."

"I need to make sure Dee gets home okay from school first."

"I'll go with you." We said good-bye to the rest of the crowd, and he walked alongside me, close enough to make my insides smile no matter what we were talking about. "Tell me about this Ed guy."

In the ten minutes it took us to get to the transit stop where Dee would meet me, I told him pretty much everything about Ed. Except the vids. I couldn't talk about that with Sal.

We got to the transit stop, and I spotted Dee on the other side of the street, looking in a shop window. At the same time I saw Ed sitting in a green transport—one that looked just like the transport that had narrowly missed me the day before. He wasn't alone, though. There was a woman in the passenger seat, but I didn't recognize her.

"Sal—that's Ed." I grabbed Sal's arm and pointed to the green trannie idling at the intersection, close to Dee. Panic rushed over me. "DeeDee!" I yelled, and threw my arms up in the air, waving. "Here! I'm over here!"

I dashed across the street. Luckily, no one was coming. The trannie screeched into gear and sped off. Sal followed.

"Neens!" Dee cried. "Are you crazy? You could've got hit!"

"I'm fine, Dee. I—I didn't want you to miss us, because . . .

uh . . ." I leaned over, panting. "Help me out here," I whispered up to Sal, who was looking at me like I'd lost my mind.

"Because Nina and I are going for a walk and she can't wait to be alone with me." He winked at Dee.

"Are you her boyfriend?" Dee said.

"Maybe." Sal grinned at her. "Does she need one?"

"All girls do," Dee said. "Especially when they're practically sixteen."

I'm sure I turned as red as my jacket. I wished someone would invent blush control.

The number 33 transit pulled up. Dee boarded first. I was getting on when Sal whispered, "So, Nina. *Do* you need a boyfriend?"

The feel of his breath on my neck and the faint smell of some kind of aftershave, maybe Orion, made me all quivery inside. I couldn't deny that it felt good. I didn't need a boyfriend—I was not a sex-teen. But maybe I wanted one? It had to be possible to like someone and not go crazy over them. I hoped so, at least.

Sal took my hand, twining his fingers between mine. Much too soon, we were home and the three of us got off the trans.

"Dee, tell Gran I'll be up in a bit to help with dinner."

Sal and I watched Dee until she got in the elport.

"Walk?" he asked.

I nodded. The Chicago River was across the street, just south of the apartment building. That's the direction Sal took.

"So are you sure that the green trannie was Ed?" Sal asked.

"No doubt. I'd never forget someone I despise as much as him."

"Okay. Don't worry, Dee's fine right now and we'll figure out something to make sure she stays that way." He gave my hand a squeeze; I squeezed back.

The river was lined on both sides with small green oases divided by grimy stretches of concrete. The one we stopped in had a maple tree with a few faded yellow leaves hanging on against the chill wind. Chipped planters held what had once been flowers, but were now brown, withered pom-poms quivering atop brittle stalks. The river rolled by, the promise of winter riding its dark choppy waves.

Thanks to Ginnie, I'd always been somewhat aware of the audio surveillance police, but ever since the recent NonCon incidents downtown, and after seeing Gran's scrambler, I'd been thinking more and more about the ASP listening in on everything. "Is it safe? Can we talk here?"

"Not a problem, this one's DZ."

A dead zone. "Really? How do you know that?" I said.

He shrugged. "I get around. You find out things when people aren't paying attention to you."

"Like when you dress homeless?" I'd never asked him about that day I'd met him.

He laughed. "Yeah. Like that."

We sat down on a metal bench, the coldness of the seat shooting like ice straight through my jeans. I shivered.

"You cold?"

"Yes." I was not going to admit where I was cold. "I need my gloves . . ." I started to retrieve them from my pockets, but Sal grabbed my hands and clasped them in his.

"Let me warm them up. What kind of work did your father do?" Sal concentrated on rubbing my frozen fingers.

"I don't know," I confessed. "He died the night I was born. Gran said he was on the debate team in high school and then in college. But after that . . . no one ever told me what he did."

"Do you know anything about his debates?"

"Just that they were pro-citizen, anti-Media. We never really talked about him. I guess it was too much for Ginnie." My ignorance about my father's life made me uncomfortable. Ginnie hadn't talked much about him and Gran and Pops focused on his childhood when they told me about things he'd done.

"Do you have any of his writings or any of his notes?"

"No." I cocked my head. "Why do you want to know?" Why did he care so much about my father in the first place?

"Just wondered." He raised his eyes—his face close to mine. I didn't want to talk about my father. I wanted Sal to kiss me. He didn't. Instead, he said, "You know that Wei's dad knew him? And mine did, too."

I dropped my gaze, embarrassed that I'd been hoping for a kiss. "She told me."

"Warmer?"

I nodded and he let go of my hands, putting his arm around me instead. "Do you ever wonder if your father's really dead?"

I stiffened. That was not a random question. Extricating myself from his grasp, I stood up, pulled out my gloves, and put them on while Sal watched.

Finally, I trusted myself to speak. "Why are you asking me all these questions? You seem to know more about my father than I do." I searched his eyes—they were as unreadable as the murky water below. "I want to know what's going on, Sal."

"I can't exactly say." He was hedging; I could tell. "I don't know much."

"Much? How do you know anything?" Then what Pops had said that morning hit me: things aren't always what they seem. "Are you only interested in me because of my dad? Is that it?" I took a step backward.

"Of course not." He reached for my hand, but I evaded him.

I felt so stupid. He was using me. I'd been craving a kiss, when all Sal wanted was information about my father. Why was Sal asking about whether or not he was dead? I hadn't said anything about what Ginnie said that night she died. Why did he—or even Wei—want to know anything about my father? Sal's parents were dead—it wasn't like he talked to them the night before about this girl he knew who was Alan Oberon's daughter. A couple strolling along the path stopped right behind us.

"Come here." Sal took my arm, but I pulled away. "I don't want other people to hear us," he whispered. "Come on."

I wanted to pull away, to run home, away from him. But I also needed answers. I followed him closer to the river.

"When my mom and dad died they were on assignment for the Media, following up on a lead about your father. Alan Oberon was the leader of the NonCons in the Americas. Rumor was that he hadn't drowned that night. He supposedly found out his family—you, Nina—was in danger and faked his own death. He'd been seen in the Hebrides off the Greater United Isles. There are supposedly a lot of NonCons hiding out there. They put my dad on that assignment because he knew Alan."

"What are you talking about?" My head was spinning.

"NonCons? You're saying my father is a criminal—no, the leader of the criminals!"

"NonCons aren't criminals." He looked at me with disbelief. "Don't you read history?"

"I'm not stupid," I huffed. "I know history."

"You know Media's version. The GC controls the Media, and shapes people's perception of what goes on. They've been doing it for at least two centuries. Your father spoke out against their manipulation and the GC's interference."

"But . . . but things are good," I said, more out of anger than true belief. I thought back to my conversation with Gran. "Life used to be awful—wars, incurable diseases, hunger, homelessness. Now everything is the way it should be."

Sal stared at me, his eyes opened wide. "You believe that?"

A voice in the back of my head, that sounded a whole lot like Ginnie, whispered, *You're lying. You know better.* I ignored it. I didn't care if it was true or not. I'd been stupid to let myself think Sal cared about me, that he was my boyfriend. My heart was breaking in two; he didn't want me. He wanted my father; he wanted information.

I glared back at him. "What else should I believe? Look around."

"I am looking around. And what I see is that the GC and Media tell you where to live, what to wear, what to want, when to grow up, how to act, and who to be. The government tags you with a GPS and then brands you like you're nothing more than property. Doesn't that make you mad, Nina?" He raised his eyebrows and stared at me. "GPSs don't keep girls safe—a GPS is called, knowing where everyone is all the time. A tattoo doesn't make you an adult. And no tattoo is going to save you in some dark alley; just the opposite, you'd be considered fair game. The only information anyone gets is from Media. Haven't you ever wondered what goes on in places when Media cameras aren't there? Do you think life really is as great as the Governing Council says it is?"

I couldn't stand the way Sal was looking at me like I was an idiot.

"Maybe I don't know everything you know." My voice was shaking, and I could feel the tears crowding to get out. "But I know who I am." It wasn't like I hadn't thought about the tattoo as a brand, a visual vert proclaiming "legal sex here." The vision of those 'letes in the park flashed through my brain. But my emotions had taken over and I wasn't about to back down.

"Media tells you who you're supposed to be, but is that who you really are? What about the you that exists outside of their parameters? I never would've thought Alan Oberon's daughter would be satisfied with Media's status quo."

A hot spike of anger rose up inside me. I was tired of Sal telling me what to do, what to think. I took a step toward him and jabbed my finger in his chest. "You listen to me, Sal Davis. The GC may not be perfect, but things are a hell of a lot better than they were during the Religion Wars and Gang Rule and even when Fems were in power. And who are you to tell me what to think?" I planted my feet and jammed my fists onto my hips.

"Whatever you say." He held up his hands and backed off.

I wasn't done. "And don't you dare talk to me about my father. If you knew all you claim to know about him, you wouldn't be asking me all these questions about him. I have friends of my own, friends that don't care whose daughter I am. I'm sorry your mom and dad got killed chasing some story about my father, but you know what? That wasn't my fault."

I'd turned to go when he said, "What about Dee?" I spun around. His jaw was set—his eyes flashing. I couldn't believe I'd trusted him—I thought he'd liked me for me. I was wrong.

"What about her?" I shot back.

"Ed, her father. What do you know about him?"

"What do you care?" I knew plenty. He was a cheater, an abuser, an exgovernment agent who was now a Chooser, a skiv who'd rather watch sixteens have sex on vids than turn them into FeLS, and a jerk of a father who wanted to turn my little sister into a Cinderella girl. But I wasn't about to tell Sal any of that. "I know that he made Ginnie's life miserable," was all I said.

"How'd she meet him?"

"At her work."

"How long did she—"

"I don't know and I don't care," I snapped. "You can quit with the questions. My life is not your business. It wasn't your business two weeks ago, it isn't your business now. If you want to know about Alan Oberon, you can put on your homeless disguise and go find out on your own."

I strode up the incline and down the street. This time when I walked away, I didn't look back.

XX

At about ten p.m. my PAV beeped. I didn't bother to look at the receiver to see who it was before clicking it on.

"Shame about your mother."

Ed. My heart nearly stopped.

"Not even a hello?"

"What do you want?" I said.

"I want to see my daughter." He laughed.

I didn't know what to say, so I said nothing.

"Is there a problem? I would have called your grandparents, but they aren't her grandparents, so it seems ridiculous for me to ask their permission to see my daughter."

Ginnie's words clanged in my ears like a fire alarm: keep Ed away from Dee. Legally, he had a right to see her. My mind raced for an excuse, any excuse. Anything to buy some time. "She's still having a hard time with Ginnie's death," I said. "Maybe it's not a good time to see her. It's a reminder—"

"I'm her father," he said. "She needs a parent."

"She's got me. I know her better than anyone. Ginnie told me to take care of her and that's what I'm doing."

"You aren't even sixteen." He snorted. "And when you do turn sixteen, the last thing you'll want is the responsibility of a kid. First time a guy looks at you, you'll be out there fu—"

"I will not!" I would never be a crazed sex-teen. Guilt about the feelings and thoughts I'd had about Sal rushed through me. "I'm Dee's sister, I will *always* take care of her." A thought occurred to me: What if Ed was right downstairs? Or worse—right outside our door. Goose bumps broke out on my arms. "Ginnie named Gran and Pops Dee's legal guardians. Even if they aren't her real grandparents, you'll have to ask them when you can see her."

"When I want to see her," Ed said, "I won't ask. And no one will stop me. Understand?" He clicked off.

For a full five minutes I was frozen to the spot with fear and rage. Then I started pacing my room, like a feral cat in a cage. It seemed like forever before I could form a coherent thought. Exhausted, I finally collapsed on my bed. Staring out the window, I watched the lights of the building across the way. They went out, one by one.

I tried to calm my racing mind. I knew Sal was right about most of what he'd said; it was the exact same thing Ginnie had said. But that didn't make me any less angry at him for deceiving me. Or at myself, for letting him get to me, for slipping so easily into sex-teen, for wanting him to kiss me so badly. I remembered our kiss in the park, and sank even lower. This wasn't working. I had to stop thinking about Sal.

I thought about my father.

Ginnie had to be right; he had to be alive. He just had to. And now I needed to find him more than ever. Gran and Pops were no match for Ed, whether the law was on their side or not. And I had a feeling Ed would figure out some way to make it "not." He had connections, at least that's what he'd always said. Even if my father had disappeared because he didn't want me, I was sure that he loved Gran and Pops. He couldn't let someone like Ed take away a granddaughter they loved. But how could I find him? I was chasing a ghost.

Wei. Her parents knew him, knew Ginnie. Maybe they could help. That was my only hope.

I lay down, but my thoughts still raced. By the time I'd fallen asleep, some of the lights across the way had come back on.

***

Next morning, halfway on the way to Dee's school, we ran into Wei.

"Hey, where you guys headed?" she asked.

"We're going by Dickens to drop off Dee," I said.

"Cool." She looked at Dee. "Can I walk with you?"

Dee, wide-eyed, nodded. I could see she was impressed that a high school girl, and a top-tier one at that, would hang out with her. They walked ahead of us. Every so often Wei would lean down and whisper in Dee's ear. I could hear Dee laugh; at least that felt good.

Mike, Derek, and I trailed behind. They talked about Derek's music show at a new coffeehouse next weekend where he was playing with his brother, Riley. I was silent. When we got within half a block of Dee's school, Maddie and a couple of Dee's other friends joined us. We watched them meld into the crush of kids waiting for the first bell.

"She's cute," Wei said. "I wish I had a little sister. Can we share her?"

"Sure." Wei and I had only known each other a few days—I wondered about her sudden interest in Dee. Then I realized Sal must have said something to her about Ed. It steamed me that Sal was broadcasting my problems around, but I liked Wei too much to be angry with her.

"How about after school we all go to TJ's? Does Dee like tofu fries?"

"They're her favorite."

"Mine, too." She stopped in front of a three-story brownstone, the really cool kind with the curved windows and gargoyles on the gutter spouts. "This is where I live. It's almost three hundred years old."

"Wow!" Derek said. "I love old things, like houses and music."

"Me, too." Wei gave him a sweet smile.

It's funny, there was such a difference between her smile and the one Sandy'd aimed toward Sal at the zoo. Sandy's had been so . . . fake and sixteen. Wei's was so . . . I wasn't sure what, but definitely different from Sandy's. They were both pretty, but Wei was *ultra*. Guys definitely noticed her, but not in a leering way, the way they noticed Sandy. Even though Wei was sixteen, she didn't act like it. At least not like the sixteens in my old school, the ones Sandy was desperate to be like. And definitely not like *XVI Ways* said sixteens acted. Was it because she was upper tier, or was it just her attitude?

A wave of longing for Ginnie washed over me. I shook it off. Sometimes I couldn't help being mad at her for dying.

"There's my dad." Wei pointed up to the second floor on the right and waved. The silhouette of a man waved back. "I'll share him with you, Nina—like you're sharing Dee with me—okay?"

"Sure." I squinted up at the dark figure in the window. I had to fight back the urge to suggest going inside right then so I could meet him. I didn't want to push it, afraid of blowing my chance at getting more information about my parents, maybe even a lead on my father's whereabouts.

"What's he doing home now?" asked Derek.

"He's a writer."

"That's cool," Derek said. "Wish my dad did something neat. He's just a tech at Onadrell.

"Wish my dad did something, period." Mike kicked a rock, sending it halfway down the block.

"My brother, Chris, is a tech," Wei said. "You've got to be really smart to be one." She looked right at Derek when she said that, and his neck turned crimson. I thought it was cute, and I hoped it meant that he found her interesting. Even though he hadn't said anything else to me about his feelings, I didn't think I'd dodged that laser yet. It'd make everything easier if he and Wei . . . well, it would keep my friendship with him on the right track.

Wei leaned in to me and whispered, "If you ever need help, someone's home almost all the time."

Her words should have made me feel better. Instead, they scared me half to death. I didn't want to admit, even to myself, that things were getting beyond my control. But Wei had noticed. And if a girl I'd just met a few days before was concerned enough to offer her house as a safe place, I couldn't deny it any longer.

***

Nothing happened at school except school. I didn't see Sal, which was good, because I was still angry—at both of us.

On the way to pick up Dee I told Wei about Ed calling me. "I didn't have time to tell Gran and Pops, and I don't want to worry them. They don't need any trouble because of me or Dee."

"We'll talk to my dad about this," Wei said. "He'll know what to do." She hooked her arm in mine. "Don't worry, no one will take Dee. I promise."

A tiny bit of optimism lodged in my heart. I hoped she was right. I'd been reckless, bold in my conversation with Ed the night before, when I'd challenged his authority to take Dee. In the past, when I mouthed off to him, Ginnie had taken the brunt of his anger. With her gone, I had every reason to believe that given the chance, he'd be more than happy to take a swing at me. Maybe Mr. Jenkins could reassure me that the legal guardianship was something Ed couldn't ignore.

We picked up Dee and went to TJ's. She'd never been to a place like that, filled with high school kids.

"Can I tune into the aud, Nina?"

"Sure, DeeDee, you pick." I swiped several credits into the music box. I was getting low—I hoped the government would start our survivor benefits soon. Dee punched in her picks and tuned her PAV into the channel.

Dee sat in the booth, eating fries, sipping a Sparkle, and moving in time to the music. Her eyes darted around taking in the scene. There were 'letes with their letter jackets acting like, well . . . like 'letes. Their girlfriends, either real or wannabes, were hanging over their booths or sitting elsewhere, giggling and making eyes at them. A group of techies drew diagrams on napkins, talking in a language only they could understand. Some music guys were drumming on their table and mouthing the words of whatever they were listening to. A couple of people had their viewers on. I thought it was more fun to look at the people instead of a vid you could see anytime. Wei and I sat and watched; it was too noisy to have any sort of conversation.

It was weird—I hardly knew Wei, but I felt so at ease with her. It wasn't like we were that similar: aside from the connection between her father and mine, we were at opposite ends of the tiers. Although I had to admit, her attitude wasn't like most high-tier girls. I wondered if she was only being friendly to me because our parents had been close.

I tamped down my insecurity. I didn't think Wei was like Sal. Wei's family wanted to meet me, and she was eager to give me information about my father, not just ask me a bunch of questions.

Sal. Why did he get to me so much? I wanted to just be able to forget about him, but I couldn't stop thinking about him. About how I'd been so eager to be close to him, and now . . . Heat crept up my neck just thinking about how I'd stood there, waiting for him to kiss me. Wanting him to kiss me. Instead I'd been grilled for information about my dad. The humiliation stung as much as it had the night before.

As we were leaving, Wei asked, "Can you come to my house for dinner tonight?"

"Sure." My pulse quickened—I could meet her family, I could find out about my dad. "I need to take Dee home first. You want to come with us and meet Gran and Pops?"

"Sure."

"You've gotta watch out for Pops," Dee cautioned. "He's kind of silly and sometimes he doesn't have his leg on."

"He's got a bio-limb?"

"Nah," Dee said. "It's an old GI leg. The government wouldn't give him the good kind. He hates the government."

"DeeDee!" I shot her a disapproving look. "He doesn't hate the government. He's just mad . . ." Ginnie hadn't been quite as careful about airing her views on the GC around Dee as she had been with me. I guessed I'd have to have a talk with my little sister before she got herself, or anyone else, in trouble.

Wei laughed. "It's okay with me if he hates the government. No one I know likes it."

"Doesn't your dad work for Media? That's like working for the government."

"Boy, is it ever. Yes, he does. But . . . well . . ." She let that trail off, and Pops's cautionary words darted through my brain: things are not what they seem. It felt like that was becoming my mantra. Maybe Wei and her family were not what they seemed. I'd just have to wait and see.

***

We were almost to the apartment when my stomach dropped. How was our low-tier retirement community apartment going to look to someone who lived in a mansion? "Uh, Wei, our place is, well . . . we just moved and . . . the government benefits haven't—"

Wei laughed. "You think I care about all that tier crap?"

I smiled at her. "Some people do." My heart swelled and I instantly relaxed. I was so used to Sandy—everything tierwise mattered to her. It could be nice to hang out with someone who wasn't so caught up with tiers and sixteen, to talk with a friend who was more interested in things like music and art. I hoped Wei would want to be friends.

When we walked in, Pops was dozing in his favorite chair. He stirred when I shut the door.

"Hi, Little Bit, Deedles." His voice was heavy with sleep. He blinked. "Who's that with you?"

"Pops, this is Wei Jenkins. We're in school together."

"Hello, Miss Wei Jenkins." He straightened up, running a hand through his shock of wiry hair.

I could almost see him collecting his thoughts, like picking out favorite AV chips. Thank goodness he had his leg on.

"Jenkins, hmm. That name sounds familiar." He called into the other room, "Edie-hon, get out here, I need your memory—and we've got company." He smiled at Wei. "I apologize for not getting up. Old bones, you know. Pretty little thing, aren't you?"

She didn't blush, like I most certainly would've. "Thank you."

Gran walked into the room, wiping her hands on a towel tucked into her belt. "I'm making chocolate chip cookies." She saw Wei. "Hello."

"This is Wei Jenkins, Gran. She's a friend from school."

"Jonathan Jenkins's daughter," Gran said.

"I am," Wei said.

Gran turned to me. "It was Jonathan Jenkins in that picture we were looking at."

"Wei and I figured that out yesterday. I forgot to tell you." I didn't tell her why I'd forgotten—the fight with Sal.

"Wei, it's nice to meet you. Would you like to stay for dinner?" Gran asked.

"I was hoping Nina could come to dinner at my house tonight," Wei said. "Is that all right?"

"Of course. But don't forget it's a school night."

"Mom won't let us. Nina will be home before nine."

"Take a coat, dear." Gran fussed over me. "It's getting cold. And take the transit. I don't want you walking alone at night."

"Yes, Gran." I went for my coat. She didn't have to worry; I could take care of myself. Hadn't I been doing that for weeks now?

Minutes later Wei and I were outside waiting for the number 33. As it pulled up, I noticed a green trannie behind it. I craned my neck, trying to make out if it was Ed's. I couldn't get a clear view, to be sure. For a second, I wondered if I should not go to Wei's to watch out for Dee. But I couldn't not go—I needed to meet Mr. Jenkins. Just then, the green trannie sped up and passed the transit. I had to figure out some way to keep Ed from seeing Dee. At least for the time being, I didn't have to worry about tonight.

XXI

"I'm a little nervous," I confessed, which was a huge understatement. My brain was wagging back and forth between jitters and paralyzing panic. Somehow I'd managed to keep my body under control as we walked from the transit stop to Wei's house.

"Don't be. My parents are really easy to talk to."

"Mine, too." For a split second I thought, I can't wait to tell Ginnie about this when I get home tonight. Then I remembered. I'd never get to tell her anything again. Just when I'd think I had it all under control, a thought about Ginnie would spring up and I'd forget she was dead. I hoped someday I could think about her without wanting to cry. I struggled to get back into the moment, forcing myself to think about getting closer to finding my father. That was the most important thing I needed to do. I was doing it for Ginnie.

"You okay?"

I blinked furiously, trying to stop the tears. "Yeah."

With every step I willed myself back to that place where missing Ginnie was almost bearable. By the time we got to Wei's building, I'd succeeded.

There was a regular security panel on the front, but Wei didn't use it. She pressed a series of numbers into a keypad hidden behind the brass house numbers. A light beam shone into her eye and a moment later the door clicked open.

"What's that?"

"Retinal scan. Dad installed it. He loves gadgets."

The foyer of the brownstone was like a museum. The pink marble steps leading upstairs had deep depressions worn from centuries of people's feet climbing up and down. The brass rail was burnished to a shine by countless hands that had gripped it. A huge crystal chandelier illuminated the whole area, throwing shadows and shimmers everywhere.

"Wow!" My breath caught in my throat. "This is beautiful. I love it!"

"Me, too. Some people don't because it's so old. My sister, Angie, hates it. She couldn't wait to move out to some neo-mod in Grand Isle. Her husband's a tier-seven. She can be a real snob sometimes." She shook her head. "They could've lived here, on the first floor, but she didn't want to. So Dad put his office down here." She pointed to the right. "And that's a guest apartment." She pointed left. "You wanna see?"

"Sure."

Wei tried her father's office. "Locked." She shrugged. "We'll try the apartment." She turned the knob, and we walked in.

"Everything in here's kind of old," Wei said. "It's mostly furnished with things we don't use anymore."

Old things? Everything I saw was ten times nicer than anything I'd ever had, or ever hoped to have. Even when we were tier five, our furniture wasn't this nice. I supposed high-tiers, like Wei, didn't think about things like that. I reddened as I imagined what she must have thought of where I lived now.

"Our whole house is safe, you know." Wei smiled. "You can say anything here and no surveillance will pick it up."

As she gestured, I noticed her tattoo. I wondered if she'd had sex."Can I ask you something?"

"Anything. I'm an unlocked text chip." She grinned at me. "Dad says people used to say, 'I'm an open book.' But hardly anyone reads books anymore, since they're all on chips or downloads."

"Ginnie did," I said. "Read real books, I mean. After she died, B.O.S.S. came to our house and confiscated most of them."

"No kidding? That's weird. I wonder if they go looking at everyone's stuff after they die."

"I don't think so," I said. Her XVI caught my eye again and I decided I'd better ask while I had the nerve. "Have you ever had, you know . . . sex?"

"No way." She put her hands on her hips. "And I won't until I'm ready. No guy better try to force himself on me, or he'll be sorry. I'm not a Cliste Galad student for nothing."

"Cliste what?" Her flashing eyes were evidence enough for me that any guy would've been a fool to mess with her.

"Cliste Galad. It's a kind of martial arts I'm learning. It's a combination of Eastern mysticism and Celtic warrior fighting."

"Is it hard to learn?"

"Not for me," she said. "But I guess it could be. I think it will come in real handy for keeping guys in their place." She laughed. "I bet you don't want to have sex yet either, do you?"

I shook my head. "I've seen—" I started to say something about Ed's sex vids, but stopped myself. I wasn't sure how much I should or shouldn't say to Wei. I didn't want to ruin what could be a good friendship by telling her how typical my low-tier life had been.

"Mom has drilled into my head that women are not sex objects, and that sixteen-year-old girls are not walking sex-bots, like Media portrays them. And those vids in Health class? If some guy tried that stuff with me, I'd send him on a one-way trip to the moon. We're supposed to like guys talking us into having sex? I don't think so. Not this girl."

I couldn't help but laugh. The how-to sex vids that we watched in school were pretty ridiculous.

"We should get upstairs," Wei said, walking toward the apartment door. "They're probably waiting for us." She shut the door carefully, and we climbed the stairs.

I had the strangest sensation as my hand glided up the brass banister. "Do you ever feel like you are somehow touching all those people from the past who used to live here?"

"Uh-huh. It's like this continual connection with history. Mom says that people carry the wisdom of the ages inside them. But mostly no one wants to look that closely at themselves. Mom practices ancient healing methods and uses herbs and charms and all kinds of things that the world has forgotten. She's got all kinds of strange stuff up on the third floor. She'd show you sometime, if you wanted to see."

We stopped in front of a pair of dark wooden doors that had huge ornate brass doorknobs. A U-shaped object hung in the middle of one.

"What's that?" I pointed to it.

"A door knocker." She demonstrated its purpose by lifting and then dropping it. There was a sharp retort that echoed down the hallway. "Before viewers and buzzers, there were these. I live in an antique. See that?" She pointed to a little brass circle with a thick glass lens in the middle, right above the knocker. "It's a peephole, a primitive viewer. You look through it and can see whoever's on the other side."

I leaned in close to try it out. Just then the door opened, jerking me off balance, and I fell inside. A man caught me on the other side.

"This must be Nina." He didn't let go until he was sure I had my feet under me.

"Hi, Dad. Yep, she'd never seen a peephole before."

"Didn't bother to tell her they work much better from the other side, did you?"

She grinned at me. "Sorry."

"No biggie." I blushed.

Wei's father surveyed my face. "You look like your father . . . but those dimples. They're your mother's. She used to blush all the time, too." He winked at me.

That was news to me. Ginnie'd always been so self-assured, nothing ever seemed to rattle her. Maybe there was hope for me yet.

"Jade," he called out, "Nina's here."

Wei's mother was the most beautiful woman I'd ever seen. Her straight dark hair swung across her cheeks as she put her arms around me and hugged me tight the way mothers do. It felt so good, my heart ached. I could almost imagine she was Ginnie.

After a moment, she held me at arm's length and, like her husband, studied my face. "You are your father's daughter." She ran a perfectly manicured finger by the corners of my mouth.

"And I see Ginnie here." Her eyes clouded. "Your mother was the best friend I ever had."

"Really?" I choked back tears. "I didn't know that. She never—" I stopped, thinking it would be rude to say Ginnie'd never mentioned her.

"Of course you wouldn't have known. We hadn't seen each other since . . . well, the last time we were together, you were this big." She held her hands about a foot or so apart.

"I was a baby?"

"Yes. It was a wonderful time and also very sad, after your father . . ." She paused, and looked at Wei's dad, who gave an almost imperceptible shake of his head. "But tonight we're going to talk about good times. Shall we have dinner now? You girls must be starving."

***

I was so afraid of making some kind of stupid low-tier mistake during dinner that I kept quiet and mostly picked at my food. Later, in the living room, I perched on the edge of the sofa, determined not to miss a single word about my father and Ginnie.

"We grew up together, about five blocks from here," Mr. Jenkins said.

"Don't forget Sal's dad," Wei said.

"Yes, Brock lived on that block, too. In fifth grade we called ourselves the Outlanders, after the Resistance in *Mars Rising*. Do you know that story?"

"Yes," I said. "The B.O.S.S. agents confiscated our copy after Ginnie's death."

"What it's all come to." Mr. Jenkins sighed and shook his head. "I remember Brock's mother sewed us Outlander costumes to wear to school on Imagination Day."

"I have a picture of my dad in a cape with a big E on his chest. What was he like?" I wanted details. I knew how he looked; I wanted to know what kind of person my father was.

Mr. Jenkins laughed. "We were crazy kids, but . . ." His eyes got serious. "That was only the beginning."

"All the girls in school were crazy about Alan," Mrs. Jenkins said. "He was so handsome. Friends with everyone, but he only loved Ginnie."

I felt a stabbing sadness in my heart. My mother had a man who loved her like that and then . . . then she chose to be with Ed. If my father was in fact still alive, why hadn't she stayed with him? More than ever, I had to know what happened, why he'd left.

"Being a charmer was not his most important quality." Mr. Jenkins laughed. "He was clever, intelligent, and definitely had a way with words. As captain of the debate team, he could persuade nearly anyone to see his side of an argument. In tenth grade the Media recruited him to be prime anchor for their Chicago network. That was a plum tier-ten job. They awarded him a full-ride scholarship to college and drew up the contracts to be ready when he graduated."

"Was he nice?" I needed him to be a good person. Ginnie deserved to have been loved by someone who treated her good.

"To a fault," Mrs. Jenkins said. "That's what got him in trouble. He helped anyone less fortunate than himself. He couldn't pass a homeless person without stopping to ask if they needed any credits or food." She turned to her husband. "Remember when he tried to start that soup kitchen?"

"I sure do," Mr. Jenkins said. "Media found out about that side of him and, even though legally they had to make good on the scholarship, there was no job waiting for him after college."

They were talking so freely that I began to worry. "Is it safe? You know . . ."

"Surveillance? Don't worry," Mrs. Jenkins said. "It's perfectly safe here."

That's what Wei had said before, in the hallway. I wondered if they had a scrambler. Before I could ask, Mr. Jenkins started talking again.

"Alan won the Chicago regional debate of 2132," he said. "His name's engraved on a plaque in the Education Administration building on State and Adams in the Hall of Winners. It's in a display case halfway down the main hallway on the left." He winked at me, as if he knew I'd go looking for it. "Media tried to have it removed in 2135, but their plan backfired. The flurry of publicity around their efforts simply put him and his ideals more in the public eye."

"That was the debate about media versus free will, wasn't it?" There was that picture in Gran's album of my dad and his medal.

"Yes. He wasn't afraid to take on Media versus the rights of citizens; he strongly believed in government by the people, not by the Media."

"But you work for Media, don't you?" I didn't understand how a person could be associated with someone, or in this case, a business that they didn't trust or believe in.

"Yes, I do." Pausing, Mr. Jenkins unhurriedly traced the

patterned fabric of his armchair. Finally, he raised his eyes and looked straight into mine. "Over three thousand years ago a famous Asian general, Sun-tzu, said, 'Keep your friends close and your enemies closer.' Those are good words to live by."

He sounded like Ginnie. The only real enemy I had was Ed. The thought of being close to him sickened me.

"Dad," Wei said, "can you give Nina a chip of her father's debate? He explains it so well."

"You know I can't," Mr. Jenkins said. "Alan's speeches and debates are so radical they're considered contraband. If you're found with them, you can be arrested. Reassimilation is the usual course of remediation."

"Alan was on the Governing Council's watch list," Mrs. Jenkins explained. "His every move was scrutinized from the time he started openly debating against Media—and winning. If he'd never won, he'd be alive. If he hadn't died, he would've been reassimilated."

Since the start of our conversation, something had been nagging at the fringes of my brain.

"Wait—there was a vert disruption downtown the other day by a guy Derek said was the Eliminator. Is that my dad? Ginnie told me she thought he was alive and in Chicago." My pulse was racing so fast I felt light-headed. "She was right, wasn't she? That had to have been him. You said you guys called yourselves the Outlanders. One of them was the Eliminator. Dad's costume had a big E on it. It has to be him." I felt like I'd just won the Interstellar Lottery.

All three of them stared at me—then looked at each other.

No one said a word. I took a deep breath and explained more.

"Before Ginnie died, she told me my father was still alive. The other night Sal asked me if I'd ever thought he might not be dead and said that my father was a NonCon leader. Gran says Alan wasn't a radical, that he changed things by talking. Whatever the truth is—I need to know. Ginnie left me something to give to him. She said it had all the answers. Answers to what, I don't know. But if you know where he is, please tell me."

"I was there the night your father drowned," Mr. Jenkins said. "Alan and I were meeting at one of the oases. I arrived first and saw your father crossing the bridge. The streets were icy; a trannie swerved and knocked him off the bridge into the river. I think it was deliberate. The trannie disappeared down the street and your father disappeared into the water. I told the police what I had seen. Alan's body was never recovered."

"Ginnie wouldn't lie. And what about Sal?" I searched their faces for some glimmer of hope, but there was none.

"I'm so sorry, Nina." Mrs. Jenkins hugged me. This time it didn't make me feel anything at all.

"If we had more time tonight I would let you hear one of your father's speeches. But it's late. Next time you're over, if I'm not here, Wei knows where they are. You'll be sixteen soon and you need to know the things your father believed," Mrs. Jenkins said. "These are the things he would die for."

"Thank you."

"Have you filled out your FeLS application yet," Mrs. Jenkins asked.

"Ginnie bought my contract," I said. "It was one of the last things she did."

"I am so glad. Keep that contract in a safe place. We don't

believe that FeLS is exactly what the GC would like us to believe it is. I know that neither your mother nor your father would want you to end up in FeLS training."

"Gran's got it," I said. "I'm sure it's fine."

"Make sure it is secure," Mr. Jenkins said. "I'm sure the government would love to have Alan Oberon's daughter in their FeLS program. As if that might give it some respectability in the eyes of those who don't trust the government."

"My friend Sandy wants more than anything to be a FeLS. She thinks it's the only way she can get out of the low tiers. She even asked me to talk to Ed for her."

"Who's Ed?" Mr. Jenkins asked.

"He was Ginnie's boyfriend. She started seeing him when I was four or five. He got her pregnant with Dee and we moved out of Gran and Pops's. When Ed was transferred to Cementville, we went, too." I wasn't quite sure how much to say, but Wei's parents had been so kind, I kept on. "Ginnie kept us away from him as much as possible. He was abusive and mean. I don't know how she stood being around him."

"He's a Chooser, too," Wei said.

"He was at my old school the other day and was asking Sandy if Gran and Pops were healthy enough to take care of Dee. Then last night he called me and said he wanted to see Dee."

"That seems normal," Mr. Jenkins said. "He is her father."

"I know, but . . ." I had to trust them; there was nowhere else to turn. "Ginnie told me to keep him away from Dee, no matter what. After school today I saw him hanging around Dee's school. I'm afraid he might want to take her as a Cinderella girl."

"Sometimes biological fathers do that," Mrs. Jenkins said. "If he abducted your sister, it would be extremely difficult for you to get her back. He could even have her reassimilated into believing she wants to be with him."

"I won't let her out of my sight. But what can I do about school? Will she be safe there?"

"He'd have to have proof of paternity to get her, which he must not have or he'd have taken her already," Mr. Jenkins said. "What school does she attend?"

"Dickens." My stomach was churning. Not only were my hopes of finding my father in ruins, but now it was confirmed: Dee was in real danger from Ed.

"I have friends who work there," Mrs. Jenkins said. "Do you have a picture of Dee?"

I beamed a digi of Dee's school picture from my PAV to hers. "That's last year's," I said. "Her hair's longer now. Otherwise, she looks the same."

"You won't need to worry about her at school," she said. "I promise."

"What are you going to do?" It felt as if they had this whole network of people I couldn't see, but who were there to do things that needed to be done. It was surreal, but comforting, too, in a bizarre way. And, somehow, being with these people made me feel closer to Ginnie. I had a feeling she would've been happy I'd found them.

"My friends will keep an eye on Dee," Mrs. Jenkins said. "They are very trustworthy and will be sure that no one gets close to her. Would she be afraid of her father if he tried to take her?"

I shook my head. "She likes him. He's always been nice to her.

She never saw him hurt Ginnie. He never hit Mom when she was around."

A large clock in the corner struck the half hour. "You can count on us for help, but it's late now. Don't worry about Dee. Wei, you walk Nina to the bus stop."

"Sure. Let's go."

"Thank you for dinner, and for telling me about my dad." The numbness that had threatened to take over my heart, after their silent confirmation that Alan was dead, was being challenged by the insistent sound of Ginnie's words in my head. He was alive. They had to be mistaken.

Mrs. Jenkins bundled me up in my coat—just like Ginnie would've done. "Talk your friend out of FeLS. It is a dangerous business, not at all what it seems. You must convince her that even a low-tier existence is better than what lies beyond the FeLS training station."

"I'll try." I couldn't imagine anything I might say that would sway Sandy's determination to get into FeLS.

When we got outside, it was cold. And Mrs. Jenkins's warning about FeLS made it seem even colder. I tried to push those thoughts aside. I'd had enough for one night. I wanted normal—even if just for a few minutes.

"How come your parents don't mind you walking around alone after dark?" I asked Wei.

"Martial arts. I can show you some moves sometime, if you want."

"That would be ultra. Then if Ed shows up to try and take Dee . . ." I made some flailing motions with my arms. Wei and

I both laughed, and for a moment I felt like a normal girl with a friend, just being silly. But that feeling didn't last. I hesitated a moment before asking, "Did you see Sal today?"

She shook her head. "He wasn't at school. Why?"

"No reason. I didn't see him either and I wondered—that's all."

"Sal and I have known each other since we were babies. Since his parents died he hasn't let himself get close to anyone. He even tried backing off being close to me. I told him, 'No way, Salzo, we're tight till the end.' I know he's afraid of being hurt if something happens to anyone else he cares about. I also know he really likes you."

That didn't help my mood. We stood under the yellow glow of the streetlights on Clark, the cold November winds whipped around my legs, cutting through my jeans, chilling me to the core.

As I sat on the number 33, heading home, my thoughts turned to Sal, like I knew they would. After what Wei'd said, I could almost feel myself softening toward him. I wanted to believe her, that he liked me, really liked me. And I could, almost. At least until I remembered that the day we met, he'd recognized my name. He'd known I was Alan Oberon's daughter from the start.

I pushed Sal thoughts aside, only to be assailed by other things I'd heard at the Jenkinses'. They wanted me to believe that Alan was dead, but Ginnie'd said different. It hadn't been the drugs talking or the Infinity machine or her injuries. She knew that my father was alive and she expected me to find him.

She also had to have known that Alan was a NonCon. And not just any NonCon, but the leader. Why didn't she ever tell me? She could have trusted me. I'm sure she had her reasons, but I was her daughter. Who else could she have trusted? A bit of anger at her leaked out and I smacked the back of the seat in front of me in frustration. The guy sitting there whirled around.

"What's your problem?" he snapped.

"Nothing. Sorry." I cut my eyes to the left.

He turned back, muttering something about teenagers.

I sat on my hands. FeLS. How was I ever going to talk Sandy out of her life's dream? As impossible as that seemed, I figured I had a better chance of doing it than finding my father. But I had to try to do both—somehow.

XXII

I got up late, with plans to go back to Robin's Roost and poke around there. I was so late, there was no time to talk with Gran about my FeLS contract before breakfast. I had to keep moving if I was going to make sure Ed didn't get near Dee between home and Dickens.

On the way to school, I was constantly looking over my shoulder, scanning the streets for Ed's green trannie. Derek and Mike came around the corner and Wei showed up a second later. I noticed that Derek got real quiet, and the way he looked at her . . . He had the same dreamy look in his eyes that he'd had when he was looking at me two weeks ago. Skivs, he had a crush on Wei! I could not have been happier. No more crushing on me. I could finally relax again.

Before Dee ran off with her friends, Wei told her, "Wait for us after school and we'll go somewhere special."

"More special than TJ's?"

"Yep."

"Okay!" She grinned and then raced to the school yard, giggling and laughing with her friends.

"Where are we going?" That put a serious kink in my own plans to visit Robin's Roost.

"Rosie's." Wei lowered her voice. "It's DZ and we can tell Dee what's going on with Ed. She should know."

Mike heard "Rosie's." "You're going there? Chocolate cake, white icing, sprinkles on top. Man, that's the best!"

"I've got credits I picked up yesterday playing music with Riley. I'll buy," Derek said. "That is . . ." He looked at Wei. "If you don't mind if we come, too."

I watched him, contemplating how I felt about the shift in his affections. There was the teeniest bit of jealousy rattling around inside me, but mostly I was glad I didn't have to deal with his crush anymore. Coming right out and saying something like *I don't want to be your girlfriend* might well have ruined our friendship. I would never have wanted that to happen. Plus, I really liked Wei. And they looked cute together, his tall blondness alongside her dark-haired petiteness. I smiled to myself. It was a good thing.

"Why don't you meet us there later?" Wei said. "Nina and I have girl stuff to talk about first." She flashed Derek her famous smile and I swear he began melting around the edges.

"Sure. We can, uh, we can . . ." His look implored Mike for help.

"Go to the Alley and check out the newest techie crap. What time you want us to show up?"

"Four."

"Save me some cake."

***

When we got to school, Sal was at the top of the steps by the doors. Derek waved to him, but he turned away, following a crowd of students into the building.

"What's up with him?" Derek asked.

"Sun was probably in his eyes." Wei squinted up at the sky.

That was a lie—there was no sun on the steps. Derek bought it, though. I think he'd believe anything Wei said.

A male voice behind us said, "Excuse me," and walked by in a cloud of aftershave. I recognized that smell: Ed. I froze.

"Where's the main office?" the voice continued. Wei stood off to the side, giving him directions, and I snuck a peek. The breath I'd been holding rushed out of me all at once, my entire body shuddering. It was just a mousy little man, probably someone's dad.

"I've gotta run," I said. "I'll be late for first period." I forced a smile at Wei and hurried off.

***

Between periods I searched the crowd of kids, thinking I'd at least *see* Sal. I wasn't sure why, because I knew that would only make me feel worse. I figured he'd turn away, like he had done outside. Even though I knew it was futile, I was hoping he'd have some reason to come by. Like maybe me.

Stop kidding yourself, I thought. Now that he knew I had less information about my dad than he did, he had no reason to hang around me. He'd probably kissed dozens of girls . . . just because it was my first wouldn't matter to him. Besides . . . I'd been the one who walked away. By homeroom, I'd settled into a state of anesthetized emotions. It was all I could handle.

"You okay?" Wei asked.

170

I shrugged.

"You want me to talk to Sal?"

"No. He probably—"

"Something you'd like to share with the class, ladies?" Mr. Haldewick's pointer was aimed right at us. "Anything of importance?"

"No, sir," I said.

That pretty much wrapped up my morning—nothing of any importance.

***

At lunch, Mike, Derek, and I snagged a window booth at Mickey's. I couldn't stop staring outside.

"What's going on?" Derek asked.

"Yeah," Mike said. "You're not yourself, Neenie Beans. Gran and Pops okay?"

"They're fine." I rarely kept secrets from these guys, but I couldn't talk to them about Sal. I didn't buy all the Media hype about girls, but the things we learned in Health and Soch about guys seemed pretty accurate. Mainly the part that they didn't like to listen to girls' drama. And I was feeling pretty dramatic about Sal. Instead, I elaborated on the other thing that was bothering me.

"It's about Dee. We ran into Ed." I proceeded to fill them in about seeing Ed the day before, and all the rest of it. "Wei's dad thought the same thing as you, Der . . . about him wanting a Cinderella girl."

"That won't happen while we're around." Derek puffed out his chest.

I thought back to elementary school and how Derek had

always been there for me. I knew he would do anything to help.

"Neens, you should have told us all of this before." Mike looked a little hurt. "I thought we were your best friends."

"You are. I'm sorry—I just, well, since Ginnie died and we moved here . . . Things have changed."

"Since you met Sal, you mean," Derek said. "It's pretty obvious something's going on between you two."

I was almost surprised that there wasn't a bit of jealousy in his voice. He was smitten with Wei. That, at least, was good.

"Nothing is obvious," I said. "He's not interested in me."

"Really?" Mike said. "That's not how it's been looking."

Mickey's buzzer, indicating that the school's bell had rung, saved me from any more discussion. We were swept out the door along with everyone else, the flow of bodies surging back to Daley. Once inside, I caught a glimpse of Sal.

He didn't see me. I watched him walk down the hall while other students jostled me from side to side. I'm not exactly sure how I got to my next class, Language & Lit, but I did. I scrolled my test page up and down, up and down. The questions didn't make sense. I couldn't focus on anything, other than how miserable I felt. I turned in the quiz without having answered one question.

Miss Gray asked me to wait afterward. "Are you all right today, Nina?"

"Yeah." As much as I liked her, I wasn't about to unload my problems on a teacher. Sal or otherwise.

"You're Alan Oberon's daughter, aren't you?"

I nodded. Since we'd moved back to Chicago, it seemed as if everyone knew who my parents were.

She took a pad of passes from her desk drawer, filled one out, and handed it to me. Then she took out her PAV and beamed something to mine. "That's my PAV number. If you ever need anything, let me know."

"Thanks." I took the pass and headed out the door. Around the corner, I spied Sal with some girl I'd never seen before. You couldn't have squeezed a sigh between them.

She was dressed a lot like Sandy, typical sex-teen, showing plenty of skin, except she didn't look cheap. Her clothes weren't Sale—they were definitely top tier, ultrachic. Her chest was pressed up against Sal, her arm wrapped around his neck. I couldn't tell if she was nibbling on his ear or whispering something. Her free hand was busy stuffing something into his shirt pocket.

He noticed me first and halfheartedly (or so it seemed to me) shook free. She inclined her head slightly, taking in my Megaworld jeans and T-shirt. Since the floor wasn't going to open up and swallow me, I fled into the nearest girls' bathroom, straight into one of the stalls. Sitting on the john, I pulled my feet up and hugged my knees. I squeezed my eyes shut so I didn't have to look at my last year's discount jeans or my value tennies. What a fool I'd been to think that Sal would want to be with me when there was someone like that girl around. She had the right clothes, the right look, and the right sex-teen attitude. I'd even been idiot enough to tell him I was afraid of having a boyfriend. It didn't matter if I believed *XVI Ways* propaganda or not. I wasn't going to have a boyfriend if I persisted in being anti-sex-teen. But I told myself, I didn't want a *boyfriend*, I wanted *Sal*. Even if he was only interested in my father. But I wasn't going to get him. Not now. Not ever.

I spent the next period in the bathroom, breathing in the smell of disinfectant and urine and feeling like it was all that I deserved.

XXIII

After my pathetic bathroom stay, I managed to sneak around Hal, the robotic hall monitor, and get into my next class. The teacher didn't notice the time difference on the pass—but Hal would've. After school I made sure Sal was nowhere in sight before I went outside to join Wei, Derek, and Mike.

"They know about Ed," I told Wei.

"So, we're all in this together." She smiled at the guys.

"Yep." Derek literally beamed at her.

A sigh of despair escaped me. I didn't want Derek, but I wouldn't mind being Wei for a while. I bet nothing even close to the hurt and humiliation I'd just endured would ever happen to her. I couldn't picture Wei running away from anyone or anything, let alone cowering in a restroom.

Turning my focus to the job of keeping Dee safe, I stuffed my Sal feelings deep inside, alongside the Ginnie tears that I refused to cry. Keeping all those emotions inside wasn't easy, and the more I tamped them down, the harder it got.

We picked up Dee outside Dickens, and she, Wei, and I split off from the guys.

"You're sure you don't want us to come with you right

now?" Mike rubbed his stomach. "It's growling."

"Come on." Derek grabbed his arm. "They said they had 'girl' stuff to talk about. "We'll see you later." They took off in the direction of the Alley.

"Get me a piece of chocolate cake," Mike hollered over his shoulder. "Don't forget the sprinkles!"

At Rosie's, we chose a table near the back of the room and placed our order. When the waitress left, I turned to my sister. "Deeds, we've gotta tell you something."

"You're not gonna talk to me about boys, are you? I know all about them from my friends."

I remembered my fifth-grade conversations about boys. How dumb had we been? "No, Dee. It's not about that at all. It's about that day I yelled across the street at you . . . I saw Ed."

"My dad? He didn't tell me he was coming to see me." No one could've missed the excitement and longing in her voice. She wanted a father as much as I did. So much that she'd even settle for a low-life bag of space trash like Ed.

"I think he wants to take you back to live with him."

"I couldn't do that." She turned to Wei. "He might be my dad, but he doesn't need me the way Pops does."

I didn't want to tell her what kind of person Ed really was. She'd gotten a little suspicious about the way he treated Ginnie, but I was sure she didn't have any idea just how awful he'd been to our mother. "If Ed comes around your school or tries to have you go somewhere with him, don't," I said.

"Why not? I want to at least see him. I'll tell him I can't live with him. He'll understand."

A tall, lean woman emerged from the kitchen and came to our table.

Wei placed her right hand on her chest and bowed her head slightly. "Rosie, these are my friends Nina and Dee."

I said hello and Dee smiled.

"Rosie is my Cliste Galad master," Wei said.

"What's that?" Dee asked.

"It's a kind of martial art," Wei said. "Around the time of the Energy Wars, a group of Scottish women combined several types of fighting and came up with it."

"What's it mean? Cliste Galad?" Dee fumbled over the pronunciation.

"It means 'agile brave girl,'" Rosie said. "Nowadays the Media tries to scare women away from learning it. There's even talk of making it illegal. The GC doesn't want girls to know how strong and courageous they can be. But that doesn't apply to the three galads I see sitting here." She winked at Dee.

The waitress came through the kitchen doors with our order.

"For my special customers," Rosie said, placing the drinks in front of us.

"Wow!" Dee's eyes widened, then narrowed. "This won't make me fat, will it?"

"Since when do you care about that? And where did you get that idea in the first place?" I stared at my little sister.

"Maddie and I were watching a *XVI Ways* vid," she said. "The earlier girls start paying attention to how they look, the better they'll look."

Wei smiled at her. "I wouldn't believe everything that comes from *XVI Ways*," she said. "I happen to know for a fact that a chocolate shake with whipped cream and a cherry on top will cure anyone's problems. See?" She took a big pull on her straw.

"Oooh! Ice-cream headache." She rubbed her forehead.

Dee laughed and took a drink.

I twirled the straw around in my glass, taking halfhearted sips. Dee noticed.

"Don't worry," she said. "My dad will understand that I can't live with him."

"Uh-huh." Her wanting to see him changed everything. Keeping them apart was not going to be easy.

The bell attached to the door jingled. It was Mike and Derek.

"Check this out." Mike handed me a chip as he pulled up a chair. "I thought you'd get a kick out of it—it's Van's newest vert. They're giving them away in exchange for your opinion about a new PAV."

"You're just like your dad," Derek said.

"Am not." Mike sounded a little hurt. "And it's not like he wants to take all those drugs they stick in him. He only does it so we have a decent place to live. I'd never let anyone put all those drugs and stuff in me. I'd rather be homeless."

"Just kidding—calm down." Derek looked at Dee. "How's everything?"

"Nina's worried that my dad might want to take me to live with him. But Pops needs me too much. I'll just tell Ed and everything will be fine. It's no big deal." The trust in her eyes made my stomach lurch.

"Hey," Mike said. "Where's my cake?"

***

After dinner, when Dee went to her room to do homework, I talked with Gran and Pops about Ed. I didn't want to scare them, but I couldn't keep all of this from them any longer. I chose my words carefully. "Dee says she wants to see him. I guess I understand a little. He is, after all, her father."

"He's a snake, is what he is. If I didn't have this damned leg"— Pops banged a fist on his stump—"I'd go out there and give that jerk what he deserves. Father or not, he'd never come around Dee again. I know some people . . ."

A wave of sympathy for Pops flooded over me. These people from all Pops's stories were probably in about the same shape he was. It must be awful to be a prisoner in your own body.

Pops went on: "I can call in some favors, you know."

"I know," Gran said. The look in her eyes was exactly what I felt, only a thousand times more. "Let's hope it won't come to that. All the same, you might want to give them a heads-up that something's brewing."

"Good idea, old woman." Pops shifted in his chair. "You want to get down the scrambler, Nina?"

I hoisted myself up onto the counter and removed the machine from its hiding place. Gran took it from me and plugged it in. "We'll leave you here to talk in private." She laid a hand on Pops's shoulder, then motioned for me to come with her.

Once we were in the living room, she said, "His friends will be glad to hear from him. After a few minutes of bluster and bravado, they'll start reminiscing; he'll forget all about Ed." The sadness in her voice cut right through my heart.

"How do you do it, Gran? I feel awful for Pops."

"When you've loved someone as much and as long as I've loved that old man . . ." Her eyes glistened. "You do whatever it takes to help them keep their pride and dignity."

Gathering up dishes from the table, she went into the kitchen. My PAV beeped; it was Sandy. I took a deep breath and herded all my worries into a corner of my brain. They'd still be there when the call was over.

By the time Sandy and I'd finished talking, we had worked out the whole weekend. She was coming to town Saturday for the first time since I'd moved. I should've been ecstatic, but I wasn't. I had no idea how she and Wei would get along. Never had I known, and liked, two more opposite people. I did still like Sandy, I told myself. She was my best friend. I shook off any thoughts to the contrary.

XXIV

Sal hadn't called and I hadn't seen him at school. By Friday I wasn't shaking every time I moved from one class to the next. And my ears weren't permanently tuned for the sound of his voice. Dull was exactly how I felt. Thankfully, none of us had seen or heard from Ed, either. Maybe he'd changed his mind about Dee. Probably not, but I could hope.

On the way home Friday, Derek told us that Riley would be playing music with him on Saturday night at Soma. It was the newest place to hang out. Patterned after coffeehouses from the mid-1900s, it featured acoustic music and espresso. I personally couldn't stand coffee—but it smelled great. I was sure Sandy would love going there, especially if there were lots of boys.

"You guys better be there," Derek said. "We need the moral support. This is our first real gig."

"Can I come, too?" Dee said.

"It's past your bedtime," I said.

Dee shot me a look and kicked a rock down the street. "Fine."

I didn't enjoy playing the role of mother, especially when Dee got peevish with me.

"How about I come by your house at seven-thirty?" Wei said to me.

"I've got some stuff to do before then." I'd been neglecting my art and I'd planned on spending the day sketching at the Art Institute. "I'll meet you guys there." At the corner of Clark and Dickens, I said, "See you tomorrow. I think maybe Dee and I will go through the park instead of taking the trans."

"Really?" Dee brightened.

"It's warm today," I said. "Last time till spring probably."

"You sure you want to do that?" The concern in Wei's voice wasn't lost on Derek. Or me.

"We'll go with you," he offered.

"Yeah," Wei said. "I haven't been by the zoo in ages. We could walk along the perimeter and maybe see the horses and cows. Okay?"

I agreed, because I knew they were right. No matter how much I didn't want to think about Ed, he was always in the back of my mind. And even though it was the middle of the afternoon, and we were in a public place, if he showed up, I wasn't sure if I'd know what to do.

***

By the time we passed the zoo, Derek and Wei had fallen behind us. They were talking low and Wei was laughing. We were close to my mountain. I didn't want to think about the last time I'd been there, with Sal.

I turned to Dee. "Mom and I used to come here," I said. "We would picnic and play games. It was before you were born. I had so much fun."

"Just you and Mom? What about Ed?"

"She didn't know Ed back then. I don't think she had a boyfriend. Though, you know, come to think of it, there was a guy sometimes. I don't remember him very well. He used to make me clover-chain crowns to wear. They'd talk and laugh together while I rolled down the hill. You wanna do that?"

"Nina." She scrunched up her mouth. "I am almost twelve. I do not roll down hills."

"Well, maybe you ought to." I reached over and tickled her. She screamed and darted away. I chased her and we tumbled down, wrestling around like we used to. It was the most fun I'd had with her since Ginnie'd died.

Wei and Derek caught up and were standing over us. "What are you doing?" Derek said.

"Playing," Dee said through her giggles. "See?" She flopped over and rolled down the hill. "You do it, too," she called up to us.

"It's getting late," Wei said. "We should make sure you get on the transit."

"We'll be fine," I said. "The stop is right over there." I pointed through the trees. "Nothing's going to happen." Having fun, for once, and being in this place made me feel almost safe.

"We'll wait here and make sure. Okay?"

"You really don't need to. I can handle it." I made an exaggerated martial arts move complete with sound effects. "Waaaah!"

Derek rolled his eyes. "I guess it's okay. You think?" He looked to Wei for confirmation.

She glanced down the hill at Dee before whispering, "I think you'd make Ed fall down laughing. That would give you plenty of time to get away." She took Derek's hand. "We'll stay here till you get across the street. How's that?"

"Fine." I laughed. "Come on, Dee."

We got across Stockton Drive and I waved to Derek and Wei. They waved back and left.

Dee and I were almost to Clark when a trannie whizzed past us from behind. It was green. I knew it was Ed.

He rounded Eugenia by Lincoln's statue and turned onto Clark, blocking us off from the transit stop. We were in a wide-open area with no place to run and hide. Derek and Wei were too far off to hear if I screamed.

My PAV beeped.

"I'm here to see my daughter," Ed said.

I clicked off and grabbed Dee's hand, "We've got to—"

Before I could get "run" out of my mouth, a yellow hire-trannie pulled up between Ed and us. The window rolled down—it was Sal.

I pushed Dee into the back, hopped in beside her, and slammed the door. "Go!" I yelled. "Now!"

"Who was that?" Dee twisted around, looking out the back window.

"Nobody," I huffed, trying to catch a breath. "Sal saw us. Beeped me. Wanted to talk. Couldn't stand in traffic."

That seemed to work for her. She turned back around and sat down. I tried to will myself to breathe.

Sal maneuvered through traffic like a Saturn 1000 driver. When I looked out the back window, Ed's trannie was nowhere in sight.

"What the hell are you two doing out here all alone this close to dark?" Sal demanded. "Are you nuts?"

"We weren't alone. We were with Derek and Wei at the zoo," Dee said. "I didn't know you were an HT driver. I thought you went to school."

"I do. I'm just test-driving this for my brother." Sal glanced over his shoulder at me. "Something wrong? I saw you guys and figured I'd stop . . ." He shrugged a shoulder toward Dee.

I couldn't believe my luck. He hadn't seen Ed and I wasn't about to say anything in front of Dee.

"Nothing. I'll tell you later."

"Secret boyfriend stuff," Dee teased.

"DeeDee, cut it out!" I immediately regretting losing my temper and reached for her. "I'm sorry." She pushed my hand away.

"Leave me alone." She crossed her arms over her chest and turned back to the window.

Great. I huddled in the corner of the backseat until we got home.

"Go on in and tell Gran I'll be right up."

Dee grumbled, "Okay," and slammed the HT's door behind her.

I watched her enter the building, and avoided making eye contact with Sal. "So you didn't see him, did you?"

"Who?"

"Ed. He was across the street—between us and the trans stop. He called me and said he wanted to see Dee." Then the tears started.

Damn! Was I was going to cry every time I was around him? He already thought I was an idiot about the government and Media.

He'd have "emotional wreckage" to add to the list. I bet that girl who'd been hanging all over him at school would never fall apart. I hated it, but I'd been so scared; tears streamed down my cheeks. I finally managed to stop.

"Sorry." I sniffed, dabbing at my eyes.

"That's just adrenaline." Sal didn't even turn around. "When a crisis is over, your body does crazy things."

"Right. Adrenaline." My tears dried instantly and in their place was a growing anger. Not just at his matter-of-fact tone but because of the remark about my body doing crazy things. Like when he'd kissed me. That pissed me off even more. Before I said things I would certainly regret, I got out of the HT. "Thanks for the ride." I slammed the door just as hard as Dee had.

I strode into the building without a backward glance.

Dee pulled me into the living room; she was white as Gran's hair. "Someone broke into our apartment. Gran had to give Pops one of his tranqs he was so upset."

"Broke in?" I glanced around the room. There were books and chips strewn across the floor. "Skivs!" I ran down the hallway. My clothes and my art supplies were everywhere. My makeshift dresser was empty. I rifled through the piles on the floor. The book was gone. I raced back down the hall and into the kitchen. "Dee's baby book! Where is it?" I grabbed Gran by the shoulders. "Someone took it! You don't know how important it is!"

Gran extricated herself from my grip. "Calm down, Nina. What about Dee's baby book?"

"It's got . . . I promised Ginnie . . . There's important . . ." I hadn't planned on telling Gran anything about the baby book until I'd found out for sure that my father was alive.

Dee had left the room and Gran was staring at me. "You are not making any sense, child. What is all this fuss about Dee's baby book?"

I clasped and unclasped my hands, trying to compose myself. "The last thing Ginnie asked me was to take care of it. She said it was important. Maybe it isn't, but because it meant so much to her, I have to keep it safe." I threw up my hands. Gran didn't have to believe me, but it was the best I could come up with.

"I don't know why anyone would take that." She rubbed her chin, studying my face. "The police think it was someone looking for meds. There weren't any here, that's why your grandfather and I were out. His scrips needed filling."

My mind was racing. I could see that Gran didn't believe what I'd said about the book, but she didn't seem to want to pressure me either. "You called the police?" I asked.

"Of course I did. They've been here and gone," she said. "Since nothing was missing, that I was aware of"—her eyes narrowed at me—"they left. We're supposed to call if we discover anything is gone. Are you sure you didn't just misplace Dee's baby book?"

"No, I'm not sure." Actually, I was sure. I knew I hadn't misplaced it. And I was sure Ed had broken in and stolen the book. How I was going to get it back, I didn't have any idea.

"You'd better check your room," she said. "When we got home everything was a mess. If you had anything important, besides that book—"

Dee came into the kitchen. "I looked through everything, Gran. I've still got all my stuff. But it feels creepy in my room now. Nina, will you come with me and help me straighten up? Please? I don't want to be in there alone."

Gran motioned us out of the kitchen. "I'll make sandwiches. I don't think any of us feels much like eating a big dinner."

I knew I didn't. I felt sick that Ed had gone through our things. I wanted to wrap myself up in a big blanket, cover myself from head to toe, anything to stop the naked feeling I had.

"Come on, Nina." Dee took me into her room. "See what a mess?" Her clothes were strewn everywhere. Like me, clothes were about all she had.

I took a deep breath, picked up a shirt, and started folding.

"I'm glad they didn't mess this up." Dee held out her baby book.

"What are you doing with that?" I snatched it out of her hands.

"What's the big deal? It's mine, isn't it? I saw it when I was looking for my brown shirt you borrowed. I took it to school for Genealogy Day."

Panic surged through me. I took a deep breath. "Dee, I promised Ginnie I'd keep this safe. Do you mind if I take it?" I put on my best sad face, which wasn't hard. "It makes me feel close to Mom." Skivs. That was low, but I couldn't let Dee traipse all over the city with the book.

Her face softened. "Okay. I don't need it anyway. But remember that it's mine."

"Of course."

I finished helping Dee get her room in order, then I went to mine. One of my rapidos was broken, but the rest I put back in their case. I found Ginnie's picture facedown by the wall; the frame was chipped, but the glass wasn't broken. I righted my makeshift dresser and put her picture on the top. Then I laid the book on the bottom. Later, I'd cover it with my clothes again.

***

After we ate, I helped Gran get everything in the living room put back in place. Then I went straight to my room. I piled every piece of clothing in the center of the floor. Taking them, one by one, I started putting them in order.

Sal hates me, I thought.

I refolded a shirt.

It was sheer luck that he'd happened on Dee and me at just the right time. I don't know what would've happened if he hadn't.

I put the shirt in the box.

It's okay that he hates me. He's an overbearing know-it-all who only wanted to find out things about my father. He never cared about me.

I grabbed a pair of jeans and folded them.

That kiss meant nothing, nothing at all. I'm fine.

I stuffed the jeans next to the shirt.

I don't need some arrogant, underhanded boyfriend.

I remembered Sal saying, *A boyfriend,* huh? I closed my eyes. I could feel his closeness, smell his scent, see his eyes . . .

I piled two more shirts and another pair of jeans on top of the others.

I called Sandy. She was at a party—I could hear music and people in the background—we didn't talk long. Besides, I wasn't going to tell her about Sal anyway.

"I'll call you when I'm on the express tomorrow," she yelled through her PAV.

I couldn't wait to see her. I liked Wei a lot, but I longed for the comfort of my best girlfriend, which I hoped she still was. Even if we never ever talked about Sal, just being around her would make me feel so much closer to normal. Closer to the way I'd been before my life had been turned upside down.

Maybe, I thought, she wouldn't get chosen for FeLS. If I got into the Art Institute, I might be able to get a tiny apartment. Sandy could come stay with me whenever she wanted. The daydream was nice, but reality took over.

I could not forget that someone, most likely Ed, had broken in looking for something. But on further reflection, he couldn't possibly know about the book. The only people in the Infinity machine room when Ginnie'd told me were me and her.

I pushed the rest of my clothes on the floor and plopped into the middle of the borrowed inflato-mat. All kinds of awful thoughts started crowding into my brain, making me crazy. I got up and went into the living room. Pops was asleep in his chair and Gran was reading.

"I'm going out," I said.

"Where?" Gran asked. "It's late."

"Just outside. I need some air." I could tell she was concerned. "Look, I'll be fine. I'll be just outside the lobby. What can happen there? I won't be long, I promise." Before she could protest, I had my coat on and was out the door.

***

I didn't stay right outside the building. I went down to the river, ending up at the oasis where Sal and I had argued. Plopping down on the bench, I stared out at the black waves slapping up against the pilings. I knew this wasn't smart, but I couldn't take it anymore. I needed to think for a little bit. Everything felt off to me. I realized suddenly that I hadn't sketched or drawn anything since Ginnie died. Ginnie. The river looked ominous and cold. I wondered how my father could possibly have survived falling into it. And if he had, like Ginnie'd said—

The sounds of people coming my way snapped me back to the present. I shrank into the corner of the bench, out of the direct glow of a nearby streetlamp. The circle of light fell on two homeless women walking down the path. I couldn't make out what the older of the two was saying, but there was something about the younger one that seemed familiar. They stopped for a moment and the covering over the younger one's head slipped down. I gasped. "Joan?"

"Who's there?" The girl clutched the arm of her companion.

I leaped off the bench and ran over to the women. "Joan, it's Nina." I started to touch her, but she pulled back.

"Do I know you?" She cowered behind the other woman.

"I'm Mike's friend . . . Nina. Remember?"

"Mike? Who's Mike?" She turned to the woman. "Do I know Mike?" Her voice began to tremble. "He's not going to come for me, is he?" She grabbed my arm and terror spread across her face.

"Mike's your brother. He's not coming for you. He doesn't know where you are. Neither does your mother. You should let them know—"

The woman grabbed me, pulling me close. I could smell the stench of garbage on her. "Sometimes she don't remember nothing except what those FeLS trainers did to her. It would be best if you don't remember seeing her here."

With that warning, she shoved me backward, threw a protective arm around Joan, and the two of them melted into the shadows.

XXVI

Thank goodness the next morning was Saturday, because I'd barely slept the night before. All I'd thought about was Joan. I couldn't forget that look of fear on her face. I still hadn't decided if I should tell Mike I'd seen her. Or if I should, like that woman had said, forget all about it.

I needed to put everything out of my mind, once and for all. After breakfast, I packed up my art tote and took Dee to her friend Maddie's, making them promise to stay inside. Which was easy considering the temperature had dipped into the thirties and it was threatening a dreary mix of rain and snow. Coat collar up, I braced myself against the wind, waiting for the number 56.

While I waited, a trannie with a couple of guys inside stopped at the light. "Want a ride, babe? Two for the price of one." I could see their XVIIIs.

I slid my coat sleeve up, showing my bare wrist.

"We won't tell." The guy doing the talking grinned.

The trans pulled up behind them and I hurried on. What was I going to do when I had my tattoo? It wasn't going to be easy turning down guys who thought the tattoo was a free pass. And

I wasn't some martial arts expert like Wei. Maybe she'd teach me some moves for real.

When I got to the Art Institute I went straight for the Twenty-first Century Postwars exhibit. I took out my paper and rapidos and spent the entire day sketching. Several people stopped to look over my shoulder at my efforts. It didn't bother me; I was used to it.

"Nice," one lady said.

"Are you a Creative?" a man asked.

"I will be," I said. Would I? I hoped so. Ginnie had worked so long and hard for me to have this chance.

"Take this." He handed me a card. "When you get your designation, come and see me. I could use a bit of help."

When he left, I read his card.

MARTIN LONG, CURATOR

TWENTY-FIRST CENTURY ART COLLECTION

ART INSTITUTE, CHICAGO

That's what it said. What I read between the lines was "hope."

***

After dinner, I helped Gran clear the table. On the way to pick up Dee from Maddie's, I'd listened to verts; their mindless chatter helped to pull me from the world inside my head back into reality. A particular one about dressing for that "someone special" stuck in my mind. It had made me question my usual jeans and T-shirt. And I wondered about Sal. Yes, I knew he hated me, but still . . . that girl in the hallway, the one who'd tucked something in his pocket (and draped herself all over him)—she obviously didn't shop Mega or Sale. She was ultrachic. Was she the kind of girl he really liked? I knew I didn't stand a chance against someone like her.

I shook my head. Why was I obsessing about this? I didn't stand a chance with him anyway. I didn't *want* to stand a chance with him . . . did I? But if I looked different, maybe he'd notice, and then be sorry that he wasn't with me. I kicked the sidewalk. Damn Sal Davis anyway.

When I got home, I asked Gran, "Did you ever dress up or fix your hair special because you wanted Pops to notice you?"

She smiled at me over her glasses. "Someone you want to impress?"

"No." I doubt she believed me. I hardly believed me.

"One time I was going to a party where I knew your grandfather would be. I wanted to get his attention, so I decided to get all dolled up. One of my girlfriends came over and we spent the entire day getting me coiffed, polished, and stuffed into clothes I'd normally never dreamed of wearing."

"Did it work? Did he notice you?"

"Oh, he noticed me all right." Gran laughed. "He walked over to me and said, 'Edith, you look like you fell into a bucket of paint, face-first, and stuck your finger in an electro socket gettin' out of it.'

"I was so embarrassed, I ran out crying. He was right behind me, braying like a donkey. He finally caught me and asked what I'd done to myself. He said I was the prettiest girl he knew—no matter what I did with my hair or what I put on my face. But that he liked me best natural—like I always was."

She started loading the dishes into the sterilizer. "I went home that night, washed the gunk off my face, shampooed the curl out of my hair, and got rid of those clothes. I never tried to change myself to impress anyone again."

I couldn't imagine Gran being any way except how she'd always been. She'd confirmed what I'd suspected all along. When two people liked each other, it wasn't about clothes or makeup or hairdos.

"You're going out tonight?" Gran said.

"I'm meeting everyone at Soma."

"Can't they come here, and pick you up?"

"I'll be fine, Gran. The trans picks us up right out front and Soma's at North and Wells. One well-lit block from the trans stop. Please don't worry about me. I'm always careful." It wasn't me I was worried about anyway; Dee was the one in danger.

"It's not your carefulness, it's other people's carelessness that worries me."

"Well, don't." I kissed her cheek and went down the hall to get ready.

I left for Soma, dressed in my usual T-shirt and jeans. Sandy'd called from the express and I gave her directions, telling her I'd meet her there. When the trans neared North Avenue, I didn't get off like I should've. Instead, I rode up to the stop by Robin's Roost. When I got off the trans, I crossed the street and stood in front of the building. I conjured up the image of how it had looked in the photograph of my dad and Mr. Jenkins. I knew it was silly, but something about this place made me feel close to my father . . . and to Ginnie. They had been here often. I bet they'd even stood right where I was standing. Tilting my head back, I looked up toward the roof. Light sleet peppered my face. I wondered if there was a way to get up there. Gran had said it was Ginnie's favorite place.

"I'll find him, Mom. I promise," I whispered up to the sky.

I realized I was running late. At least Soma was just a few blocks down Wells. I hurried around the building and slipped on a patch of ice. I reached for the wall when someone grabbed my shoulders.

"Thanks . . ." I looked up—right into Ed's face.

XVII

"Well, well . . ." Ed tightened his grip and put his face close to mine, the smell of tobacco and garlic and his aftershave almost gagged me. I tried to wrench myself free, but he had a secure hold.

"What are you doing here?" I glanced around, hoping someone would come down the street, but it was empty.

"Looking for you. I want to talk about Ginnie."

"What about her" I tried jerking free again. "You didn't call or come over after she was killed. Why the sudden interest now?"

Ed laughed, and I could feel the blood rushing to my face. "She's the mother of my child," he said. "Maybe she left something for me. Maybe you found it. Maybe I want it—now." He shoved me against the wall, hard, but didn't let go of my arm.

The streetlight shone on his face and I recognized the look in his eyes—the same one he'd get before Ginnie'd send Dee and me to Sandy's. Instinct took over and I rammed my knee up between his legs. He yelped and loosened his grip enough for me to struggle free. I took off like a veljet. He lunged at me, catching the pocket of my coat. It ripped as I kept on running, narrowly avoiding crashing into a couple of guys as they exited an apartment. Ed wasn't so lucky. I heard the collision and the ensuing curses and accusations, which grew fainter as I raced up the street.

Instead of going straight down Wells, I ducked into an alley that cut through to Clark. Slipping and sliding on the sleet-slick pavement, I somehow managed to get out the other side. Racing to North and Wells, I didn't stop until I was inside Soma.

Bent over, hands on my knees, my lungs screamed for air. I saw Wei about the time she saw me.

She rushed over. "What's wrong? Are you okay?"

"Bathroom," I gasped.

We went down a narrow hallway and through a door marked "Fems."

"Are you all right?"

Still breathless, I pointed at the door, making a locking motion. She secured it. "Nina, what on earth's happened?"

"Ed." I gasped for air.

"What about him? Dee's okay, isn't she?"

I finally managed to fill my lungs. Exhaling, I collapsed onto the stool in one of the stalls. "She's fine. I was coming here . . . and I ran right into him . . . got away . . ."

"Did he follow you?"

I shook my head. "I dodged a couple of guys; he wasn't so lucky. I don't think he knows where I went."

"We need to tell the others. Are you sure you're okay? He didn't hurt you?"

"I'm fine." I looked down at my ripped pocket, "My coat, however . . ." I flipped the flap of ripped material back and forth.

We both stared at the torn pocket. I started to giggle. After a moment, Wei joined in. Then all my emotions burst out in uncontrollable laughter. I clutched my sides and Wei was rocking back and forth. We didn't stop until someone banged on the door, yelling for us to get out.

As soon as we stepped into the main room, I scanned it for Ed. Wei spotted Sal and Mike. Sal. I didn't realize he was going to be there. I took a breath.

"Forget your good coat?" Mike asked, pointing at my pocket.

I sat down in the chair facing the door, and tried to ignore Sal. "I ran into Ed. Literally."

Sal raised an eyebrow at Wei. "Everything okay?"

"No. Ed attacked her when she was on her way here."

Even in the dim light, I could see Sal's jaw muscles tighten. However, any hope that he might still care about me was dashed when, without even looking at me, he said, "Guess you're okay."

"Yeah, sure I am."

"What happened?" Mike asked.

With only a slight alteration of the truth, I said, "When I got off the trans, I turned the corner onto Wells and there he was." I recounted the details and concluded, "That's it." I didn't say why I was on that particular corner in the first place.

Then all the what-ifs started racing through my mind: What if I hadn't caught him off guard, what if I hadn't kneed him as hard as I did, what if—

"I wonder why he followed you?" Wei asked.

"Yeah. You're not his daughter," Mike said.

"I don't know." I really didn't want to start dissecting things now. Soma wasn't the place to be telling my secrets.

"Did your mother leave you anything valuable?" Wei said.

"Maybe he gave her something and wants it back."

Startled, I stared at her. It was as if Wei knew, but she couldn't possibly.

She cocked her head and looked at me like she was reading my thoughts. I stuttered about for a second, gathering my thoughts, then said, "Ginnie didn't have anything worth much. All her jewelry was fake and her designer stuff was knockoff. The only things Ed ever gave her were cuts and bruises."

Sal had been quiet the entire time we were talking. It threw me when he said, "This Ed sounds like a great guy, I can't wait to meet him."

"There's no reason you would," I said, and quickly looked away.

"I'd like to," Wei said.

"Yeah, the Cliste Galad girl." Sal's mouth curled into a half smile. "He wouldn't know what hit him."

"We can't go out there looking for him now," Mike said. "Sandy's not here and Derek hasn't played yet."

"I'm sure he's long gone anyway." I made eye contact with Mike, purposely avoiding looking at Sal.

A sigh of relief escaped Mike—he was about the most nonviolent person I knew. Not a scaredy-cat, just not someone who'd go looking for a fight. Especially not against a former government spy and grown man. I didn't blame him.

"You're right," Sal agreed.

"What I want to know," Wei said, "is why he went after you, Nina. We all thought he was after Dee. Did he say anything, give you any clues?"

"Our apartment was broken into the other day, but nothing

was taken. And Ed said maybe Ginnie gave me something that he wanted." A chill ran through me. I thought back to those last few minutes with Ginnie—her certainty that my father was alive and her instructions to get the book to him. I had had enough of keeping all of this to myself. I needed help. But as much as I wanted to tell my friends about what was really going on, I couldn't, not in public, where anyone might hear. I was contemplating when and where I could spill all my secrets when Sandy walked in.

Riley and Derek were on the stage, which consisted of two chairs set up in front of the tables. Derek was tuning an antique guitar he'd found in a junk store and restored. Riley was hitting a note here and there on his accordion. But no one was paying them any mind—all eyes were on Sandy. Even Sal watched as she approached our table.

Sandy's Saturn blue plether pants were so tight there was no way could she have gotten them on over underwear—and it was obvious she hadn't. She wore black thigh-high sueded boots and a cropped faux-fur jacket over a skimpy little top. Her hair was the only thing about her that looked familiar.

"*Skivs!*" Mike exclaimed. "What the hell did you do, Sandy? You look like—"

"A model," I blurted out before Mike could make things worse. *Yeah*, I thought, *a model for sex-teen of the year*. The outfit made me cringe. I sincerely hoped the Sandy I knew and loved was under the Media-hyped crap she was wearing.

"I've missed you sooo much!" she squealed, yanking me out of my chair.

She hugged me and blew air kisses, and though I wanted

everything to be like it used to be, it wasn't. I tried to forget about her sex-teen look, but it was impossible. I pulled away and introduced her to Wei. They chatted for a minute before realizing that they both adored raw galactic music.

Sal stared at me as I sat back down. I could feel my neck getting hot. He cocked his head toward the door and got up. I don't know why, but I followed him outside. It was freezing and I'd left my coat back at the table. Hugging my arms around me, I waited for him to say something.

"What do you think you're doing, putting yourself at risk like that?" He glared at me.

I could hardly believe it. He was mad at me. "It's not like I did it on purpose."

"It was stupid of—"

"Stupid?" My finger shot right up into his face. "I am not stupid and I am not going to listen to your insults. I may not be some top-tier, ultrachic sex-teen who fawns all over you, but I am sure as hell not—"

"Nina. Stop." He grabbed my outstretched arm and pulled me up close to him. "You are not stupid. *I* am." He kissed me. It was like electric currents racing through my body. After what seemed like a much-too-short eternity, we came up for air, but he still held me close. "I will never let anyone hurt you, ever." It felt so right, being in his arms. I ignored the bit of doubt in the back of my head—this didn't feel like he was only interested in me for my father.

His hot breath on my neck sent little tremors though my whole body. I was shivering, but not from the cold.

"Skivs, I'm an idiot." He ripped his jacket off and threw it over my shoulders. "Let's get inside; you must be frozen."

When we were back at the table, Sandy made no secret of scrutinizing me and Sal. He'd scooted his chair next to mine and was holding my hand under the table. She grinned, pretty smugly, and said, "Sixteen's right around the corner, Nina. Told you . . ."

I felt a blush rising up my neck and started to pull my hand away from Sal's, but he wouldn't let go. And I didn't mind.

"Oh, come on, it's not like you can stop it from happening." Flouncing her hair, Sandy gave a quick glance around the room. "By the way, have you heard from Ed?"

Sal squeezed my hand; Wei and Mike stared at Sandy.

"What did I say?"

I grabbed a napkin and wrote, Can we find somewhere DZ to talk? I pushed it into the middle of the table.

"Not until after Derek plays," Mike said. "He's counting on us being here. Besides, we couldn't leave him out of this."

Everyone nodded in agreement, except Sandy, who still looked confused. "What's going on?"

Wei whispered something to her and she didn't say anything else.

Mike was right. I wasn't too eager to leave anyway; Ed might still be out there.

Derek and Riley started their set. They weren't playing the electro-tech that everyone listened to, which didn't surprise me. Media owned all the popular broadcast stations, so all music was government sanctioned. Occasionally a rogue broadcaster would tap into PAV airwaves and play old protest songs from the 1960s and the 2070s. The GC really hated that. Ginnie'd always said that they persecuted the rogues because the music they played made people think about what freedom really was. Those underground broadcasters were always on the run from the Audio Media Management agents, so there was no telling when you could hear them.

The guys were great. I was glad I hadn't insisted we leave. I wouldn't have ruined Derek's moment in the spotlight for anything. When a string on his guitar snapped, he and Riley took a short break. While the room was relatively quiet, I listened in on Sandy's conversation with Wei. She was rattling on about the guys in her school, all the XVIIIs.

Sal nudged me to look at Mike. His elbow was on the table, his chin firmly seated on his hand; he was hanging on Sandy's every word like she was giving directions to the lost treasure of San Cabalo—or the nearest free all-you-can-eat buffet.

As he leaned close, Sal's lips barely touched my earlobe. "Looks like he's smitten," he whispered.

That can't be, I thought. Mike being infatuated with Sandy would not be good, not at all. Even though she herself was low tier, she looked down her nose at welfare families. No matter how low you are, you can always find someone lower, I thought. Two of my best friends on a collision course with disaster; I knew which one would be crushed.

I noticed Wei's eyes were glassed over and her smile looked more than a little forced. Sandy's babbling on about FeLS and boys definitely had that effect on people. I started to intervene, but Derek and Riley took care of interference by playing again.

The crowd loved them so much they did three encores. When they finished, Riley went to the table where his twentieth-century music clique was sitting. They were going nuts, pounding him on the back and yelling like he'd just won a free trip to Galacticaland.

"Well . . . ?" Derek avoided direct eye contact with all of us, he was so nervous. "What'd you guys think?"

"I loved it!" Wei said.

"It was cool," Sandy said, leaning forward so her shirt gaped open more. Then she tossed her hair just like the girls in the *XVI Ways* how-to guide.

"What kind of music is it, Derek?" I hoped to steer Sandy off course.

"Zydeco. From New Orleans."

The blank look on all our faces demanded an explanation.

"Oh, come on, guys. The city that was totaled after the Cat Six hurricane in 2025. What was it called? Hey, Ri," he yelled across the tables. "What was the name of that storm that took out New Orleans?"

"Sandra!" Riley yelled back.

"That's the one—Sandra."

"That's my name," Sandy squealed.

"Huh?" Derek shook his head and went on: "It was like the third hurricane to hit in a couple of decades. It washed away so much land, there wasn't anywhere left to rebuild."

"After that storm and the multiple oil disasters in the Gulf, that's when they finally got serious about alternatives for oil, wasn't it?" Sal asked.

He, Derek, and Mike started to talk about fuels, which I knew would lead to a discussion of transports. We'd be there forever if I didn't interrupt.

"Can we go?"

"What?" Derek asked.

I held up the napkin so he could read it, and mouthed, "Ed."

"Is Dee okay?"

"Yes, but we need to, you know . . ." I gestured toward the napkin. "Come on, let's go."

"I've gotta put my guitar away."

"Just do it, then." No sooner were the words out of my mouth, and I saw his reaction, than I felt awful. It was his big night and I had just ruined it by being a bitch. "Derek, I'm sorry," I called after him as he walked back to the makeshift stage and put his guitar in its case. He either didn't hear me or he didn't want to.

Wei's eyes followed him as he packed up his music.

"I should've been nicer," I said.

"Yeah," Sandy replied. "That was über-B. What's got into you?"

"You need to hear the whole story first." Wei turned her back on Sandy. Reassuring me, she said, "He won't mind once he finds out what happened."

Over Wei's shoulder I saw Sandy's eyes narrow and I knew what was coming next. The last thing anyone needed was Sandy losing her temper.

"I'll apologize, okay?" I directed my words at Sandy.

She shrugged and proceeded to fuss with her hair and straighten her jacket. I noticed a couple of guys checking her out. I glanced at Mike. The look on his face was unquestionably fanaholic.

Derek's shoulders slumped as he walked back to us, guitar case in hand.

On the way out I whispered, "I really am sorry. You were great. Everyone loved you guys."

"Yeah, thanks." He repositioned his guitar between us, eyes intent on the sidewalk.

Tangling with Ed had been bad enough, but hurting one of my best friends felt worse. Derek had always been there for me, and I'd just stomped all over him. I'd have to make it right, somehow.

"Where can we go?" I asked.

"The park," Sal said. "Not far from your moun—by that place where we met. There's a vert tower near there, it's not total DZ but it scrambles everything."

"Not like anyone's paying attention to us anyway," Derek said, scuffling his feet along.

Wei caught up to him. "I wouldn't be so sure . . ." She began whispering to him.

Sandy tried to catch up with them, but the best she could do was a precarious wobble in her stiletto-heeled boots. It was pathetically sweet when Mike grabbed her arm to steady her.

"Hey," he said, "they got some new calves at the zoo. Want to go see them tomorrow?"

"Yeah, maybe." She leaned on him, her gaze intent on Derek's and Wei's backs.

XXVIII

No sooner had we gotten to the park than a police trannie cruised up in front of us—and stopped. Two officers, one male, one female, got out.

"You girls, over here." The female officer pointed to a spot by her. "Boys there, with Officer Gorton."

Sal squeezed my hand quickly and then we separated. Wei sidled up next to me, Sandy was on my left. She looked over her shoulder at the policeman and sighed. I would've thought it was funny if I hadn't been a trembling mass of jelly inside. Ed might have sent them looking for me. I had, after all, attacked him. I'm sure they'd believe a government Chooser's word over mine.

"This way!" the female officer barked. "Where are you all going?" Before we could answer, she added, "Get your IDs ready."

She trained her LED on our faces. I could see Wei's expression, as cool as the marble in her home. She put her hand out. Sandy, meanwhile, had dropped her purse, spilling the entire contents of makeup and who-knows-what all over the ground. I turned my hand over, hoping the cop didn't notice how badly it was shaking.

"Wrists." The officer sounded bored.

We all turned our arms over. She shone the LED on them. One

bare and then there was Wei's. The colors of the thistles popped in the light.

"A Creative?"

I detected a note of derision in the woman's voice.

"Yes, ma'am," Wei said. "It's on my ID."

The officer squinted into her scanner. "Huh. Like I asked. Where are you going?"

"Down by the horses." Wei was in complete control. "It's cool to see them at night. Don't you think?" She had one of her most charming smiles on—and it seemed to have the desired effect.

Sandy'd been kneeling on the ground collecting her things. When the policewoman got to her, she jumped up, flipping her hand. "My dad was a policeman. Killed in the line of duty."

"Uh-huh." The officer made a cursory glance at scan. "Wrist."

Sandy turned her arm over. "He was on a foray when he was—"

"You better pick that stuff up," the cop said.

Sandy knelt down again, busying herself with getting everything back into her purse. I could tell her feelings were hurt.

"Oberon?" The woman read from her scanner and shined her LED on my face again.

I was beginning to hate my name. I tried to smile, but the result was probably more of a grimace. I really wished I had some of Wei's composure.

"Are you related to . . ."

I felt my insides shrink. What was I going to say? If they had a portable DNA reader, they'd know in a second who my father was. I took a deep breath and held it, waiting.

". . . the Oberon who was hurt in that explosion down in Florida? It was years ago."

I hid my relief as best I could and exhaled, saying, "That's my grandfather."

"Shame how he and that other guy had to fight to get what was due them." She turned off her LED. "My uncle was on that job. Lucky for him it was his day off."

Leaving us standing there, she joined her partner. It was our first chance to see what was happening with the guys.

Like us, they were standing in a line. The policeman had apparently asked to see inside Derek's guitar case, because it was lying on the ground, open.

The two officers conferred for what seemed like forever. Eventually the policewoman returned. "Everything seems to be in order. There was an incident earlier, some thug accosted two men over on Lincoln." She pointed in the direction of Robin's Roost. "He got away. A big guy, over six two, if you believe those wimps he beat up on." She snorted. "Anyway, be careful, he's still at large. And you . . ." She motioned me over and lowered her voice. "Tell your grandfather some of us think he deserved better."

They got back in their trannie and sped off.

"Well, that was fun," Sal said.

"Yeah." Derek glanced over his shoulder at the disappearing trannie. "That cop messed up my music, and I think he swiped one of my picks."

"At least he didn't take any of us," Mike said. "Stupid checker—"

I poked Mike in the ribs. "Remember Sandy's dad," I whispered.

"Oh, uh . . . yeah." He cleared his throat. "Need some help with that?" He knelt down beside Sandy, who was still squatting on the sidewalk, retrieving a comb and some lipstick.

We had to step off the sidewalk and into the grass, which made

Sandy's progress even slower. Her stiletto heels kept sinking into the ground. For a moment, I thought Mike was going to carry her. He didn't, but he stuck with her. I'd only seen that side of him when he was working with the zoo animals, particularly baby calves that needed to be hand-fed. He was just as gentle with them. Sandy kept directing questions at Derek, but he and Wei were too far ahead of her and too engrossed in each other, for answers.

Something rustled behind me. My fingers tightened on Sal's arm. Lights from an apartment building at the park's edge cast a pale beam on some shrubs from where the sound originated.

Sal pushed me behind him and grabbed Wei. She, in turn, grabbed Derek and they stood like a shield in front of me. Sandy and Mike bumped right into my back.

"What the heck?!" Sandy exclaimed. "Why'd you—"

"Shhhh," Wei hissed.

"Don't sh—"

I stuck my hand over Sandy's mouth. "There's someone over there," I whispered, pointing at the silhouetted bush. "It could be Ed."

As I peered between Sal and Wei, the bushes crackled again.

XXIX

"You guys stay with Nina," Sal whispered to Derek and Mike. He motioned for Wei to circle around the bush on one side; he took the other.

Their reconnaissance became unnecessary when two sets of legs kicked partway out from under the bushes. One pair was bare and obviously female. The other pair had jeans pushed down around the knees. It didn't take a gallacticon scientist to figure out what was going on under the dark branches.

I was glad Sal couldn't see how red my face was. Or had been able to read my mind. Not that I wanted to be having sex with him . . . just thinking about it made me quiver. I had to stop myself.

***

We sat under the shadow of the vert tower on a huge concrete pad. Our presence was partially blocked by a row of trees to one side and fencing that surrounded the tower on the other.

At first, no one said anything. I wondered if anyone besides me had had those embarrassing thoughts after seeing that couple in the bushes.

"Well, that was pretty crazy, wasn't it?" Sandy said, readjusting her boots. "I'd never do anything like that. Euwww! Think about all the crawly little things in the grass." She swiped imaginary insects off her pants. "Yuck!"

In a moment of huge collective release, everybody laughed. That was one of the things I loved (and sometimes hated) about Sandy. She spoke her mind about how she felt—about anything.

We were in a circle, Sal and I next to each other. On my right, Sandy was absorbed in straightening her clothes and sneaking glances at Derek. Couldn't she tell he was with Wei? Or didn't she care?

Mike was by Sandy's side. He hadn't taken his eyes off her since she'd walked into Soma. Derek and Wei were toying with some pebbles on the concrete. It felt like a bunch of friends hanging out—almost normal, except for the whole Ed thing hanging over my head.

Sal's fingers intertwined with mine. "You were at Robin's Roost, weren't you? When you ran into Ed?"

"Robin's Roost—" Wei's pointed look made me feel the tiniest bit guilty.

"What's that?" Derek asked.

"It's an old condemned hotel at Lincoln and Wells. It was really special to my mom and dad. I wanted to feel close to them," I said.

Sal squeezed my hand reassuringly. I had to tell them. Out tumbled the whole story about Ginnie, the Infinity machine, and Dee's baby book. "Because of what Ed said tonight, about me having something he wants, I don't think it's just Dee that he's after," I said. "It sounded like he knows what Ginnie said to me in the hospital. But we were alone when she told me about the book."

"He might have known something about it before. Maybe Ginnie let something slip when she was with him," Wei said.

"Maybe . . ." I wasn't convinced. "But I don't think so. Ginnie was careful. I've looked all through the book for clues, but there's nothing except dates, first words, Ginnie's thoughts about being a mother, doodles, stuff like that. I don't know if it's important or not."

"You know, it could be written in code," Wei said. "You should let my mom take a look. She's amazing with codes. She started using them when she was a kid. Media even tried to hire her as a code writer and translator. She turned them down. They were so insistent that she made up some excuse about hitting her head in an accident and how she couldn't focus on sequences and patterns anymore. They made her take a ton of tests to prove she wasn't lying. A friend had to give her some kind of synapse interrupter that temporarily rerouted her cognitive skills. It worked, and she got off the hook."

"Even though my grandparents and Wei's parents both say my father's dead . . ."—I hoped Wei didn't take this wrong—"Ginnie was certain he's alive."

"My parents thought that, too," Sal said. "My mom and dad were . . . NonCons."

I cringed at the hesitation in his voice. I bet he was thinking about that night by the river and our argument. He didn't know my true opinion about NonCons, especially now that I'd found out about my parents and their views. I squeezed his hand, hoping that conveyed my support. He squeezed back. "What about your brother?" I asked. "Is he a NonCon?"

"Yeah, and"—he looked me straight in the eye—"I am, too."

Sandy gasped. "I don't believe this." She struggled to stand up, hobbled by her tight pants and unwieldy boots. "NonCons killed my father. They're a bunch of lawless—"

"Oh, sit down and shut up," Derek said. "Anyone with half a brain knows that the Governing Council supplies Media with all sorts of fabricated stories accusing NonCons of being the bad guys. I'm sorry about your dad—but where's the proof? I've read all about that foray and lots of people are sure it was a setup."

Sandy's jaw dropped. I was taken aback, too. I didn't know Derek had that kind of fervor in him for anything except for music. Sandy sat back down and kept quiet. I doubt her reaction would've been the same if that speech had come from any of the rest of us.

I could only take so much of the silence that followed Derek's outburst. "Wei, do you think your dad knows where my dad is but didn't want to tell me? Didn't want me looking for him?"

She hesitated a moment. "Maybe. Nina, I don't know what I should or shouldn't say." I could see the conflicted emotions on her face. "My dad's gone until Sunday. He's been summoned to an emergency meeting in Amsterdam with his Media bosses. It's so hush-hush that they've blocked all outside communications. I can't even call him."

"Do you think your mom would know anything?"

"If Dad knows but didn't say, then Mom knows and won't say."

"Back up a sec," Sal said. "About Ed. What exactly is he? Government? B.O.S.S.?"

"He's a Chooser." Sandy didn't look at any of us; instead she pawed through her purse, looking for who knows what. "After tonight he'll never pick me," she muttered. I hoped I was the only one who heard her. I also hoped that whatever she was hearing she would keep to herself. For the first time since I'd known her, I wasn't sure I could trust her.

"So he's government, but not B.O.S.S.," Sal said.

"I think he used to be an agent, but I'm not sure with who. I remember a big blowup he and Ginnie had when she was pregnant with Dee. It had to do with his job. But I was like five. I don't remember."

"Why'd your mother stay with him? Did she love him?" Sal asked gently.

"I don't think so," I said. "At least not after he started beating her up. Sometimes she'd swear she was leaving him, but then she always went back. It's like he had some kind of hold over her."

"Fear maybe." Sal's jaw muscles tensed. "That's what keeps my brother from leaving his wife. Fear that she knows what he and I are really doing and would expose us."

Wei tossed a couple of rocks aside. "I'm sure this has something to do with that book. Otherwise, why would she have said you had to get it to your father? With Ed's connection to the government, they have their ways of getting information. Even if you were alone with Ginnie, the room probably had some kind of surveillance."

Sal jumped up. "Let's go look at it. Sounds like that book's the link between you, your mom, and Ed."

***

On the way to my place, I caught up with Derek. "I'm really sorry I messed up your big night. I didn't mean for any of this to happen. And I would never hurt you, ever."

"It wasn't totaled. Besides, you're more important than any old show. "

"Still friends?"

He grinned down at me. "Always."

"What are you two whispering about?" Sandy'd teetered up alongside us.

"Apologies."

"Oh." She did her signature hair toss. "I hope you accepted." She smiled up at Derek, her blond hair sweeping seductively across her shoulder.

"He did." I took her firmly by the arm, steering her away from Derek; leaving him to walk with Wei. I figured that was best for everyone. Handing Sandy off to an eager Mike, I joined Sal, hooking my arm in his.

We headed down LaSalle Street like a small army marching into who knew what.

A green trannie whizzed past us. I stopped breathing and clutched Sal's arm. The transport didn't slow down, turn, or stop. I watched its lights disappear into the night.

The green trannie was the only thing we saw, between the park and the apartment, that could've had anything to do with Ed.

"Why don't you go up and get the book?" Sal said. "We can take it over to the oasis. That way we won't disturb Gran and Pops or Dee."

Sandy and I went upstairs. While we were there, I made her change out of her ridiculous boots so Mike didn't have to serve as her crutch.

"Listen, Sandy." I didn't quite know how to say what needed to be said, so I just said what I felt. "You can't say anything to anyone about what you heard tonight, okay?"

"Nina, how could you even think that?" She stopped looking through my meager cache of shoes (all three pairs) and stared at me. "You don't honestly think that I would get you in trouble, do you? You're the only friend I have, the only person who actually cares what I think or feel about things. Now . . . have you got some socks? These shoes are way too big, but if I stuff the toes . . ."

I didn't know what to say, so I just helped her get my low-decks on. It amazed me at how one minute she was a sex-teen queen, and the next, she really was a true friend.

I grabbed Dee's baby book and we slipped out of the apartment. I tucked the book under my coat.

At the traffic light, I noticed the green trannie again, halfway down the cross street.

"Don't look," I whispered to Sal. "That's Ed's on Wacker." I tilted my head in the direction of the street.

Sal pulled me into an embrace. What the . . . ? I started to protest when, instead of anything romantic, he whispered, "Pretend to trip on the curb. Fall down like you've hurt yourself."

The light changed. I lurched forward, yelped, and then collapsed, clutching my ankle. I didn't have to pretend; like an idiot, I'd accidentally twisted it for real.

Wei rushed over, kneeling beside me. "What happened?"

"Ed's across the street. Sal told me to fake it, but I actually twisted it."

"It's her ankle. Come on, guys, we'd better get her home."

Sal and Derek each grabbed an arm and hoisted me to my feet. Sandy retrieved the book, which I'd dropped.

"Don't forget this." She waved it in the air.

Wei snatched it from her. "Way to go. Now he's seen it for sure."

"'Scuse me?" Sandy planted a hand firmly on one hip.

"If you'd use that head for something besides growing hair . . ."

"Stop," I said. "Somebody just take it, okay? My ankle's killing me."

Wei stuck the book in her bag. Sandy gave her a dirty look and stormed back to the building.

I put one arm around Sal's neck and grabbed Derek's arm. I hobbled back between them. I felt ridiculous for actually hurting myself.

Wei made small talk, like, "Does it hurt much?" and "Be careful, guys." I guessed she was doing this in case Ed had a listening device. We didn't stop the ruse until we were all in the elport.

"That really did hurt." I rubbed my ankle. "If that's Ed out there, we can't use the oasis. We'll have to look at the book in my room. If we're really quiet, we shouldn't disturb anybody."

"Not a good idea," Sal said. "You know . . . listening . . ."

"It'll be fine," I replied, winking at him.

When we got into the apartment, they all went down the hall to my room while I hobbled to the kitchen. Several minutes later, I returned with the scrambler and plugged it in.

"Is that what I think it is?" Wei said. "Those are illegal."

"They are. But if you knew Pops . . ." I grinned. "It's lucky they didn't find this during the break-in, but Pops has his hiding places."

Wei pulled the book out of her bag and handed it to me. "I hope Ed didn't see exactly what it was," she said.

"Look, he was all the way across the street and it was dark. It's not like I did anything wrong." Sandy plopped down on the inflato-mat and started plucking at the blanket, obviously still upset. I figured it had a lot more to do with Derek and Wei than with the book.

"You also shouted at full voice. And he could've had some kind of nightscope," Wei retorted. She shot a withering look at Sandy, who fortunately was so busy looking at Derek that she didn't see it.

"Give her a break," Mike said. "If he saw it, he saw it. We already know he knows that Ginnie gave something to Nina and he wants it. And has been looking for it."

Sal, Derek, Wei, and I congregated in a circle on the floor. Mike perched on the edge of the bed close to Sandy and leaned over Sal's shoulder. Sandy was lying on her back, staring at the ceiling. I'd definitely have to be smoothing things over later.

On the page that contained all the pertinent information, Wei noticed the same things I did. "I wonder why Ed's name isn't written in after 'Father.'"

"I don't know," I said. "I wondered the same thing. Maybe Ginnie just wanted this book to be about her and Dee."

Following that was information about the hospital, how much Dee weighed, and all the normal baby statistics. The next page with writing on it said Mother's Thoughts at the top.

Ginnie had written how beautiful her new baby was and how much she loved her. How she hoped I would love my little sister and watch out for her. Then she'd signed her name and put a little squiggle after it.

"What's that funny mark after your mother's name?" Wei asked. "Is it just part of her signature? Like the way some girls dot their *i*'s with hearts?"

"I've never seen her sign her name like that before. Although she did doodle all the time."

"It looks like a flower," Derek finally said.

"You're right," I agreed. "Unfortunately, that doesn't make it mean anything."

The next page, Father's Thoughts, was blank. As I flipped through the book, I noticed a photograph of me holding Dee when she came home from the hospital.

"Weren't you adorable," Sal teased.

I could feel the blush starting up my neck.

"Little-kid pictures are the worst," Wei said. "My mother is always . . . what's that?"

A quiet beeping emanated from the scrambler, and the light was blinking red.

"It must have a timer," Sal said. "Do you know how to reset it?"

"No." What if I'd broken it? Would Gran be furious?

"When the light stops blinking, if it stays red, I bet it won't be scrambling anymore," Sal said.

The beeping stopped, and sure enough, the light burned a steady red. We were already deep in discussion about zydeco music, hurricanes, and guitars. Well, everyone else was. I was silent, picturing Ed, hunkered down in his car, listening to everything we said.

XXXI

Sandy had fallen asleep while we were all still talking. I covered her with a blanket and shortly after that, everyone left. I went to sleep on the sofa. Next morning, when Gran got up, I knew I had to tell her about the baby book. She had to know that I wasn't the only person who suspected my father was alive. But Sandy appeared and I didn't want to go into it while she was there. I was glad to see her snit from the night before was over.

"Hi, Mrs. Oberon." She gave Gran a hug. "Can I help with breakfast?"

"No. I'm sure you and Nina still have a lot of catching up to do. I'll let you know when it's ready."

Sandy and I went back to my room. We sat down cross-legged on the inflato-mat.

"I don't think your friend Wei likes me."

"She's just being protective."

"Of Derek?" Sandy scanned the top of my "box" dresser and picked up a couple of my text chips. "Can't blame her; he's gotten pretty cute."

"Derek looks like he always has. You never thought he was cute before."

"Yes I did. But he was crazy about you. Bet he still is. If you wanted him . . ." She snapped her fingers in front of my nose. "All the guys like you. Zeb asked about you just last week. And that ultrahot guy from your art class . . . you know the one, he's got purple streaks in his hair . . ."

"Grayson?"

"Yeah. He told me to tell you he was sorry about your mom."

"Tell him thanks." Grayson and his friends had never talked to me the entire time I was in school with them. Weird. "You know, Sandy, you could've been a little nicer to Mike."

"Yeah, yeah, he's kinda sweet, in a . . . well, you know." She must've thought better about making some rude remark regarding him. "I did tell him I'd call him about going to the zoo sometime. It's cool that he can get us into the barns and stuff. And I do like that he knows all about cows. I guess he's not so bad." She pondered Mike for a moment, then tossed one of my chips at me. "You're taking L & L? We're reading stupid plays by some guy named Shakespeare who's been dead for over five hundred years. What did he know about anything, huh? And I guess it's completely out of the question for you to ask Ed to pick me for FeLS?"

"Sandy, are you crazy?" I slapped my hands to my head. "How can you even ask that? Weren't you listening last night?"

"What? That you guys are all Non—"

I dove across the bed, landing on top of Sandy. "What's wrong with you? Do you want the entire world to hear?" I whispered.

"Where's that ma—"

I clapped a hand over her mouth. "Where's what? My math homework? You want to see what we're studying here?"

"I'm not going to tell anybody anything, Nina. Didn't we go through this last night?"

"Sandy, sometimes you say things without thinking." I was waiting for an outburst—none came.

"Sometimes I do, don't I? *XVI Ways* says a little ditziness is charming to guys."

"It can also get you in big trouble," I whispered.

She ran her fingers through her hair and flounced it around for a minute. "Look, Nina, I intend to get into FeLS, one way or another. I'm not smart enough to get a scholarship, and FeLS is the only way out of low-tier hell, okay?"

"It's not everything it's supposed to be," I said, remembering Mrs. Jenkins's warning. "How come girls who go into it never come home again?" I thought about Joan.

"What do you mean never come home again? Jolianna Whitcomb came to the school right after you left. She said it was the most amazing experience she ever had." Sandy's eyes widened. "And you should have seen what she was wearing. Ultrachic all the way." She clutched her arms around herself. "I'm going to look like that, too. And guys . . . she had tons of digis of her with the cutest guys in the solar system. She ate lunch with some of us, and told us, strictly secret, that she has sex whenever she wants to, with whomever she wants. She said her first was Tylo! Can you believe that?" Sandy flopped back on the bed. "Having sex with the Tylo."

"Sandy, there's more to life than having sex with vid stars. And what does Tylo need a Female Liaison Specialist for? He's got tons of people who are always with him. And one girl coming back out of how many? At least fifty that have gone from our school in the past year. Where are the rest? Like Mike's sister, Joan, where's she?" I almost said I'd seen her, that she was homeless, but that whole encounter still freaked me out. The vibe I'd gotten from the woman who was with her was that Joan wasn't just messed up; she was in danger, too.

Sandy propped herself up with one arm. "Who cares? Don't you see? If I'm a FeLS, I'll get to wear ultra clothes and hang out with vid stars and have all kinds of money. Nina, I don't want to live in Cementville all my life and marry some tier-two loser and end up like my mom. If I get the chance to leave, I'm never coming back."

She was right. Girls like us didn't have choices. We were either super smart or artistic and got scholarships so we could enter a profession, or we ended up stuck in the kind of life we grew up in. Unless we were lucky enough to get some tier-three or -four guy to fall in love with us. Even then, they probably wouldn't marry below their tier. Sure, they'd have sex with anyone, but they married into their own, or higher if they could.

Then there was FeLS. Whatever secrets they were keeping, most low-tier girls wouldn't care, they just wanted out of their lives. I shuddered when I thought about how "out of her life" Joan was.

Sandy kept going on and on about FeLS and all the places she would travel to and how she'd send me digi-cards of all of them. "You'll be so sorry you didn't even apply," she said. "You still could."

I shook my head. "It's not for me, Sandy."

She covered the small details of all of her boyfriends and everything that they'd ever said or done until Gran called us for breakfast. Afterward I was going to walk to the station with Sandy, but Gran insisted I let Pops and Dee do it.

"I need Nina's help with something."

"What's that?" Pops asked.

"None of your business, old man. Now, you three get out of here or Sandy will miss the express."

"Can we stop at Toy Planet on the way back?" Dee asked.

"Sure nuff," Pops said. "Let me get this leg on good 'n tight."

He didn't see Sandy wrinkle her nose as he made a few adjustments. I hugged her and whispered, "At least think about not getting chosen, okay?" She promised to talk to me later and that was that. Pops grabbed his cane and they went out the door.

"I do believe that leg is bothering him more than usual," Gran said to me when they were gone. "He takes that cane almost all the time now. Then again"—she sighed—"maybe he's just getting older—like me." She went to the chiller and reached above it for the scrambler. I panicked.

"Gran," I confessed, "I borrowed the machine last night. I think I broke it. I put it back, but. . . ."

"Here's how to take care of that." She showed me a tiny button on the bottom. "Do this." She jabbed it with the tine of a fork. "Now it's good as new." She switched it on. "We need to do some talking, don't we? About Ed."

"How did you . . . ?"

"I don't think he's back for Dee—he could've taken her from Ginnie at any time. After Alan died, the government refused to give Ginnie survivor benefits because his body hadn't been found. You and she were living with us and the financial burden was difficult. All we had were Pops's disability payments."

I wondered if Dee and I were too much of a burden now.

Gran must have noticed the expression on my face because she said, "We get survivor benefits. When they finally declared your father dead—eight years after his disappearance—Ginnie signed the credits over to us to put in trust in case anything happened to her."

"She was afraid something would happen to her, wasn't she?"

"I think she was," Gran said. "She got a job as executive assistant to the vice president, at Rockford Stone's headquarters in Achelon Towers."

I couldn't help interrupting. "I know. It was a tier-five job. What made her become a tier-two service worker in a cafeteria?"

"Patience, dear, I'm getting there." She eyed the light on the scrambler; it was still green.

"She had a respectable job and didn't go near any of her and Alan's old friends."

"Jonathan Jenkins."

"Yes, Jonathan, Jade, Brock and Elise, they all kept their distance for obvious reasons. Although this little baby"—she patted the scrambler—"got plenty of use for a while. Ginnie was never seen in public with them, but they did talk—often."

"But . . . Ed?"

"He and Ginnie met at an interplanetary conference on the moon. He was working for the government on a deal with Rockford Stone on mining ocribundan from Mars. She was so beautiful. I'm sure he fell for her on the spot." She cleared her throat. "It had been four years since Alan's death. I'd told her that she was too young to pine for him forever and you needed a father. I just was never sure about Ed."

"But he was married and has kids. Why did she even go out with him in the first place?"

"She didn't know about his family until after she was pregnant."

"He was so mean, Gran."

"He never hit her until after Dee was born." She shook her head. "I urged her to leave him. I was afraid for her and for you girls."

The scrambler started its low beep and the light was blinking red.

"It has to cool down," Gran said. "One reset won't keep it going long enough. These old scramblers are about as temperamental and cantankerous as me."

"There are things I have to tell you, Gran. Important things. Can't we try?"

"If they're that important, we can't risk being heard. Patience, dear."

I had no patience.

Gran promised we could try again after lunch, so I wolfed down a nut butter sandwich and some chips. As if eating fast would speed things up. I couldn't stop thinking about everything that was going on.

What ended up taking my mind off the scrambler was a call from Sal.

"I'm delivering a dual trannie to a customer out in the country. Want to come along? We can take the express back." I mentioned it to Gran, and she practically shooed me out the door.

Fifteen minutes later I was in the lobby, hiding behind one of the fake plants that flanked the doorway. I scoped out the street. When I didn't see anything resembling Ed or his green transport, I went outside.

Standing in a sheltered patch of sunshine, shielded from the legendary Chicago winds, I was warm. It felt more like spring than almost winter. I basked in my little bit of sun until I heard a beep. It was Sal in a shiny blue dual transport.

"Wow! This is really cool," I said.

Sal hopped out. "We modified the engine—it goes to one-twenty in sixty seconds. And the exterior . . . you like?"

He paraded me around the vehicle, pointing out the gold flecks in the Hawsworth blue paint. And showed me that when the light reflected a certain way you could see a deep pink flower with a thorny stalk encircling the transport.

I felt an overwhelming urge to trace it with my finger, but I didn't dare touch. "It looks like Wei's tattoo."

"Yep, it's a thistle." Sal opened the passenger door. "Madam . . ." He bowed low with a sweep of his arm.

I giggled, sliding into the seat, which immediately conformed to every curve of my body.

"Comfort Style," I murmured. I'd heard about the features of Comfort Style in verts, but never imagined I'd ever get to sit in a tran that had it. I felt guilty about enjoying the luxury. It didn't seem fair to relax when I had so much to worry about.

Sal got in on the other side. "Give it a sec, it will warm you up, too. Ready?"

While Sal wove through traffic, I alternated between exploring all the luxuries surrounding me and checking out the window for green trannies. Inside there were individual entertainment devices, a dashboard chiller, and separate light diffusers in each window. Outside, there was reality—Cinderella girls, FeLS, sex-teens, and Ed.

Out of the corner of my eye I caught Sal watching me. After I'd ooh'd and aah'd over every little gadget, he said, "Then there's this." He pressed a dial marked *temp*.

I looked around to see what had happened—nothing. "And?"

"And," he said, "we are now shielded from any listening or tracking devices." He beamed with pride.

"You mean, we can talk about anything and no one can hear us?"

"Click on your PAV."

I tried. It didn't work. "A traveling DZ." We were driving down State Street, where every store's verts tried to outdo the others'. The verts were inescapable, even when you were in a trannie. But there we were, sitting in complete silence.

"No verts—Mike would hate it." I laughed. "Whose car is this anyway?"

"My aunt Rita's, we're going to her place."

Rita—it took me a second to connect. That was the name on Ginnie's list. Before I could ask him anything about her, we merged onto the Cementville expressway and a wave of sadness washed over me. "This reminds me of going home." There was a catch in my throat.

Sal reached over and squeezed my hand. "We'll only be on here for a few miles; then we switch over to Angola Works West."

I turned to the window, watching the countryside fly by. We sped past Mill Run Farm. I remembered the last time I passed it, the night Ginnie died. I caught a glimpse of the horses, tails flowing out behind them as they galloped across the meadow. We turned west and I forced myself to concentrate on the present.

"Want a Sparkle?" Sal pressed another button on the dashboard and the chiller in front of me popped open. A metal arm held up the drink. After I removed it, everything closed up again. I relaxed into the seat, which was practically cuddling me. This is tier ten all the way, I thought.

Sal steered past a little old couple in a 2100 DT. They reminded me of Gran and Pops, and I thought of my conversation with Gran earlier. "I found out more stuff about Ed." I filled him in on everything Gran and I had discussed.

"I've been doing some investigating, too, and I think Aunt Rita will be able to fill in a lot of the gaps. That's one reason I wanted you to come along."

"What's the other?"

He glanced over at me and his eyes met mine. "To have you close by."

A rush of warmth spread over me that had nothing to do with the Comfort Style seat. After last night, I no longer had any doubts about Sal's motivations—I knew he liked me for me, and not my father.

Sal scanned the traffic. "Hang on." He flipped a lever under the dash and we shot down the road like a comet. The g-force pinned me to my seat.

Eventually he slowed down to just under eighty miles per hour. "Wanted to make sure the engine would do what we modified it to do. Besides"—he grinned impishly—"it's fun."

"Yeah, it is! I haven't felt like this since moon travel simulation in fifth grade."

He caught my hand and kissed the tips of my fingers. "You're my kind of gal."

That kiss traveled to my toes faster than the trannie had taken off. I was blushing, but didn't care. He made me feel so good.

"Tell me about your aunt. Could she have known my mother?"

"She knew your mom really well. Rita's my mother's sister. She, uh . . . 'died' in high school. Like several people back then, she deliberately disappeared to join the NonCons. Only two people, besides my mom and dad, knew about it—Jade and Ginnie. They helped fake her death. She got a new identity. She has a big farm that's also an NC."

"NC? NonCon?" I asked.

"No, it stands for 'nook and cranny,' which is slang for a safe place. There aren't many NCs near cities. Most are in the mountains or deserts; it's easier to conceal them in rough terrain. This one is right in the middle of Easely Woods."

"Easely Woods! Doesn't that belong to a big Media corporation?"

"Sort of. EnviroManagement owns Easely. They're Resistance sympathizers. There's even a rumor that they run a rogue radio station from somewhere in Easely Woods. But no one's ever been able to track it down."

What was so matter-of-fact to him was hard for me to take in all at once. People—his aunt and hopefully my father—who died, but weren't dead. There were safe places for NonCons to go. Some big corporations sympathized with the Resistance. There was so much I didn't know. I felt foolish for my ignorance, particularly because my mother had apparently been right in the middle of it all. Media, government . . . my head was spinning.

"Where did he come from?" Sal jerked his thumb over his shoulder.

I looked out the back. A green transport. "That can't be Ed. Can it?"

"I'm not taking any chances." Sal reached over, checking my safety restraint. "This could get rough."

With a quick twist of the steering wheel, we flew across the median strip, then bounced over a fence and into a field. Granted, we were a foot or so off the ground, but at the speed we were traveling the resonance tractor was having difficulty keeping us stable off-road. The seat embraced me like a mother holding a baby. Even so, I thought my teeth were going to rattle right out of my head.

Sal veered into a patch of woods. I slapped my hands over my eyes, bracing myself for the imminent collision with one of the trees. He steered the trannie through more twists and turns than the Martian rocket ride at Lands o' Fun. I was so scared I didn't look through my fingers until we slowed down.

"You okay?"

"I think so." I felt my head, then my arms and stomach. "Yep, everything seems to be in place."

He gave me a half smile. "I don't understand; this trannie has an antitracking module." He turned off the engine. "How'd he find us?"

"Maybe he didn't need a tracker. He could have been waiting outside my building."

"Huh? I hadn't counted on him not using technology. That's got to be it. All the same, I'd better let John know when we get back." Sal got out of the transport and walked around it, checking the tractor underneath, and all the outside surfaces. "Dammit!" He swore and kicked the dirt.

My legs were shaking as I joined him. We stared at the scrapes that raked down the side of the transport. They'd cut all the way through to the composite below.

"I'm so sorry. This is my fault. If I wasn't here . . ."

Sal hugged me. "It's not your fault. It's a by-product of war."

"War?"

"Us and them; the Resistance versus the government; good versus evil—that kind of war. You're safe; that's what matters to me." Scanning the area, he said, "If that was Ed, I'd say we lost him. Let's get out of here."

While Sal fed coordinates to the GPS, I thought about the Resistance waging war against the government. It was impossible to imagine how anything or anyone could fight and win against something as powerful as the Governing Council. Finally, we emerged from the woods into a field, but my thoughts were still lost in a forest of confusion.

"There." He pointed ahead.

I couldn't see anything, but watched the horizon as we continued moving forward. Eventually, I made out a ribbon of black snaking through a field of soybeans. At least, I thought it was a field of soybeans.

"It's an old construction road, but it'll do."

No matter what kind of road it was, its surface was smooth as Telite compared to the detour we'd just made in the trannie. As we zipped along, I kept checking over my shoulder, watching.

XXXII

Sal drove up a narrow gravel road lined with trees. At the end was a clearing and a sprawling house like nothing I'd ever seen before.

"What are those?" I asked. The golden-hued sides of the structure appeared to be made of trunks stacked sideways. A porch ran the entire length of the front; hanging planters with the remains of flowers hung between the posts. One or two faded red blooms still survived.

"Repro logs," Sal said. "Recycled wood and paper."

"A log cabin like Abraham Lincoln."

"How'd you know that?" Sal asked.

"I've always been kind of curious about Lincoln. Ginnie had a book about pre–Governing Council history. There wasn't much of it."

"Ever wonder why that is?" Sal asked.

"No," I admitted, and colored a bit, thinking back to the last time he and I had talked about life before the Governing Council, when I'd falsely claimed how much I knew. "Ginnie tried to get me to study it further, but I preferred L & L to History."

"Some of the ideas people had were really good. Individuals' rights such as freedom of speech, equal rights for everyone, reproductive rights for women—stuff like that—all wiped out of the history books. That's why your dad got in so much trouble with his debates. If he'd just decided to become a pre-GC scholar in some university, no one would have bothered him. But he wanted to change things. He wanted all those freedoms back."

Sal pulled up in front of the house. Outside of the transport it was cold, but the air smelled different.

"Mmmm," Sal said. "Take a deep breath. This isn't city air."

I breathed deep, filling my lungs like I was drinking water. After two deep breaths, I felt light-headed. Sal grabbed my arm to steady me.

"It's not like that filtered stuff in Chicago. You'd better take it easy." He laughed. "Aunt Rita will think I gave you a shot of Grindy's home brew. By the way, I forgot to mention, Rita's pretty straightforward, not much small talk."

The front door opened and a woman walked out onto the porch. She looked about the same age as Ginnie, except for some gray streaks in her hair. She wasn't much taller than me and wore jeans, sturdy boots, and a bulky sweater. A clip held her long hair to one side; the rest cascaded down her back. I could see the family resemblance between her and Sal.

"Aunt Rita!" Sal crossed the porch and threw his arms around her.

"How's my favorite nephew?"

"Good."

"This must be Nina. I'm Rita Dugan." She took my hand firmly and looked me straight in the eye. "You look a lot like your father." First Sal had said that to me, then the Jenkinses, and now Rita. It was odd meeting people who knew my father. I liked the idea that I resembled him.

I met her gaze—those same deep dark eyes as Sal's.

"I'm glad you came today. I'm so sorry about your mother." She looked out across the treetops. "Personal sacrifice lies at the center of change for the better."

Sal was certainly right about his aunt being blunt. "The police said the murder was random," I said.

"Ginnie sacrificed a normal life with her daughters, and her happiness and peace of mind. She gave everything to the cause—everything." She touched my hand, in a surprisingly gentle gesture. "I don't believe her death was random at all."

That was the same thought I'd had. I wished Rita had been with me the night of the murder to make Officer Jelneck listen to that idea.

While I was pondering this, Sal said, "We had a little problem on the way here. That guy Ed, the one I told you about, was following us. I gave him the slip, but . . . the paint job got kind of messed up."

"Oh, honey, that can be fixed. You're both okay?" She searched our faces.

"Yes." Sal put an arm around my shoulder.

"I'm going to take my new dualie for a spin. You two go inside and make yourselves at home. We'll talk more when I get back." After a cursory walk around the trannie, stopping for a moment in front of the scratches, Rita got in and drove off.

"You okay?" Sal asked.

"I suppose." I didn't even sound convincing to myself. "My life hasn't been anything like what I believed it was. Everything that

I've thought was true was a lie." I rubbed my hands together—it was cold outside. "You knew all this?"

I sensed that he was reluctant to answer. He pulled me down to the top step. "I knew some of it."

"Why didn't you tell me?" As if I didn't know. After my outburst at the oasis, I couldn't blame Sal for not saying anything.

"I was afraid you wouldn't believe me. That you would've still thought the only reason I was hanging around was because of your father." He cupped my face in his hands. "Nina, I want to be with you because of you—not because of Alan. I didn't dare take a chance by telling you what I knew. I couldn't have stood it if you'd walked away from me again."

"Sal, I—"

He kissed me and I kissed him back. It was different from our other kisses. We were generating an inner heat I'd never felt before. I couldn't have stopped kissing him if I'd wanted to—which I didn't. My fingers twisted his hair as I tried to get closer to him than my own skin. When we came up for air, he buried his face in my hair—his breath like hot spurts of steam on my neck.

Whispering my name, he traced his tongue along the edge of my ear. I slung my leg over his, straddling him; his hands grabbed my butt, pulling me close. It wasn't close enough. We kissed more, completely lost in each other. There was nothing else in the world but the two of us. His hands moved up under my jacket, touching bare skin. A tiny moan escaped me.

Sal pulled back. "We'd better stop. Before we do something neither of us is ready for."

I hid my face in the crook of his neck. I was so ashamed. I'd been not just willing, but eager to go further. That line between love and lust was thin as a whisper. And I'd been ready to cross it without hesitation. Typical sex-teen. If he hadn't stopped—I didn't want to think about that. What was going on with me? Where was Ginnie when I needed a mom to talk to? For a millisecond I was furious with her for dying. If I'd let that feeling last longer, I'd have been furious with her for a whole lot more.

XXXIII

When I finally got up the nerve, I lifted my head ever so slightly from Sal's neck and said, "You must think I'm—"

"Amazing, Nina Oberon—absolutely amazing."

I slid off his lap onto the step beside him. I was too embarrassed to even look at him.

He reached over, pushing my hair aside, and kissed my cheek. "We should go inside. Aunt Rita will be back any second."

As if on cue, the dual transport flew into the driveway.

"I love it!" Rita strode up to the porch. "You and John are trannie geniuses. And what are you two still doing outside?"

I looked at the porch floor, sure that she must've known exactly what we'd been doing. I kept my head down as we followed her inside.

She ushered us into a sleek spare room. It was modern and airy, with a vaulted ceiling and skylights. The sun poured in, bathing everything in warmth and light. There was a cheery fire in a fireplace that formed part of the wall between that room and another.

"Sal, sweetie, you get some snacks for the two of you to take along on the express."

When Sal left the room to do as his aunt suggested, Rita sat down on a mammoth sectional that curved around in front of a panoramic view of the valley. She motioned for me to sit down next to her. "We need to talk."

I sat down, not knowing what to expect.

"There's not a lot of time for explanations, Nina. I know Ginnie sheltered you from the truth about her life. She was a NonCon. I'm sure you've figured that out by now."

I nodded.

"Do you know much about Ed?"

"He's a Chooser, Dee's father, and a horrible person."

"He's also an ex–B.O.S.S. agent who's been trying to prove that your father's alive ever since that night he allegedly drowned in the Chicago River. Ginnie took up with Ed to keep Alan's secret safe. And to keep you from any harm."

Relief flooded through me. "I knew he was alive. I knew Ginnie wouldn't lie to me about that." I blinked back the tears that rose up. "And I knew Ed was a government agent, but I didn't know he was ex-B.O.S.S."

"It was B.O.S.S. who put your mother on the machine at the hospital. As soon as we found out B.O.S.S. was putting Ginnie in the Infinity machine, our operative at the hospital fixed the audio so that nothing your mother said was recorded. But someone was listening and told Ed what Ginnie said to you. Do you remember anyone there in the room with you?"

"A nurse." I nodded. "A nurse was in the doorway when Ginnie told me that my father was alive. Even though Ginnie had me sing to her so no one would hear what she was saying."

"What else did she say?"

"That all the answers are in a book I'm supposed to give to my father."

"Where's the book now?"

"In a safe place." I'd been so eager to hear about my father that I'd let down my guard and was blabbing everything Ginnie'd told me to a woman I'd just met. But there was no turning back. I had no more secrets, not anymore.

"Hmm, Ed must not have told anyone else about this or else you'd have more than just him following you. Probably wants all the glory of catching Alan Oberon for himself. If the GC knew, they'd have picked you up by now. Ed believes you're a direct ticket to your father."

"The night Ginnie died she had an envelope with your name on it," I said. "Had you been in touch with her?"

"Often," Rita said. "We met the night she was murdered. I never would've left her alone if I'd thought she was in danger."

"You were with her?" And here I'd thought Ginnie didn't have any friends. There was so much I didn't know about my mother. "Do you know what happened? Do you know who killed her?"

Rita shook her head. "I have an idea, but without proof—or even with proof . . ." She sighed. "No one cares about the death of a tier-two woman, do they?"

I told her about B.O.S.S. taking Dee and me home from the hospital after Ginnie's death, and ransacking our house. "I guess they were looking for anything they could find about my father."

"Nina, B.O.S.S. believed that Alan died in that accident. Ed did not. They thought he was obsessed, on a wild-goose chase. That's what got him demoted from agent to Chooser. He'd give anything to prove Alan is alive."

"And he is, right?" I didn't even need to wait for the answer. At least some of the puzzle pieces were falling into place. My dad was alive. He and Ginnie were NonCons. "What should I do? Ed knows I have something he wants—and I'm pretty sure he knows it's the book. I have to get it to my dad."

"For the time being, stay close to Sal or Wei. She's a good friend to have. I'll work out the best way to get that book to Alan."

"Uh-huh." I didn't feel so great. My head was exploding from all the new information I was learning about my life. And my body was still humming from Sal's touch, about which I was feeling very conflicted. I wanted him and I didn't. Too confusing.

Rita checked her chronos. "Sal," she called, "time to leave."

We both stood up. "I know this has been a lot for you to take in, Nina."

I may have been confused about everything else, but there was one point I was very clear on. "I'll give my father the book. No one else but me is going to do that. How do I find him?"

Rita sighed. "I told him you would feel like this."

"Told him? You've spoken to him? About me?"

Sal had returned to the room and was watching us. "I'll go get Max." He raised his eyebrows as he walked past me. I didn't even stop to wonder who Max was.

"When can I meet him? Doesn't he want to see me?" I couldn't believe I was so close; my heart was pounding.

"Of course he does," Rita said. "Knowing he has you is what's kept him going."

"Does he know about Ginnie's death?"

"Yes."

"When can I see him?" I was about to burst.

"It's too dangerous right now. Not just for you, but for Gran and Pops and Dee. If Ed, or the GC, gets wind of the fact that Alan really is alive, you will all be in danger. You have to be patient . . . and careful. Many lives depend on you. I know you can do this. You mustn't say anything about this to anyone."

"I'm sure Gran suspects. I've told her Ginnie said my father was alive. She dismissed it at first, but I think she knows Ginnie was right."

"Does she know about the book?" Rita put her arm around me and we walked out onto the porch.

"Sort of . . ."

"Well, the less she knows, the safer she is. Poor woman has been through so much." She squeezed my shoulders. "I feel for the families. You have no idea how difficult it's been for those of us, like your father and me, who disappeared, leaving our families behind grieving for us. I know it's hard for you. But Ginnie raised you well. You won't let her down."

I bit my tongue. No, I wouldn't let her down. I was okay with not telling Gran about the book, but I was determined to get it to my father, and sooner rather than later. Now that I was positive he was alive, I would find him. With or without Rita's help.

Just then Sal showed up in front of the house with an older-model multitransport. "Max is on his way."

A man emerged from a building I hadn't noticed before. "What's that?" I asked.

"The Lodge. NonCons who need to lay low for a while stay there. That other house"—Sal pointed behind the log home to a smaller version of it—"is where Grindy and Mobley live. They're the horse handlers. Dammit . . . I forgot." He turned to Rita. "I was going to show her the horses."

"That will have to wait until next time," Rita said. "I have things to take care of. And so do you." She gave Sal a peck on the cheek and me a hug, then disappeared into the house.

Sal and I hopped into the back of the multi and Max got in on the driver's side. I stared out the window until I couldn't see the house or the valley anymore. I felt further from my dad and Ginnie than ever.

***

We hopped a trans outside the express station. When we got to my stop, Sal looped his arm in mine. "Let's walk to the river. I don't want to let you go yet." We ended up at the DZ oasis.

"This isn't as nice as where we were," I said.

"Nice enough for me. You're here."

He pulled me close and kissed me. His lips were warm and soft. I wanted to get lost in his kisses, but I couldn't stop thinking about my dad.

Sal must've been able to tell I was preoccupied. We just sat together, my head on his shoulder, watching the murky green water of the Chicago River until the sun disappeared and night crept in.

"Can I meet Gran and Pops?" he asked.

***

When we walked into the apartment, I could hear Gran, busy in the kitchen preparing supper.

"Is there enough for one more?" I called down the hall.

"Yes."

"Who's that?" Pops looked up from his zine. His artificial leg was propped on the floor beside the chair.

Oh great, I thought. The leg, right off the bat. I took a deep breath. "Pops, this is Sal."

"Excuse me for not gettin' up." Pops chuckled. "Ain't got a leg to stand on. Do I, now, Little Bit?"

I could feel my face reddening, but I forged ahead. He was, after all, my grandfather, and I loved him.

"Doesn't look like you do, Pops. So, you'd better stay sitting."

"Smart girl—just like her father." He and Sal shook hands. "Sit, sit." Pops motioned us to the couch. "We've got company, Edith," he yelled.

Gran came out of the kitchen, dish towel in hand. She plonked Pops right on top of his head with the towel. "Don't go hollering at me, old man. Think this pile of reconstituted sand and sludge is soundproof? I heard 'em come in, I'm not deaf. But I will be if you keep shouting every time anything happens around here."

She tucked the towel in her waistband. When she saw Sal she paled, reaching for the arm of Pops's chair.

I leaped up and grabbed her. "Gran, are you okay?"

"Fine, I'm fine." She shook free and waved me back to my seat. When she regained her composure, she said, "You've got to be Brock's son. My Lord . . . the spitting image. He and my son, Alan, were friends in school. I thought I'd stepped back in time."

"I'm sorry, I didn't mean to startle you."

"It's not your fault—you had no way of knowing how the resemblance . . . well, uncanny, that's what it is." She wiped her glasses on the towel, adjusted them on her nose, and studied Sal.

"I knew I looked like him," he said. "But it's been ages since I've seen his high school pictures."

"I heard the news," Gran said. "Four years ago—wasn't it?"

"Yes. They were on assignment, researching Nina's father."

"Lost in the ocean, wasn't it? Leviton went down—no survivors."

"That was the story." I was startled by the bitterness in his voice.

"Damn lie," Pops muttered.

"What? Speak up," Gran prodded him.

"Lies, I said. Everyone knows that Media used a suicide robot for that flight. No one was supposed to survive. Anyone gets too close to the truth about Alan . . ." He made a cutting motion across his throat.

Sal was half smiling, but I saw his jaw muscles working beneath the surface. Pops could be as bad as Sandy sometimes, blurting out things that hurt other people without thinking.

Gran looked at us and almost imperceptibly shook her head. I realized there could be surveillance.

I jumped off the couch, grabbing Sal's arm. "Let's go to my room? You don't mind, do you, Pops?"

"Go on with you." He waved us away. "Kids don't care nothin' about nothin' anymore, anyway." He reached for his zine, burying his nose in it.

Gran accompanied us partway down the hall. "Ignore the crazy talk from that old man. His leg's been bothering him so much lately. I gave him some pain medicine half an hour ago; it obviously affected his head. I am very sorry about your parents,

Sal. Go on now." She motioned toward my room. "I'll call you when dinner's ready"

"Where's Dee?"

"She's doing her homework with a friend."

I panicked. "Gran! You let her go out?'"

"She's on PAV in her room." Gran pinched my cheek. "Wasn't born yesterday, dear."

Even if Ed was after me, and not Dee, I wasn't taking any chances where she was concerned. I peeked into Dee's room and waved to her, just to be sure she was there.

***

Dinner was minus Pops. The pain meds had knocked him out for the night. Sal helped me get him into bed after we ate. Then I walked Sal to the elport.

"I have so much to think about," I said. "I don't know what to do, what to think . . ."

The doors opened, Sal kissed me and stepped inside. "I have just one thing to think about," he said. "You."

The doors closed.

When I got back to the apartment, Gran was waiting for me. "Nina. Something was taken during the break-in." Her voice was strained.

My thoughts flew—Gran hadn't said if she and Pops had a second scrambler, or something else illegal. Something that could mean really big trouble for Pops if the authorities found it. And Gran had filed a police report. My "what?" came out more like a squeak than a word.

"Your FeLS contract is missing. I doubt I would've even

noticed, but I had this feeling that I should put it in a safer spot. When I went to get it—it was gone."

The tiniest shiver of fear started at the base of my neck. "Maybe you just misplaced it, Gran." I didn't mention her advanced age and that old people sometimes forget things. "Besides, the FeLS agency will have a record of the buyout, right?"

I could see the relief spread across her face. "Of course they will. I didn't think of that. I'll call first thing on Monday." She patted her cheeks. "Silly to get all upset now. Everything will be fine."

She breathed easier, but I didn't. I didn't want to think about what could happen, what might be . . . It all felt too much, almost too much to handle.

When I went to my room, instead of going to bed, I took out my pad of paper and a special rapido Ginnie'd given me when I started art classes. I sat at the window and drew the shapes of the buildings outside. Rectangles and squares stacked side by side and up to the sky. Neat, orderly, controllable. The complete opposite of my life.

If the FeLS agency didn't have a record of my contract buyout, I would have to apply to the program. Unless I was able to get my Creative designation before the Choosing. My birthday was coming up, but I didn't know when the Choosing was going to be, or when I'd be able to get my designation. I stacked the last square on the paper and went to bed.

XXXIV

woke up to the tones of my PAV. It was Wei.

"Wanna go to the zoo?"

"I'll be ready when you get here."

By the time I'd scarfed down breakfast and dressed, she'd arrived.

"See you later, Gran."

"Homework done?" she asked. "Tomorrow's a school day."

"I don't have much. I'll finish it when I get home. I promise."

"I'm holding you to that. Now go on, you two, so you can get back." She shooed us out the door. "And be careful."

"I'm always careful," I said.

"Don't worry, Mrs. Oberon, she's with me."

We goofed around while waiting for the elport. Wei demonstrated a headlock on me and then showed me how to break away if someone grabbed my arm. We were downstairs before I managed to free myself from her grasp by jerking through the thumb side of the hold. "Keep practicing," she said. "You'll get it eventually." I wasn't so sure of that.

Outside it was bleak and gray. The sky spat hard little balls of white that bounced off the concrete. Automatically, I scanned the street for Ed's green trannie. Nothing.

"I'm not ready for snow. I hate being cold." I pulled my gloves on. "Is your dad back from Amsterdam yet?"

"No—tonight. You want to walk or take a trans?"

"Let's walk. I need to toughen up to the weather." I was envious that the cold didn't seem to bother Wei at all.

We'd gone two blocks when the wind picked up and the sleet pellets turned to snow, soft and flat, falling faster and thicker. "Maybe we should take a trans," I said. "I can toughen up later."

We braced our backs against the wind gusts and waited for the number 33. I noticed a green trannie idling at the corner; I nudged Wei, nodding in its direction.

"Get in that doorway," she said. "I'll be right back."

I was so intent on watching her that I didn't notice that another green trannie had pulled up in the alley behind me until it was too late. Ed's hand was over my mouth and he'd twisted my arm behind my back before I knew what was happening. Wei turned around in time to see him force me into his transport.

Quick as she was, Ed was quicker. He pulled out into traffic before she could reach us. I pounded on the door, but it wouldn't open while we were moving—damn safety devices. I was trapped. I swallowed the urge to scream, forcing myself to turn and face him.

"Let me out," I demanded. No way would I let him know how scared I was. I'd seen the damage he'd done to Ginnie. I was sure he wouldn't hesitate to hurt me if it served his purpose. And at last I knew what his purpose was: Dee's baby book. He needed me to get that. My heart quailed, but my resolve stood firm.

"Not even going to say hello?" He smirked. "That's the least you could do—show some respect to the man who supported you for the last ten years."

"Supported me?" I couldn't disguise the sarcasm in my voice. "You never gave me anything at all."

"Well, I'll give you something now." He backhanded me across the mouth. The pain was sharp and sudden. I tasted blood. I would not give him the satisfaction of seeing me cry. I felt a fury boil up inside me—ready to explode.

He watched me, his eyes hard and soulless. "And here's something for the knee you gave me last time we met." His closed fist slammed into my face.

I actually felt my brain rattle in my head and shooting pain spread from my hairline to my chin. Little silver dots floated in my line of vision and my rage turned to nausea. It took everything I had just to stay conscious, but I knew I had to if I was going to escape.

"I think we're even now," he said. "Let's get down to business. You have something I want. A book. I wasn't sure what until your blond girlfriend practically waved it under my nose the other night."

I thought my head would explode. How Ginnie survived all the times he'd done this to her, I didn't know. I murmured, no words, just sound.

"I'm not one for making deals, but I'm feeling generous today. I'm finally going to show them. All of them." He glanced into the rearview and gave a self-satisfied smile. "So, Nina, how do you like this: you give me the book, or I make sure you're chosen for FeLS. I heard your contract disappeared. Shame. And to make the deal even sweeter, while you're out there in training, Dee will have to come and live with me. No doubt she'll want to stay forever. That's how Cinderella girls are . . . so I've heard."

"I . . ." I stalled, pretending I was still dazed while I scanned the dash in front of me, looking for something I might use to get away. His trannie had a chiller, just like the one in Rita's. I wondered . . .

Snow was falling faster now and the streets were getting slick. Even though trannies hover about a foot above the pavement, their tractor system relies on sonic contact between the vehicle and the ground; I'd learned that in Mechanical Science. I'd also learned that if a transport isn't winterized, you can be in for a slippery ride.

Ahead of us, directly in our path, three trannies had swerved to miss a transit that had stalled.

"Stupid-ass drivers!" Ed eased up on the accelerator, his attention leaving me for a moment and focusing on the road. That's when I saw my chance.

I pressed the chiller button and out burst a Sparkle—just like I'd hoped. I shook it, aimed, and popped the top—exploding the sweet, sticky liquid right into Ed's face.

"You goddamn little bitch!" He smacked both hands to his face, frantically wiping his eyes, trying to get the carbonated soda out of them. He spluttered and cursed, momentarily blinded.

Reaching over, I jerked the steering wheel, causing our trannie to plow into the back of a transit. His side of the transport crumpled and my door automatically flew open. I bolted, skidding and slipping on the snowy streets, not daring to look back. People jumped out of my way as I raced blindly on. My sides were splitting and my lungs screamed for air, but I kept on running. I didn't know how long I ran, but I didn't stop until my legs refused to go any farther.

Crouched in an alley behind a stack of wooden crates, I called Wei.

"Where are you?" she cried. "I'm with Sal and Derek. We didn't know what to do to find you."

"I. Got. Away." My breath came quick, shallow and painful. "I don't know where I am. On the south side somewhere . . . I think."

I strained to see through the swirling snow, looking for anything that might be familiar. I saw a transit sign outside the alley. It was for the number 47 line.

"I'll get to Union Station," I said. "Meet me there."

I skulked in the doorway of a nearby building, not venturing out into the open until I heard the transit approach. As I scanned my pass, the driver gave me a funny look. The trans lurched forward and I stumbled down the aisle. A woman put a package she was holding down on the empty seat beside her as I approached, so I took the seat behind her, sliding over by the window. The pain in my face had settled into a dull throbbing. I hesitated before touching my lip; it was swollen and crusted with blood. I automatically reached up to brush the hair out of my eye. A little cry escaped when I bumped my cheek. The woman in front of me half turned in my direction. I put my head down to avoid her glance.

I skimmed my fingers along my cheek—I could tell it was swollen, too. No wonder the driver and the woman had stared; I bet I looked awful. By pulling the collar of my jacket up and letting my hair fall over my face, I was able to partially conceal my injuries. I didn't want to draw any more attention to myself than I already had.

The few people brave enough to be out were merely dark apparitions in the driving snowstorm. It took an eternity to get to Union Station. The familiarity of the worn marble floors and wooden benches was somehow reassuring. I sat down, facing the front, waiting for my friends.

When they finally got there, I tried to keep Sal from seeing my face. But it didn't work.

"What—?" He lifted up my hair. Then he spun around and slammed his fist into a wooden pillar.

We all heard the familiar whir of a security cam changing direction, to focus on the disturbance he'd made.

"Control yourself," Wei whispered to him. "We don't need any cops showing up."

"I'll kill him," he muttered between clenched teeth.

"Sal . . . don't." I laid a hand on his arm. "I'm okay."

"Okay?" he practically shouted, pointing at my face. "That is not okay!" He looked at Wei. "Do something." Then back at me. "Does it hurt?"

"Of course it hurts, pigeon brain," Wei said, exasperated. "Come on." She took my arm. "Let's get out of view of that thing and get you cleaned up. Don't do anything stupid," she said to Sal. "Wait right here. Derek—watch him."

"I'll kill him," Sal repeated under his breath. "When I find him, I'll kill him."

"You'll do no such thing," Wei said. "We need to talk to my parents. They'll know what to do, and who to go to in order to get it done."

Derek, who'd been standing there staring at me the whole time, finally spoke. "We'll go outside. Sal needs to cool off. And, Nina . . . red is not your color."

I thought about smiling, but even the thought hurt.

Wei dragged me off to the bathroom. Nothing could've prepared me for my reflection. I hardly recognized the girl staring back at me. My lips were swollen, way beyond collagen-pumped, and bloody. My entire left cheek was as big as an orange and bright red to boot. I had to touch it to make sure it was really me.

Wei dabbed at the blood from around my lips.

"Ouch!"

"Sorry." She continued cleaning my face with wet tissues. "I'm trying to be careful."

A couple of white-haired ladies entered and peered at us suspiciously. I wondered if they were security—you could never tell.

"My friend slipped and fell on the steps outside," Wei said. "Looks awful, doesn't it?"

They obviously weren't security or we would've been questioned on the spot. Wei's explanation brought out the grandmother in both of them. One dug around in her purse and offered up a couple of Band-Aids. The other handed me a bottle of OTC pain meds.

"Keep them, dearie." She gently patted my hand. "I have plenty more at home. Government issue, don't you know." She winked at me.

We thanked them and they left. But not before making dire predictions about how much worse I would look and feel in the morning.

Wei doctored up my lip with the Band-Aids and I swallowed a couple of the pills.

She stood back, surveying her handiwork. "That looks a little better. I can't do anything for the bruising, though. That's going to take a major makeup job or some of Mom's concoctions."

"Great story about me falling on the slick steps. I think Gran will buy it, too. I can be a real klutz sometimes. I can't tell her what really happened. I don't want her worrying about me every time I leave the house."

"No, I'll be the one doing that now." Wei's hands were firmly set on her hips.

"Oh . . . you want me to check in with you before I go anywhere?" I mimicked holding my PAV receiver. "Wei, this is Nina, I'm leaving for school. Wei, this is Nina, I'm going to the store for Gran. Wei, this is Nina, I'm going to the bathroom. Oh, wait—that's not outside, is it?"

We both started laughing, which wasn't too bright on my part. "Ouch, ouch!" I grabbed at my face, tears trickling down my cheeks. "I really can't laugh."

We finished up and went outside where the guys were waiting.

"Nina, are you all right? I will make sure he regrets he ever laid a hand on you . . ." Sal said. I knew he would, if he had the chance. I even fantasized for a second that he, or someone, would "take care" of Ed.

"So much for a day at the zoo," Wei said.

"I need to get home." The pain pills hadn't kicked in yet, and I was exhausted, plus I was feeling nauseous again. "Ed wanted the book. The accident looked bad, but if he was able to get to the apartment . . ." Images of Ed terrorizing Gran and Pops came to me and my stomach churned. I ran back to the restroom, making it just in time before throwing up. I fought the vision of Pops trying to defend Gran and Dee against Ed. Pops wouldn't stand a chance.

Wei'd followed me in. "Come on, Nina. We'll get you home. Ed's trannie slid into a transit, right?"

I nodded.

"Even if Ed wasn't hurt, he'd be tied up with CTA investigators for hours."

We went back outside to where the guys were.

"I've got practice with Riley. We've got another show coming up at Soma. I think we were a hit the other night," Derek said. "If you need me, though, I'll call him. We can do it later."

"I'll be fine." It was getting painful to talk. "But don't say 'hit' again." I tried to smile, but that hurt, too.

"Are you sure you're going to be okay?" Derek said. "Wei and I can take you home. You need protection."

"You guys go on." Sal put his arm around my shoulder. "I'll make sure Nina gets there safely." I could get used to this kind of attention from him, but not under these circumstances.

When we got back to the apartment, instead of taking me right upstairs, Sal pulled me into the emergency stairwell.

"You've got to be careful, Nina. I couldn't stand it if anything happened to you." He wrapped me in his arms.

"Stop." I pulled back. When I saw his confusion, I quickly added, "You were crushing my face, it hurts."

He moved my hair aside and barely brushed his lips across my cheek. "I would never hurt you." He traced a finger lightly around the reddening on my face. "He will pay for this. I should have been there to protect you. I shouldn't have let you be alone."

"Sal, I wasn't alone, I was with Wei. It was my fault." I ran my hands up and around his neck, pulling him closer to me. "You can't exactly move in. And I'll be fine. I won't be that careless again."

"I'll pick you up in the morning. It's not that far out of my way."

That wasn't true—but I knew he would be there. And that he would be there every day until he was sure I was safe. I kissed him—I didn't care that it hurt. He took the elport up with me, not leaving until I was inside the apartment.

Gran didn't believe my slipped-on-the-snow story. She removed the Band-Aids, washed the cuts with hydrogen peroxide, which really stung, and put a spray-on protectant over them.

"That should help." She leaned on the bathroom doorjamb. "You want to tell me what really happened?"

"I was careless," I said. "But I'm okay."

She pointed to my wounds. "I wouldn't call that okay."

"Gran, I'm almost sixteen. I have to be able to take care of myself. And I'm learning." One more lie wouldn't hurt. "Wei's teaching me some of her martial arts moves. This won't happen again."

Cold packs helped with the swelling, but it was impossible to sleep on the side of my face where Ed had hit me. Banged-up face or not, I tossed around, replaying the day's events. Ed knew my FeLS contract was missing, so I was right, he had been behind the break-in. Even if he wasn't the Chooser at my school, he still had the authority to have me chosen. And the minute I left, he'd take Dee. The book was at the center of all of this. I couldn't keep it safe any longer. And that meant finding my father, as soon as possible.

Despite the pain, I felt sleep overtaking me. Before I drifted off, I thought that even if Ed had my contract, the FeLS agency had to have a record that Ginnie'd bought out my contract. Gran would call them in the morning. That would be one less thing for me to worry about.

XXXV

andy called first thing next morning. "So what time are you coming this weekend? I can't wait to celebrate my birthday with you! I have my appointment for my tattoo already, and I know exactly what I'm going to wear—"

"Sandy—I . . . I can't come see you this weekend. I fell last night, landed right on my face."

"But, Nina, it's my birthday!"

"I'm sorry, it's really bad." I winced, and gently touched my cheek. "Here, I'll send you a digi so you can see. It hurts like you wouldn't believe"

I heard her fumbling with her PAV. "Nina! What'd you *do?* Skivs, you can't go out looking like this! Anyway, I'm coming to town next time Derek plays." She gushed on about how great he was. "Oh, yeah, and Mike called. I said I'd go help him at the zoo when I'm in town. It sounds like fun. Besides, I won't have to worry about losing my virginity to him, and I've gotta stay virginal for FeLS. Do you have any idea how hard it's going to be? Guys are already betting on who'll be my first."

She rambled on this way for about five minutes, until I couldn't take it anymore. "I gotta get ready for school," I mumbled, clicking off.

Things were becoming way more complicated than I wanted them to be. I didn't see how I could keep Sandy and Wei from clashing over Derek. And I sure didn't want Sandy to lead Mike on; that would be so unfair. I wasn't sure I could handle relationship drama on top of everything else, but I figured I'd come up with some kind of plan. After all, these were my friends.

***

Before we were out the lobby door, Dee spotted Sal. "What are you doing here?"

"Waiting for you." He winked at her.

"I like that. Kind of like a big brother. I always wanted a one." She quickly looked at me. "But I love having a big sister, too. See Nina's face? She fell down yesterday."

"Yeah, I know," Sal said.

I wished I could hide the purple-black bruise that spread upward from my jaw to my eye, but there was no way. It covered my whole cheek.

"I was there—sort of," he said.

"You should've caught her," Dee said. "Then she wouldn't look so awful and hurt so bad. She's really grumpy when she's in pain. She couldn't even eat breakfast this morning. Gran had to make her a protein shake. I hate those. Ugh!" She wrinkled her nose.

"Was it awful?" he asked me.

"Better than nothing . . . maybe," I muttered. It hurt whenever I opened my mouth. Gran had suggested going to the medical clinic in the building. But I didn't want stitches in my lip. I said

I'd keep my mouth shut; not an easy thing for me.

Derek met up with us at the usual place, but Mike was nowhere to be seen.

"He's running late," Derek said. "His dad got real sick from the last batch of meds. Mike had to help his mom get him to County General."

"Hey guys!"

We all turned around at the same time. Mike was running down the sidewalk.

He was out of breath by the time he reached us. "What the hell happened to you? Kiss a trans?" he asked me.

"Long story," Derek said.

He started to explain, but I managed to catch his eye and shook my head vigorously. Not the smartest thing to do when every muscle in half your face is bruised and swollen. I nodded toward Dee, who was busy telling Sal about her class's upcoming field trip to the Museum of Science and Industry.

I'd worked out a way to speak by keeping my lips still and talking very slowly. "She thinks I fell," I whispered as best I could.

"Huh?" Derek just stared at me.

I repeated myself, just a little louder.

He still didn't get it.

"Fell?" Mike said. "You fell?"

I nodded.

"Klutz." He grinned at me. "I hope it doesn't hurt too much." I knew he felt bad for me, but that was the best Mike could manage for sympathy.

After we dropped Dee off at school, Wei said, "I scanned the news last night. There was a six-transport pileup with a bus on the south side of the Loop. No one was seriously injured."

"Too bad," Sal said. "If I get ahold of Ed, he will be seriously injured."

"Will you stop with the threats, already? It's not helping." Wei said, "Dad's not back from Amsterdam yet. I think we need to figure out what to do if something happens before he returns."

Sal inclined his head toward a group of approaching students. "We can talk about this later. At your house, Wei?"

She nodded.

"I don't know what you guys are talking about, but I can't come," Mike said. "Zoo duty."

"Me either," Derek said. "Practice with Riley. I'm really sorry, Nina. You know . . ."

" 'S okay," I murmured. "Your music's important."

"We'll be fine," Wei said.

***

After homeroom, Wei was waiting for me. "Come on," she whispered. I followed her down the hall.

We went through a door, down some stairs, and ended up in a corridor in the basement. I followed her to a small room at the end. "This is the old detention room. It's DZ, 'cause they never wanted anyone to know what really went on in here."

Sal was inside.

"We've gotta be quick—here are some hall passes to get you back to class." He handed them to us. I noticed Miss Gray's signature at the bottom. "I can't make it this afternoon. John's got something going down; I have to be there to back him up." He squeezed my hand. "You understand, don't you?"

I nodded. There were obviously things going on all around me that I knew nothing about. I was more than a little nervous about finding out what they were.

"Wei, talk to your dad, okay?" Sal said. "I think there's only one way to take care of this."

"You don't mean . . ." I left the awful conclusion he was leading to unsaid.

"Nina, if Ed gets you he'll go straight to the Governing Council—or worse. You wouldn't stand a chance with GC interrogators."

Icy shards of fear shot up my spine. "Are you saying it's him or me?"

"Of course not." Wei gave Sal a withering look. "We just can't let anything happen to you. Your father needs you; the Resistance needs you."

"But I don't know anything about the Resistance. How can they need me?"

"We don't have time for this now," Sal said. "First things first. We have to take care of Ed, or you'll never be safe."

"Can't we just scare him? Or capture him and take him to, you know . . . uh, someplace . . ." My voice trailed off. I meant the Lodge, but wasn't sure if it was all right for me to mention it.

"Look, hopefully my father will be home after school," Wei said. "Nina and I will talk to him. We'd better get going or we'll have a hard time explaining these passes and we don't want to get Miss G in trouble."

I left first; Wei and Sal followed. I peeked through the door on the main level. It was all clear. I didn't look back as I hurried down the hallway to my next class.

XXXVI

Wei and I hardly said a word on the way to her house. She seemed preoccupied and my jaw hurt too much to make small talk. When we got inside there was a message from her mom. While Wei was listening to it, I tried to call Gran, but my PAV wouldn't work. Of course, Wei's house was DZ. I caught Wei's eye and motioned that I'd be outside.

I was able to get reception at the sidewalk. "I'm at Wei's, Gran. I'll be home by dinner."

"Nina . . ." Her voice sounded strained. "The FeLS agency doesn't have any record of Ginnie's payment. You're still available to be chosen."

I hung up and heard Ed's voice in my head: . . . *while you're out there for training* . . . Joan's face flashed in front of me. I'd bet my life that Ed knew what really went on at FeLS training. And I was more certain than ever that it wasn't good. Especially since he'd seemed to get such a kick out of the thought of sending me there.

***

"Dad's leviton set down in Greenland," Wei said. "Supposedly because of engine trouble. He never reboarded."

"Maybe he just missed it. Where's your mom?"

"She's out shopping for something to wear in Tokyo. She's going there for a couple of weeks to visit her brother. Whenever anything is going on, we keep our routines normal so it doesn't look like we're worried. She thinks Dad's probably being questioned about you being here the other night."

"They wouldn't do anything—" I stopped midsentence. "We can talk freely, right?"

"Yes. The whole building is *always* a dead zone. Actually, Dad's such a techno-geek, it's even better than DZ. It sends out phony normal conversations whenever there are people inside talking. We can say whatever we want and all they'll hear is whatever kind of talk would most likely be going on between whoever came in. Since it's you and me, they are hearing talk about school or boys."

"Who's holding your dad?" I couldn't have been anywhere close to as calm as Wei seemed. "Is it B.O.S.S.? They wouldn't hurt him, would they?"

"Probably B.O.S.S. And, yeah, they'd hurt him if they discovered he was a NonCon. After they'd gotten whatever information they could out of him, they'd either reassimilate him or kill him. You want something to eat?"

"You're not worried?" I followed her down the hallway, hardly believing the matter-of-fact way she'd talked about her dad possibly being killed. "I would be insane if it was my dad."

"Of course I'm worried. But it doesn't do any good to get upset and emotional. I've grown up knowing that at any time my whole family could be taken from me—or me from them. That's one reason why I took up Cliste Galad; it keeps me sane. Sparkle?"

I took the can from her. I'd have given anything to be as

composed as she was. But I didn't think it would ever be possible.

We sat at the counter. I sipped my drink through a straw.

"How's your grandmother?" Wei asked. "She wasn't worried about you, was she?"

"No, but she had some not-so-good news. Remember that break-in about a week ago? At first Gran didn't think anything was missing. She thought it was someone looking to steal Pops's pain meds. But yesterday she discovered that my FeLS contract was missing."

"The agency—"

"Doesn't have a record of Ginnie buying it. I'm back on the available list. It's Ed, I'm sure. He said he'd make sure I was chosen for FeLS; he knows my contract was missing." Then I told her about seeing Joan. "Something really bad happened to her, and I think it has to do with FeLS training."

"We have to find your contract, or get money to buy it," Wei said. "I know things about FeLS. I listened in on a conversation that Mom had with Rosie. From what I could hear, the government is using FeLS as a cover for sex slavery."

"I don't get it—any sixteen-year-old-girl is already legal to have sex. Why would they—"

"You know how FeLS recruits have to be virgins? They're more valuable. And it gets worse."

My stomach was already twisted into knots.

"The training is led by Governing Council members. They get the virgins. Then FeLS makes sure there's a fresh run of girls for upper-level government officials."

"But what happens to the girls, after the government is done?"

My voice shook, but not as bad as my insides. "What happens to all the girls?"

"They consider them 'used' and send them to Mars, as wives for the ocribundan miners."

"That can't be," I said. "It sounds just like *Mars Rising*, but that's fiction. People make that kind of stuff up, they don't actually make it happen."

"*1984* was fiction," Wei said. "And it came true decades ago."

She was right. *Women Scorned* and several other books had been banned after society accepted their premises as a normal way of life. I only knew about them because of Ginnie. And B.O.S.S confiscated all of her books already. The GC wouldn't . . . the look on Wei's face was more than proof that they would. "But I ran into Joan on Earth—how could she have gotten back here?"

"The Resistance has some people at the training station. They manage to sneak out some girls and get them back to Earth. The girls on Mars, though, they're infected by the same viral disease that keeps ocribundan miners from returning. I think a lot of those girls commit suicide. That's part of why FeLS keeps sending the used girls there. The miners demand them. The girls who sneak back, well, the homeless community is the only safe place for people like Joan."

"What about the girls who talk up the program at school? They go through the program and end up as models or get high-tier jobs in Media."

"Mom and Rosie didn't get into that. They must have more than one training station, though, to keep up appearances. Then it seems legit, but most of it isn't."

My head was reeling. My contract was gone. FeLS was sex slavery. "Can we talk about something else? Please? I can't think about this right now. My head will explode."

Wei and I stared at each other for the longest time. Then she reached over and gave my hand a squeeze. "We'll figure something out, I promise. Mom and Dad won't let you go."

"Wei," I said. "Sandy . . . What about her?"

"I bet you can talk her out of it."

"I've been trying for the past year. She figures it's the only way to get out of being low tier. That's how they talk it up in school and in *XVI Ways*. You probably noticed she's not scholarship material." I felt guilty talking this way about Sandy, but it was true. "And there's a ton of girls for every higher-tier guy. Not much chance of getting out that way."

"Maybe we could hook her up with some guy?" Wei said. "She seems awfully eager to, you know . . ." She gave me a sideways glance.

"Have sex? Yeah, I know. But she knows that FeLS recruits have to be virgins. And, honestly, I think she's really into flirting, but nothing else."

"Maybe we find her some guy that she can't resist." Wei twisted the soda can in her hands. "Like Derek."

"Derek? No way. Derek isn't anything to her. Besides, I can tell he really likes you."

"Really?" The only emotion she showed was a brief smile that danced around the corners of her mouth. "But if she did want him to . . . I wouldn't mind if it kept her out of FeLS."

"You wouldn't?" If Sandy wanted to have sex with Sal, I didn't think I would be so nonchalant about it.

"Nina, I like Derek." She tapped the edge of her Sparkle can. "A lot, actually. I don't think he wants Sandy in a sex-teen way. He's not that kind of guy."

I knew she was right about that. The word that popped into my mind about him and girls was "gallant." The way he'd always been around to stand up for me. "Yeah? So . . ."

"I don't want to see any girl go into FeLS. Someone's life is more important than any insecurity I might have about a boy. Although, Derek is a pretty special guy." She took a sip of Sparkle.

We talked more about Derek and that led to his music and then to more normal things. The threat of being chosen retreated to the edge of my thoughts, hovering there, waiting to return faster than a wing beat.

***

Mrs. Jenkins arrived home, and after one look at my face, she took me firmly in hand. "Come with me. I have some salves for this."

"Mom knows herbal secrets that have been around for millennia," Wei told me. "They really do help."

I went with Wei's mother to her room. She brought a small chest out of the closet. It was shiny black with silver and gold designs covering it.

"This chest has been passed down through my family for centuries, since the Heian period in Japan, around the year 794."

I did some quick math in my head. "That's over thirteen hundred years ago! Can I touch it?"

"Of course. It's maki-e, a technique that layers gold and silver powders in the tree sap that forms the lacquer." Mrs. Jenkins watched as I ran my fingers over the surface.

It almost seemed as if the surface was responding to my touch, in the same way there'd be a slight quiver when I'd run my hand along Pepper's flank. I looked at Mrs. Jenkins. "It feels like it's alive."

"You feel that?" Her eyes widened. "It is rare that anyone notices. The lacquer continually interacts with its environment. The greatest maki-e artisans knew their work would live forever. You are very sensitive to life." She blinked and then turned away. "I am the last healer in my family. Wei has no desire to learn— she is more interested in getting bumps and bruises than fixing them."

"Are there other healers?"

"A few, but they must practice in secret. The Governing Council insists that people rely on conventional forms of medicine. Disease and pain are big business. Media makes a fortune advertising cures, all the while filling people's minds with fear of the very diseases the doctors claim to heal, which causes the very illnesses people are afraid of getting. It's a vicious cycle that lines the pockets of health care providers and drug companies."

While we were talking she'd taken three squat stone jars out of the cabinet, uncovering each and smelling the contents.

"This will do." She took a small amount of greenish cream from one of the jars and mixed it in the palm of her hand with a dab of yellow from another. Even with her butterfly touch, I winced as she applied it to my cheek.

"Have you heard from Mr. Jenkins?" I asked. "Is he okay?"

"Yes, he is fine. He will be home tonight."

I could see where Wei had gotten her self-control. I would have been at the door, waiting, pacing. But Mrs. Jenkins continued to tend to me in the same slow and gentle manner as she had done before I'd mentioned her husband.

She took a small amount of cream from the third jar and put it on the fingertips of my right hand. "Massage this on your lips. I'll send some home with you. Mix everything as I did and apply before bedtime and when you get up in the morning."

"What are these creams?"

"Arnica and goldenseal; the lip balm is my own special recipe." She cupped my good cheek in her palm. "Maybe you should become my apprentice." Wiping her hands, she closed the chest. "Let's go tell Wei about her father."

At the same time as we entered the living room, Mr. Jenkins walked in the front door.

"Dad!" Wei ran into his arms and held him tight.

When she finally let him go, he turned around in a circle. "See, no bullet holes, no neutralizing ray singes, no bruises . . ." It was then he caught sight of me. "Good Lord! What happened to you? Jade, have you . . . ?"

"Yes, dear. The full treatment; she will be fine in a few days."

"What happened?"

"Ed kidnapped her. She managed to get away." Wei dropped her voice. "I'm afraid I let this happen. I was there, but I—"

"It was my fault," I protested. "I thought—"

"There's no blame, girls." Mrs. Jenkins interjected. "We have lessons; we learn. Let me get you the salve to take with you."

"Dad, Ed stole Nina's FeLS contract," Wei said.

Mr. Jenkins glanced at me, then back at Wei. "Don't worry. I'll look into it. But now is not the time. I don't mean to sound unsympathetic," he said to me, "but there are several things that need my immediate attention. You still have a while before you turn sixteen, right?"

I nodded. "December tenth."

"Still a couple of weeks away. Good. And your school is not set to have the Choosing until after Holiday Day, which gives us even more time. Wei will see that you get home safely, and I'll be sure you have protection." He disappeared behind a set of ornate pocket doors.

"Don't worry, Nina," Wei said. "Dad always keeps his word."

Mrs. Jenkins returned with three smaller versions of the stone jars that held her medicines. Kissing my good cheek, she whispered, "You will be fine."

At that moment, I wasn't so sure.

XXXVII

Early Thursday morning, I was in the kitchen with Gran.

"Your face looks so much better," she said. "Mrs. Jenkins's salves must be the reason it's healing so quickly."

It felt better, too. The swelling had gone down considerably and my left cheek had changed from the initial dark purple to that horrible greenish yellow that bruises turn when they are healing. My fear was subsiding a little, too. There had been no sign of Ed since the day he kidnapped me; no PAV calls either. Although I kept a constant lookout for him just in case

"Your sixteenth is less than two weeks away," Gran said. "I've made the appointment. Shots first, then the tattoo."

"I don't think I'm ready."

"You know the law, hon. There's nothing I can do." She put her arm around me.

I sighed, letting my head sink onto her shoulder.

Dee appeared in the doorway. "What's going on? Are you okay, Nina?"

I straightened up quickly. "Yeah, I'm fine. Just thinking about turning sixteen."

"That's so cool." She took a rapido off the counter and started drawing an XVI on her wrist.

"Stop it!" I grabbed the pen and she stuck her tongue out at me.

"You'd better get going," Gran said. "You don't want to be late."

Dee scooted out the door in front of me. Her reaction was still on my mind as we exited the elport. I'd never looked forward to turning sixteen, not even when I was Dee's age. Mostly because of the way sixteens act when they can finally have sex without concern about what anyone will say. Then, after seeing that sex vid Ed had left at our house, I was positive I didn't ever want to do that. Now, with all the things I'd been finding out lately, I dreaded it even more. Not just for myself, but for girls like Joan and for Sandy and, eventually, for Dee.

And then there was Sal. I loved being close to him, kissing him. I got a warm feeling just thinking of his lips on mine.

"How come you don't want to turn sixteen, Nina?" Dee suddenly asked. "All my friends' older sisters have sex, some even did it before they turned sixteen." She jutted her chin in an I-told-you-so manner.

"Is that so, Miss Encyclopedia? You know if you get pregnant before you're sixteen, you can't keep the baby."

She wrinkled her nose. "I wouldn't have an abortion."

"Not your choice. If you were paying attention in class, you'd know that before they're sixteen, girls don't have choices. Even after you turn, guys get to make the decision about babies, if they want to."

At Dee's age I hadn't had a clue what sex was really about.

Not like I was an expert now, but back then it seemed gross and funny. Mostly Sandy and I had snickered and told jokes about it. Now there was Sal, and I wasn't quite as sure about my feelings on the subject.

We boarded the number 33 and made our way to the back.

"Why isn't it my choice?"

Dee wasn't going to give up this conversation. So I explained. "If you're sixteen, the baby's father has a say, if he wants to. And that's just part of being sixteen, Dee; it's not all about sex."

"How come it's called 'sex-teen,' then? All the verts tell you how popular you'll be if you dress and act so boys want to have sex with you. What else is there about it?"

"It's about control, Dee." The memory of that afternoon at Rita's crossed my mind—I didn't have any control then. In that moment, Sal's kisses and my response to them were all that had mattered to me. Even now, my body involuntarily tingled at the thought of his hands on my skin. Had we not stopped, I was sure that I would have gone further, maybe even had sex with him. I ignored the memory as best I could and continued: "The tattoo— it's a way for anyone to tell that you're sixteen. You're considered an adult then . . ."

Obviously bored with my explanation, Dee fiddled with her PAV and curled her feet up under her. "So are you going to have sex with Sal when you turn sixteen?"

"Of course not." I folded my arms across my chest and stared up the aisle, thinking about that day at Rita's again. I wondered if my body was listening to my words.

XXXVIII

" **I** 'm not ready." I stared out the window of Wei's living room, where I'd ended up after dropping Dee back at home after school. Dee had been complaining about a sore throat, so I had a free afternoon.

"It's not so bad. The thistle tattoo took a lot longer and hurt more."

"It's not the pain I'm worried about. It's all the pressure that comes along with being sixteen, and with this whole FeLS thing . . . I don't think I can do it. I thought it was bad enough before, just not being able to talk to your family for two years, but now? Wei, what if Ed does what he said? What if I get chosen and I don't end up in the safe group?" I looked to her for reassurance.

"Remember, they won't be choosing until after Holiday Day," Wei said. "I know Dad will have figured out some way to get your contract by then."

"I hope so." I took hold of her arm and studied her thistle tattoo. "You know, I love this design. It's more ultra than ultra."

Wei laughed. "When I turned, I wanted it to be for me, not just a government brand. I was the first Creative to do anything like this. The school authorities called in government people to make sure it was all legal. It's ridiculous how the GC tells us we have freedom of speech and expression when we really don't."

"What will you do when the XVI starts fading?" The tattoos started deteriorating after about three years and were supposed to be completely gone in five, although mostly they just turned a sickly shade of pale green.

"The guy who did this is going to tattoo another thistle over the XVI when I turn twenty-one."

Wei pointed out a tiny scar behind her right ear. "I got my GPS taken out, too. It amazes me how many girls, and even some guys, keep theirs. Dad says the government gets Media to run stories that keep us scared about could happen and then tells us that by keeping the GPS implanted they can keep us safe. Mom calls it passive brainwashing. It's a bunch of crap. What it really means is that the government can track you wherever and whenever they want."

I touched mine, wondering if it was a little traitor. "That could be how Ed found me that day," I said.

"I thought that, too, but Dad doesn't think so. He doubts a Chooser would have access to the government's tracking systems."

I hoped she was right. He'd found me somehow. "Maybe he's given up. It's been almost two weeks."

"Don't let down your guard." I could tell she wasn't convinced. I wasn't either.

"Can I see it again?" I asked.

Wei turned her wrist over and I admired the thistle tattoo. Deep pink flowers and gray-green leaves circled the obligatory XVI and fanned around to the other side of her arm. There they met and snaked up the back of her hand toward her fingers. A thistle in full bloom took up the majority of the skin. The leaves continued up her knuckles and spelled out free, one letter per finger.

"Was it really expensive?" As if I didn't already know the answer.

"Not so much. There's a guy who does these for . . ." She hesitated. "You know, this is a special symbol."

"What do you mean?"

"In ancient times, in Scotland, there were secret knights that guarded the true king. They were called the Order of the Thistle. The thistle is a symbol of danger and protection."

"The Order of the Thistle. Sounds serious. Are you—" My PAV alarm interrupted. "I've gotta go. Gran and Pops have an appointment at the doctor's for Pops's leg. I have to watch Dee."

"I'll walk you to the bus stop."

"No, don't. I haven't seen any suspicious trannies lately. And it makes me feel like such a baby whenever anyone purposely walks me somewhere, especially in the middle of the day."

"Are you sure? Dad thinks I should stick close to you."

"I'm sure. It's only two blocks."

***

Wei let me go, but only after we made a quick contingency plan—I would dash into the little boutique by the trans stop and pretend to be sick if Ed should happen to appear on either of those two blocks; but it wasn't necessary. When I got to the apartment, I flopped down on the floor with Dee and watched some anime with her. Shortly before Gran and Pops were due back, Sal came over.

"I wish we had a porch to sit on," he whispered to me. "I'd like it to be just you and me for a while." His breath tickled my neck and I felt it down to my toes.

"Me, too."

We could've gone to my room, but Dee would be able to hear anything we said, or if we laughed. And then she'd come see what we were doing. Not that I planned on doing anything, but I didn't want her to see me and Sal kissing. And I was sure kissing was going to happen no matter where we ended up.

I glanced at the time. Sal and I could go sit somewhere for a while and be together. Dee was wrapped up in her show and wasn't going anywhere.

"DeeDee, Sal and I are going across to the river oasis. Gran and Pops will be home in a minute. Don't answer the door or your PAV unless you know who it is. And if it's Ed, don't talk to him. Okay?"

"Yeah, sure." She didn't even look up from the AV.

"I mean it, Dee. Promise?"

"I promise! Be quiet, I can't hear." She waved her hand at us. "Go already."

A minute later we were at the elport. Sal twined his fingers in mine. "You sure she'll be okay?"

"Remember, Ed's not after her," I said. "It's me he wants."

"I suppose that's true." He tickled the inside of my palm with his finger. It gave me chills, the good kind.

"And Ed hasn't called her since the wreck," I said. "Besides, she knows not to open the door to anyone. She's almost twelve. Ginnie left me alone sometimes when I was eleven."

"But you were exceptional, right?" His eyes were twinkling.

"Right." I smiled at him. But I wasn't feeling as lighthearted as

I wished. I had something on my mind, and I needed to get it out, before it started eating away at me. As soon as we reached the DZ oasis, I said, "My sixteenth is coming up real soon."

"It's a lot bigger deal for a girl than for a guy."

"I know. I wanted to tell you . . . let you know . . . something . . ." I felt like a huge glob of nut butter was stuck to the roof of my mouth. I was terrified that whatever I said would come out wrong.

"What?" He bent over and kissed me, warming me to the tips of my toes. "What about sixteen?"

"I don't want you to think that just because I'm sixteen . . . and because of what happened . . . you know . . . at your aunt Rita's . . ." I shouldn't have mentioned that, because when I did, I wasn't sure about the truth of what I wanted to say next. This wasn't going at all like I'd hoped. Sal was so close and his kisses sent summer running through my veins. Before I got lost there, I blurted out, "I don't want to have sex."

The minute the words were out, I knew they were a lie. I hadn't been able to stop thinking about that afternoon on Rita's porch. When I lay in bed at night I could almost feel Sal's hands on my bare skin and I wanted them there again. Not just around my waist either. Thinking about this made it difficult to breathe.

"Who said anything about having sex?" His voice was husky and he was kissing my neck. "I just want to be close to you. Kissing you. Touching you."

"I want that, too." I closed my eyes and leaned into him. Then a flash of Ed's sex vids came into my head. I sat up. I did not ever want those vids and Sal in the same thought.

"Did I do something wrong?" He moved a lock of hair out of my eyes.

"No." I couldn't tell him about the vids. Just the thought of putting what I'd seen into words made me feel sick. I forced myself to concentrate on the moment. "It's the whole sex-teen thing . . ." I stumbled around for more words. "I don't want to."

"I know that. I would never try to make you either. If it happens, it will be because we both want it to." He pulled me close. "Sex is not why I'm here."

"I have to know it isn't a big deal for you." I gazed in his eyes.

"You are the big deal for me, Nina." He wrapped his arm around me, and we sat together until the streetlights came on—which wasn't nearly long enough for me.

"We'd better get back," I said.

As soon as we left the privacy of the oasis, my PAV beeped—Gran.

"Nina. Where are the two of you? I've been calling for half an hour. It's supper time."

"I'm almost home. We were down by the river. Didn't Dee tell you?"

"Dee? No. Isn't Dee with you?"

XXXIX

I grabbed Sal's jacket. "Dee's gone!"

"Gone? How can she be . . ." His face turned pale.

It was as if all the blood drained out of me, and I sank to the ground. "No, no, no . . ." I shook my head, moaning. Ed couldn't've. "It's all my fault. I shouldn't have left her. I knew better. He'll . . ."

Sal knelt beside me. "Nina, it's okay. We'll find her. He won't do anything to her. Remember, it's you he wants. Besides, he's her father. He wouldn't hurt her."

I couldn't even look at Sal. Pushing him away, I bounded up. "You don't know that! He could use her to get to me . . . he . . . This never would have happened if I hadn't been . . . if I wasn't so stupid sex-teen! I hate it!" I pushed him again. "I don't want this body. I don't want it to feel so good when you kiss me, when you touch me. It's not fair."

He snatched my arms, pinning them to my sides. "Nina, stop it! Now's not the time. We've got to figure out what to do, okay?"

I looked up, and saw all his feelings right there in his eyes. I knew mine were in my eyes, too. A shudder ran through me. He was right—it was not the time. We had to find Dee, find out what happened.

"We'd better get upstairs," he said.

In the elport, Sal and I fashioned a plan. He would call his brother while I got a hold of Wei. Between the four of us, we'd figure out what to do next. When the pod stopped three floors below mine, Sal and I fell silent. Even if it was just some old folks heading upstairs for a card game with friends, we couldn't take chances.

The door opened and there stood Dee.

I yanked her inside. "Where have you been? We've been worried to death! You were supposed to stay in the apartment." All the time I was talking, I alternated between holding her at arm's length and hugging her. She finally managed to get out of my grasp.

She ducked behind Sal, looking at me like I was insane. "What's the matter with you? I just went to Harriet's. She came over to borrow some sugar, and since I was alone she invited me for some cookies. Gran says Harriet's is a safe place to go."

"It's all right, Nina." The elport had stopped on our floor and Sal was holding the door open. "She's fine. It's okay."

I felt like I'd been sucked into a black hole and jettisoned out the other side. All the what-ifs in the galaxy whizzed through my brain—mostly what if Ed had gotten his hands on Dee? I didn't know how much more of this I could handle. I wasn't Dee's mother—and I hated feeling like I was. Gran was her guardian. But I was her sister. And Ginnie'd told me to take care of her. Even though there was no one to take care of me.

Doesn't matter, I told myself. *I'm almost an adult. I can handle this.* I willed myself calm.

My insides were awhirl, but I managed to keep my voice from wavering when I spoke. "Dee, you're almost twelve. You know better. Never go out like that again without leaving a note on the message center."

"Okay. Sorry. You're not mad anymore, are you?"

"No, I was worried, that's all." *Liar,* I thought. I was angry, but not at her. With myself. I'd wanted to be with Sal so much, I put Dee in danger. I'd let my feelings for him take over, and ignored what was most important. I couldn't let that happen again.

Dee hurried into the apartment. I could hear her apologizing to Gran before the door closed behind her. I turned to Sal. "I shouldn't have—"

"*We* shouldn't have," he corrected. "We were both stupid. It won't happen again. Don't worry." He kissed me, and while it wasn't toe curling, it was close enough.

***

After dinner, Sandy called. "I haven't talked to you in forever! You have to see my tattoo, Nina! And Mike has beeped me almost every night." Even through the PAV, I could tell she was eating something. "He even called on my birthday; which, by the way, was lame because you couldn't come out. How's your face now?"

"See for yourself." I clicked a digi on my receiver and sent it. I ignored her comment about the tattoo. That was the last thing I wanted to think about. "You know, you and Mike have a lot in common." A thought was forming in my brain. "You both love cows . . ." I couldn't think of another love they shared, unless it was Sandy herself. Saying that would be cruel, and besides, she really was sweet when she wasn't being sex-teen of the century.

"He told me Derek's playing at Soma on Saturday. I plan on being there. I'll take the six-fifteen and meet you guys like before. I suppose Wei will come, too?" I heard her huff. "Oh well. We'll party anyway. She's sixteen, too, isn't she? Doesn't act like it. Wait till you see my tattoo. It didn't hurt at all."

She made her XVI sound like a badge of honor.

"Wear shoes you can walk in, okay?"

She laughed and then told me every single thing she'd have on. Exactly how she was planning to do her hair, etc., etc., etc. Eventually, we were both laughing and being as silly as we used to be. I missed those times in Cementville. Even with the stress of Ed in my family's life, I'd been close to happy. I loved Sandy, even in her craziness.

XL

We'd only had a half day of school on Friday, and I was home, in my room, sketching my makeshift dresser. I noticed the corner of Dee's baby book jutting out from under my clothes. It had been well over three weeks since Sal and I had been to his aunt Rita's and told Rita about it. I'd been waiting for some kind of word from her so I could get Dee's baby book to my father.

Sal had tried getting in touch with her earlier in the week, but didn't have any luck. Wei'd asked her parents about my dad again the other day, but they hadn't heard anything since before her dad's trip to Amsterdam. With everything that had happened, I still hadn't been able to get away to listen to my dad's debates, or risk bringing the baby book out to Wei's to have her mom take a look. The longer I waited for other people to get me and my father together, the more I felt like I was the one who needed to do something. I'd been waiting almost sixteen years—maybe it was time to do it myself.

I called Wei. "Is your mom back from Tokyo?"

"Yes. She got back yesterday."

"Remember how you said she knows all about codes?"

"Uh-huh."

"You think she would she be willing to take a look at that thing we talked about?" I wasn't taking any chances about audio surveillance by speaking more precisely.

"Let me ask." After a few moments, she said, "Mom can look at it in an hour. You want me to come get you?"

"No. I'll be there."

I didn't want to risk carrying the book in a bag that could be grabbed from me, so I stuck it under my waistband and pulled my longest sweater on and shrugged into my bulkiest jacket. I'd worry about how to sit down on the trans when I had to.

The elport slid to a stop on the third floor and a tall man in a black Turino coat and a wool hat pulled down low on his brow got on. Maybe I should have taken Wei up on her offer. He was not one of the building regulars. I hugged my stomach.

"Cold?" He cocked his head, looking down at me, at my belly in particular, I was sure.

"Kind of." His expression sent chills up my spine. I shivered and hugged myself even harder, to keep my arms from trembling. Trying to not be obvious, I scooted close to the buttons, in case I needed to press the alarm.

When the elport reached the lobby, he exited. I mumbled something about forgetting my gloves and pressed the button to close the doors, in case he was thinking about getting back inside. Up on my floor, I got out and watched the elport display. It went down and up several times, stopping at many different floors. I waited, giving him sufficient time to leave if he wasn't trying to follow me. I went down to the first floor again. I didn't see the man anywhere, so I went outside and stood by the corner of the building, where I was shielded from the wind. I heard some noise behind me and jumped. It was a small group of homeless going through the refuse bin. One of them was Joan.

The women scattered like pigeons when I approached them, except for Joan and the woman who'd been with her before.

"Joan? Are you doing okay?" I ignored the obvious answer.

She looked up at me, and for a second, I thought she recognized me. But then the spark was gone.

"Your family says they haven't heard from you. I know your mom must be worried." I hadn't said anything to Mike yet about seeing Joan. How could I do it without crushing him? Mrs. Trueblood had been so thrilled when Joan was chosen. I couldn't imagine how she'd feel seeing her daughter the way she was now.

"Can't," she replied, staring at her feet. "Dangerous."

"Is there something I can do? You want me to call them for you?"

Joan's woman friend pushed herself between the two of us. "You can leave her alone," she said. "GC's done enough to her and everyone else like her."

"She's got a family," I said. "And friends. We can help."

Joan reached past the woman and grabbed my arm. "Tell Mike . . . I miss him." A tear rolled down her cheek, and she turned back to the bin.

"Hey, girl. Tell him at your own risk. His, too." The woman glared at me before putting her arm around Joan. She led her away like a little child. They rounded the refuse bin and disappeared.

I was torn. I wanted to tell Mike that his sister was back, but I didn't dare. Not after that warning. If everything Wei'd told me about FeLS was true and the GC was involved, it was probably safer for him not to know anything.

Walking out of the alley, I spotted the man in the coat, leaning against a light post across the way. It'd been at least twenty minutes since we were in the elport together. Luckily, the transit was just pulling up. I hurried over to the transit stop, and squeezed between two ladies waiting for the number 33, ignoring their irritated looks. When we boarded the transit, I swung into the seat behind the driver and carefully sat down. I saw the man in the coat through the transit window, still standing in the same place, watching me as we drove off. The bottom edge of the book dug into my thighs. Fortunately, the ride was short, otherwise I was sure my legs would've fallen asleep. Wei was at the stop waiting for me.

"I'm so glad you're here." I stuck my hand in my jacket, arranging the book.

"What are you doing? Got an itch?"

"It's in here. We have to hurry, there was a man at the transit stop . . ."

Wei started laughing. "Nina, you didn't need to worry. Dad's friends, you know." She nodded toward a blue trannie parked on the street. Inside was the man in the coat. He nodded to me. I felt the heat rush to my face, a combination of relief and embarrassment. *What an idiot I am*! I thought. Wei pulled me along to her house.

"I'm helping my brother, Chris, in the kitchen," Wei said, opening the door. "Mom's waiting for you in the living room." She gave me a quick hug and left. I pulled the book out of my waistband before going in.

"Here it is." I handed it to Wei's mom, and another wave of relief washed over me.

"Take your coat off. Do you want some hot chocolate or tea?"

Mrs. Jenkins had a tray with two covered pots and a plate of what smelled like freshly baked cookies. I slipped out of my jacket and sat down. "Hot chocolate, please."

"Take a cookie, too." She handed me a mug and I snagged a still-warm cookie. "Now . . ." She opened the book, perusing the pages.

I stopped mid-chew, holding my breath, watching her face.

She raised an eyebrow. "Come with me."

I set down my cup and stood.

"No, no. Bring it along. Maybe the cookies, too?" Her smile warmed me to my toes. I didn't hesitate snatching up the plate as I followed her out the door. We took the stairs to the third floor.

Mrs. Jenkins inserted a long metal key into the lock of a pair of doors that were identical to the ones on the floor below. I heard a click and the doors swung open.

I'd never seen such sumptuousness. Silken fabric stitched with golden threads hung on the windows. Pillows of red, yellow, and purple plumped the corners of oversize sofa and chairs. Everything looked so inviting, I wanted to snuggle into a seat and stay there forever. It seemed like the sort of place where nothing scary or bad could ever happen.

Mrs. Jenkins didn't stop there, but continued down the hallway. We entered a room with bookshelves along three walls. They were filled to capacity with leather-bound volumes, many of which had crackled spines and worn corners. I'd never seen so many real books in one place before. It made Ginnie's few paperbacks look paltry. The fourth wall was taken up almost entirely by a cabinet with the same lacquer finish as Mrs. Jenkins's box of herbs and potions. A large intricately patterned carpet covered the floor, and in the center of it was a massive wooden table with carved legs.

She placed Dee's baby book on the table and went to the cabinet. When she returned, she was holding two paintbrushes and several small bottles.

She uncorked two of the bottles and poured some liquid from each into a saucer. She dipped in a brush and said, "This will tell us what she had to say."

I stood transfixed as she swept the brush across the blank inside cover of the book. Within moments, I could make out the neat contours of Ginnie's handwriting.

"That's unbelievable. How did you—"

"When Ginnie and I were young we sent each other secret notes in school. Sometimes we used code, but mostly we wrote with invisible ink. Code was fine for typical schoolgirl notes, such as 'I really like so and so, what do you think of him?' However, if we had to communicate information of great importance, we would write in invisible ink."

"But how did you know there was writing in this?"

"That little flower by her signature. Of course, there had to be a sign so we could let each other know when a note contained a hidden message."

"The flower."

"Yes, the moment I saw it, I knew what to look for."

She pulled a lamp close and shone it on the faded brown letters.

Dearest Alan,

How I hope and pray I am beside you as you are reading this—otherwise, I suppose I must be dead. For only death could keep me apart from you any longer. If only . . . I dare not indulge the luxury of those thoughts . . .

or I shall cry enough tears to make all the deserts of Venus bloom.

Don't be angry with me. I did what needed to be done.

Ed had been pressuring me for months for information about you. He suspected we'd been meeting secretly. If he'd discovered I was pregnant . . . I'm sure you can imagine the consequence of that. Nina needed me, our unborn child needed me, and the Resistance (and humanity) needed you. It was a small sacrifice—to let him think Dee was his.

In these pages are the good times with our children. I had to share them with you, to let you see them through my eyes. I know you will cherish them, as I have.

All my love to you, forever and always, dearest, dearest husband.

***

Below that was a P.S. dated a week before she died.

***

I've tried to leave Ed many times, but he continually threatens to choose Nina for FeLS if I do. I finally have the credits to buy out her contract. When I get it, I will send it to your mother. I have been stealing evidence from Ed's files, collecting the proof we need to show what the FeLS organization really is. If anything happens to me, it's hidden in our secret place.

***

My cheeks were hot with tears. Mrs. Jenkins put her arms around me and I sobbed until there were no tears left to cry.

I reread the letter—three times. "Alan is Dee's father, too. Did you know that?"

Mrs. Jenkins shook her head. "After Ginnie became pregnant, she cut off all communication with everyone—except, apparently, Rita. It is possible that Rita knew."

"Then why didn't she . . ."

"For your sake, Nina. It wouldn't be difficult for the Bureau of Safety and Security to get information from a child."

"But I didn't know anything! What would I have known?"

"Are you sure? There must be something. Think back, dear."

I went through the people in Ginnie's life. "No one but Ed ever came to our modular. When we lived on Wrightwood, before Ed, there was Gran and Pops. Ginnie also had a couple of girlfriends from her work." I sighed, and then it hit me. "There was a homeless man who made me clover chains, who we saw at the park . . ." Then it hit me. "That was my father, wasn't it?"

Mrs. Jenkins nodded.

I couldn't take my eyes off my mom's writing. Dee was my full sister. There wasn't any connection to Ed at all. My father was her father. The family I thought I'd lost when my mother died . . . it was still there. We would all, somehow, be together again. In a very few minutes, though, those good feelings turned to ice.

Ed. He was still out there, still thinking that Dee was his daughter. I shuddered to think what he might do if he ever found out the truth. I wondered if he suspected anything, since he was obsessed with finding my father.

"Do you know where Ginnie would have hidden this evidence?" Mrs. Jenkins asked.

"No." Something horrible was going to come from this. I knew it. "I need to go home."

"First we must take care of the message." She opened the second bottle and brushed over the page again. In moments, the writing disappeared. "There is probably more written throughout the pages. It is best if I don't let you take the solutions back with you. Too much temptation. You can't risk this falling into the wrong hands."

I nodded—my mind was numb with dread.

"Do you want me to keep the book here? I can lock it up."

"No." I took it from her. I couldn't bear to know someone else held my family's secrets. "Ginnie entrusted it to me. I have to get it to my father. If you or Mr. Jenkins hear anything, please let him know I have to see him. Tell him how important it is."

"I will. Be careful, Nina."

I retrieved my jacket from downstairs, stuck the book back in my waistband, and left. I didn't even say good-bye to Wei.

***

Thankfully, the trip back was uneventful. When I got home, Dee met me at the door.

"Whatcha got under your coat?"

"Nothing."

"You're lying. You're hiding something."

She tried to unzip my jacket and I pushed her away.

"Quit being a jerk," she said. "I was just fooling around. But since you're being that way, I won't tell you about Ed." She flounced off and headed to her room.

Racing after her, I spun her around. "Dee! What about him? Tell me now!"

"What's all the commotion?" Gran called from the kitchen.

"Nothing," I called back while dragging Dee into my room. "Now, what about Ed?"

"You're hurting me!" She struggled to get away.

"Dee. This isn't a game." I pulled her down on the bed next to me. The book dug into my gut, but I didn't dare remove it or she'd start questioning me. "I'm sorry. Just tell me about Ed. Please. I'm afraid he'll try to take you away, or maybe even hurt you."

"Nina, he won't hurt me. He's my dad."

I had to stop myself from blurting out the truth. If Dee knew she wasn't Ed's daughter, she'd act differently around him, or worse, she might slip and tell him. I couldn't put her at more risk. I couldn't tell anyone. "Dee, what exactly happened?"

"He called me. He said he missed me and he wants to see me. Maybe even go to the zoo with me, like fathers and daughters do." She smiled. "He said since Mom's gone, I need a father."

I couldn't breathe. My whole body shook and fear overwhelmed me. The edge of the book dug into my leg, and I grabbed my blanket pulling it tightly around me, keeping the book hidden away. "When, Dee. When did Ed say he wanted to see you?"

"He said he wanted to talk to you first. He tried to call you, but you must have been in a dead zone since you didn't pick up."

I stopped and focused for a moment, controlling my breath,

trying to act casual. "Yeah, I must've been. There's dead zones everywhere. I guess he'll call me again. Hey . . ." I stood up, still wrapped in the blanket. "Promise me you won't talk to him again until I do, okay? For Mom's sake?" I was pulling out everything I could to keep things under control. I could hardly believe I'd said that—that I'd use Ginnie's memory to manipulate my little sister. But it got the desired result. Dee promised and sulked off to her own room.

Dropping the blanket, I pulled the book out of my jeans and stared at the cover. Ginnie'd been right about it containing answers. But the answers were far more dangerous than the questions. At least I'd moved closer to finding out all kinds of truths. Now, if I could only figure out where Ginnie and my father's "secret place" was . . .

My PAV beeped. For a moment, I thought it might be Ed, but it was Sandy. Her shrieks were deafening. "He chose me! I'm in! I'm going to be a FeLS! Can you believe it?! Of course you can. Ed was the Chooser. I knew that he'd choose me because of your mother. He came and I reminded him that you and I were the best of friends. I hope that doesn't bother you, Nina."

"No. Sure, Sandy. That's okay." I felt as though the wind had been knocked out of me. No, Sandy, no . . . I had forgotten that the Cementville Choosing took place before my school's. I listened as long as I could stand it, all the time seeing Joan's face, thinking about what Wei had said about the program. "There's no way out?"

"Way out? Nina! Why would I want to get out? I'm going to be rich and famous!" She laughed. "The only thing left is the physical. And I'll pass that, no prob. Finally, I get to be in FeLS! It's—it's just the ultra?! Oh, Nina, I wonder if we get to have sex during training? Speaking of that, how's Sal? Have you had sex yet? If Sal was my boyfriend—"

"Sandy, I—" My stomach churned. "I've gotta go. See you tomorrow."

I ran down the hall and puked my insides out into the toilet. When I stood up, Dee was in the doorway.

"I knew you were sick. You were acting so weird. I'm getting Gran."

I grabbed her arm. "It's okay, Dee. I feel better now that I threw up. If I lie down for a while, I'll be fine."

I knew she wasn't entirely convinced, but we both went to our own rooms and shut our doors.

I stuck the baby book under my mattress and flopped onto the bed. Staring at the ceiling, I thought about how Ginnie'd loved my dad and me and Dee enough to give up her whole life for us.

I thought about the way I'd acted with Sal down by the river, what I'd said about the government, NonCons . . . I knew I'd been wrong, but I didn't realize how wrong.

I thought about Sandy, heading off to who knew what. At least there was a chance she could go to the right training center. If only she wasn't a virgin . . . Could anyone persuade her to have sex before the physical? I ran through the list of guys we knew in my head . . . Mike, Derek . . . A little voice in my head squeaked, Sal. My heart sank. What about Sal? She'd been so hot for him before, I was sure it wouldn't take much . . . But I wasn't sure I could make that kind of sacrifice, or ask him to.

XLI

The next morning, I was up early and had coffee ready when Gran came into the kitchen. I needed to find my father and Ginnie's favorite place, the "secret place" Ginnie referred to in the letter. I was afraid that coming straight out and asking about it might set off alarm bells, but couldn't think of any other way.

"Did my dad and Ginnie have any favorite places besides Robin's Roost?"

Gran poured herself a cup and sat down at the table. "No, I don't think so. Ginnie particularly loved the view from the roof. The minister who married them was terrified of heights. You should have seen the look on his face when Ginnie insisted that he stand near the edge of the roof so that she and Alan could look out over Lincoln Park as they took their vows. Poor man." She took a sip of the coffee. "You're getting pretty good at making the real thing." She smiled at me. "It helps to know how to do some things without the help of cookers and chillers and all these other kitchen gadgets."

I ignored her compliment. "Did they go up on the roof a lot?"

"I think they did," Gran said, narrowing her eyes at me. "Why the sudden interest?"

"No reason," I lied. "I'm just trying to learn all I can about my father."

"Sometimes too much knowledge is a dangerous thing." Gran put down her coffee cup and got up. "Time to get breakfast going. Your grandfather will be up soon." She took some ingredients from the cook center. "You know, I do remember that every year on their anniversary, Alan would rent the roof of Robin's Roost for the two of them. He and Ginnie would spend the night dining and dancing above the city lights. It was very romantic."

That settled it. I needed to get to the roof of Robin's Roost, and soon, before they demolished it. But first things first. I'd already promised Gran I'd help her clean the apartment, and we'd take Dee to the aquarium. Though I was worried about Ed—as always—knowing that Wei's parents had people keeping an eye on me made me slightly less nervous. By the time I got home from the aquarium, it was nearly time to go to Soma.

***

Wei showed up early. I could tell by her expression that she wanted to know what we'd uncovered in the book. But I knew that if I told her, she'd be in danger, too.

As we passed Dee's door, I glanced in. "Remember . . ."

"Gah, Nina. I promised, didn't I?"

It was freezing outside and Gran insisted on wrapping a tensalite scarf around my neck before she'd let us leave. I felt like I was five again.

Wei and I got on the trans and headed to the back.

"I'd better call Sandy and tell her we're going to be a little late meeting at Soma." I tried her PAV several times, but there was no answer. I left a message. "There's somewhere we have to stop at before we get there."

"It has to do with your meeting with Mom?"

"Yep. Are your dad's friends still hanging around?"

"I don't know—I don't think so, since we're together."

At Lincoln and Wells, Wei and I did a thorough scope-out to be sure no one was watching us, then snuck around back of Robin's Roost. I knew there had to be a way inside, other than the front door. I was prepared to break a window, but luckily the door at the bottom of the stairs swung open easily.

Wei stuck her head inside. "This is cool!" She dug around in her pocket. "We can use this for light." She clicked on her PAV receiver and shone the light on the floor of the storage room.

I pulled her inside and shut the door. "I think it's DZ here." I tried calling Sandy again. No tone at all. "Yep. Definitely DZ. Listen, we've got to get up on the roof. I'm sure Ginnie left something up there for my father. We have to get it."

"Wait, is that what was you and my mom found in the book?"

"Yes." I explained, leaving out the part about Dee being my real sister. "Come on." I pulled out my receiver and turned on the light, too, leading the way down the narrow hallway. The door at the end opened into what had been a kitchen. The place was a mess. Cabinets had pulled away from the walls and were hanging by who knew what. Things were strewn all over. Old cook centers, prep tables, and debris littered the room. A chiller lay faceup on the floor; its door was nowhere to be seen. Up by the ceiling a row of grime-covered windows let in a sickly bit of glow from the late afternoon. There was no reason to worry that anyone outside would see our pathetic PAV lights.

I shuffled through the dirt and pieces of pipe and plasticine until I reached the door on the other side of the room, with Wei close behind me. Through it and up a short ramp was a banquet room where the skeletons of chandeliers, with broken bulbs and loose wires, were hanging from the ceiling. There were no windows in the space. One of the doors to the lobby hung by a rusty hinge and light filtered in through the opening. When I pushed on it, it fell with a crash.

Wei and I held our breath until we were sure no one had heard.

"Look!" On the dusty floor in front of us I saw footprints. They looked relatively fresh, considering the years of grime that covered everything. "Those have to be Ginnie's." I put my foot over one. My foot and the print were the exact same size. Just like my feet and Ginnie's had been. I started to run into the room, but Wei grabbed me.

"People can see in those doors." She gestured toward the front, where a month earlier Sal had surprised me when I first found Robin's Roost. "Turn off your PAV light. We don't want anyone outside to see. We have to be careful."

"We have to follow those footprints," I said.

"Okay. Just keep behind things so if anyone looks in they won't see you." Wei took over, leading the way through the lobby. First behind the front desk, then a large sofa, an oversize table, and other pieces of furniture. Eventually, we made it to the other side. We followed the footprints to a door near the elport, which opened onto a stairway.

"The building is only ten stories high," I said. "Come on."

The stairwell was as black as the Chicago River at night. If we hadn't had our PAVs, it would have taken a lot longer to get to the roof. The door at the top of the stairs wasn't locked, but it was a bit harder to open than the one in the basement. It took both Wei and me ramming ourselves against it, but it finally gave way. A drift of snow on the other side had been the problem. When we walked out onto the roof, I checked my PAV—still no signal, still DZ. Of course, like Gran had said, this used to be a B.O.S.S. building; they'd have it rigged to keep it a DZ, and keep out any kind of surveillance.

"There are no footprints," Wei said. "The snow has covered everything."

"Ginnie left something up here. I'm sure of it. We just have to figure out where."

"I'll take this side," Wei said. "You take the other."

I walked over to the edge of the roof. Streetlights were coming on everywhere and Lincoln Park twinkled like a fairyland. I stopped for a moment and looked out over the skyline and the city. This was the view Ginnie'd loved, and I understood why. I went and got Wei; she had to see it, too. When we got back to where I had been standing, my foot caught on something. I knelt down and felt around. My pulse quickened. "There's something here."

I swiped the snow aside and there was a metal cover. I snatched at it with my fingers, nearly tearing them to shreds. It had no intention of giving way. "I need something to pry with."

Wei searched the roof and eventually returned with a rusty length of metal. "Here, try this."

I worked it under the cover and tried to lever it with all my strength. I felt a few wet flakes of snow—we had to hurry. At the same moment as the piece of metal broke, there was a *pop* and the cover opened.

I shined my PAV into the hole. Inside, wrapped in all-guard, was a packet. Wei and I sat down in the snow and I opened it. There was a note in Ginnie's handwriting and three chips. The note said, Here's the proof. FeLS is a cover for sex trafficking. I know you can stop this . . .

I didn't read any further because the heavy wet flakes of snow started coming down harder. I wrapped everything back up and stuffed the packet in my jeans.

"Let's go," I said. "We've got to get this to my father. Do you think your father's been in touch with him lately?"

"I hope so." Wei went back into the building first. "Be careful on the steps," she said. "My shoes tracked in some snow and it's slippery."

She wasn't kidding. My foot nearly skidded off the first step. I grabbed onto the banister to keep from falling and felt the metal give under my weight.

We hurried down the stairs as quickly as we could, Wei in the lead. I'd just rounded a corner when I heard a thump in front of me.

"Wei?" I hissed. No answer.

"Wei?" I stepped carefully down the flight of stairs. Wei was lying at the bottom of the landing.

"Wei, are you okay?" Nothing.

Skivs! I put my hand on her neck, felt her pulse, and breathed a sigh of relief. She was still alive, but my PAV light wasn't bright enough for me to see how badly she was injured. I wasn't strong enough to carry her. Besides, I was afraid to move her. What if she'd broken something? I started to call Sal before I remembered we were in a DZ. I tried to calm myself and think of what to do next, but my heart was near pounding out of my chest.

"Wei . . ." I tried waking her again. Still nothing, not even a moan. I didn't want to leave her, but I had to get help. "Wei, I'll be back."

I didn't even think about anyone seeing me as I crossed the lobby. When I got to the kitchen, I heard a noise and froze. Prickles rose on my arms. Then I heard someone say, "Damn cheap piece of shit! Fucking worthless!"

Ed! For a second I was paralyzed. Then a voice in my head screamed, *Move!* I ran to the hallway door and tried turning the lock, but it was rusted fast. I could feel the panic rising up through my body. Think, Nina, think. I looked for a chair to shove under the doorknob, but there weren't any. Grabbing a small table, I flipped it over and thrust it against the door. Then I threw some other debris on top of that. Enough to maybe buy me a second or two.

Not daring to turn my PAV light on, I stumbled around the room, tripping over several things. Somehow managing to keep my balance, I fumbled around and grabbed a metal pipe from the floor and ran to one of the counters. Scrambling up on top of it, I tried to reach a window. If I could break one, I could scream for help or climb out. No sooner had I stood up than the countertop gave way beneath me and I tumbled to the floor. I heard the doorknob rattle. I stood stock-still, not even daring to breathe.

"I know you're in there, Nina."

My heart was going to beat right out of my chest. The table scraped along the floor as the door slowly opened. Ed was getting in.

"Dead zone, isn't it? How nice—no one will ever know we're here. Maybe you and I can have some fun."

The sick AV images of his vids popped into my mind. I choked back my terror and ducked behind one of the counters, the metal pipe still in my hand.

"Might as well show yourself, Nina." Ed's voice echoed through the ruins. "There's no way out of here except through me." He grunted and I heard a dull thud, and next thing, the door was completely open. The table tumbled onto its side. "You think some junk is going to keep me out of here? You can't escape me, Nina."

I heard him scuffling through the pile of debris I'd thrown in front of the door. Every inch of me wanted to scream, to run, to do something . . . but I waited, clenching the pipe tighter and tighter until my hands hurt.

"Don't be stupid like your blond friend. Would you believe, she actually thought I was taking her for her physical. It didn't take much for her to tell me where you were."

Sandy. The only friend of mine that Ed knew was Sandy . . .

"As soon as she said 'Wells,' I knew you'd be here. You know, your mother had a thing for this building, too. Or so I heard."

Panic burbled inside of me as his voice grew louder.

"Come on, Nina, don't you want to know what happened to your friend? I could tell you all the details. She had those sexteen ways down pat, but you know, she really was a virgin. Bonus for me."

I pressed my lips together to keep from screaming.

He kept on, like we were having some kind of normal

conversation. "You one, too? Or has that scrawny boyfriend of yours already gotten into your pants? Doesn't matter to me. I'll enjoy myself either way."

Nausea gripped me. I swallowed down a bit of vomit.

"You know, Nina, we've got some business to take care of before the fun begins." He waved the light randomly around the room and I heard him trip over a pile of rubble. "Goddamn cheap LED!" Dust swirled like a whirlwind in its faint beam. "There are only so many places you can hide in here, Nina. I am going to find you."

One of the cabinet doors creaked as he opened it. "You in there?" He slammed it shut. A second later, it clattered onto the floor.

Every muscle in my body ached. Panic clawed at my insides, trying to get out. What if Wei came to and walked in on this? I shut my mind to all of the crazy thoughts.

"Ginnie told you to give a book to Alan. Her idea of having you sing that nursery rhyme was clever, but not clever enough. That nurse made out enough of Ginnie's words. I know your father is alive. What's in that book? I suggest you give it to me, or I'll take your sister and you'll never see her again."

I couldn't let him take Dee—all he needed was one DNA screen and he'd find out she wasn't his daughter. My eyes followed the dim glow from his LED. The dust was filling my nostrils and I prayed I wouldn't sneeze.

"Nina . . . just give me the book, Nina. Are you listening to me?" His voice became strident. "You know that it's because of your father that I'm a Chooser. I used to be top-level B.O.S.S. People worked for me. I told them he never drowned, but they said I was crazy. I spent ten damn years trying to get the truth out of your mother. But when I give the GC proof that Alan's alive, they'll have to reinstate me."

His voice lowered. "I really loved her." There was something close to tenderness in his words. "She despised me," he went on. "You think I didn't know that? Even after having a kid with me, she still loved your father. Funny, ain't it? He's alive, she's dead. How unfortunate for her." His voice lowered to a growl. "Even with that knife to her belly, she wouldn't give him up. Almost couldn't go through with it, though," he said. "That woman turned me on—what a waste."

Then there was silence, horrible silence. I could hear my heart pounding in my ears. The taste of bile filled my mouth. Ed had killed my mother. I think I'd known all along that he'd killed her. I clenched the pipe more tightly, my rage growing.

"I'm getting tired of this, Nina. You know what, Nina? I don't think I need you to get that book. I think Dee knows where it is, and you know she loves her dad. That leaves you . . . well, now, I can't just leave you, can I? Not with all you know, now. That just won't do." He kicked some rubbish. "But what to do with you, now . . . There's an old saying 'like mother—like daughter.' What do you say we find out if that's true? And if I like what you do, I might not kill you, least not right away."

Pervert! I wanted to scream so badly. Scream and scream and scream, until I'd screamed him into oblivion. I knew if I made a sound it would be all over for me, for Wei . . . And after he got to me, he'd go for Dee. I couldn't let that happen, no matter what. I had to keep focused.

The faint beam of his LED trailed along on the other side of the counter.

This would be my only chance to get away. I watched the light getting closer and closer. Pressing my back against a piece of countertop, I braced myself. He stepped closer to my hiding place, his LED shining right in front of me. I held my breath, waiting.

The moment the light moved past me, I leaped up and the full force of my rage and every other emotion I'd been holding inside surged out. I let loose one horrible shriek and with both hands brought the full force of the pipe down on Ed's head. I heard a sickening crack and Ed crumpled into the rubble.

XLII

Ed's LED wobbled across the floor, the light throwing shadows everywhere. I grabbed it, then raced to the storeroom and out into the night.

I pulled out my PAV and called Sal. "Sal—I need help, NOW! Wei and I are at Robin's Roost. Come through the alley. Come now!"

Wei—I had to get back to her, but what if Ed came to? I began to shake and it wasn't from the cold. I couldn't leave Wei in there, alone with him, unconscious. I had to risk it. I turned to go back inside when the door creaked open. I pressed against the building, paralyzed, hoping I blended in with the shadows. If Ed found me, I knew what would happen.

"Nina?" Wei's voice was weak and thready; she slid down the doorjamb into a heap.

I ran to her. "Get up. Come on."

She tried to sit, but only managed to slump forward, holding her head.

"Wei, come on, we've got to get out of here," I said. "Ed's inside. I knocked him out but he's gonna come to. If he finds us . . ."

She struggled to her feet, and I half carried her up the steps to the alley. We had almost reached the entrance to the street when I saw Sal and Mike.

"Sal, Mike, over here! We've got to get Wei some help. She fell . . . and . . ."

"I'll be fine," she said. "I'm just a little woozy." Her legs kept giving out under her. "No worse than other falls I've taken. I just need to sit for a minute, okay?"

The guys supported Wei as we snuck out of the alley and crossed the street. A three-story walk up, with large bushes on either side of the steps loomed in front of us.

"You girls get behind those." Sal pointed to the bushes. "We'll keep watch until Ed comes out."

***

Ten minutes passed . . . nothing. Twenty minutes later, Ed still hadn't come out. Wei and I stayed hidden behind the bushes. Much as I ached to call Sandy and make sure she was all right, I couldn't. Ed might have come to and would, no doubt, be looking for me. He might be able to hone in on my PAV signal. I dared not take that chance.

Everything Ed had said inside Robin's Roost ran through my mind. He'd killed Ginnie. What was to stop him from . . . No. I refused to believe Ed had killed Sandy, too. Maybe he hadn't even raped her—maybe it was just talk to scare me. *She's probably at Soma already,* I thought, *talking to some guys.* That had to be it. I checked my PAV receiver for the millionth time to see if she'd called while I'd been inside Robin's Roost. She hadn't.

"Ed couldn't have gone out any other way, could he?" Sal asked.

"Maybe we should go take a look?" Mike said.

"You can see through those windows into the basement if you get close enough." My voice was trembling as bad as my insides.

"You guys stay here." Sal walked nonchalantly across the street to Robin's Roost. He took something out of his pocket and dropped it. Kneeling down, he pretended to search for it, but I saw a flash of light—must have been an LED—and figured he was looking inside for Ed. Eventually, he stood up and continued walking toward the corner. When he got there, he glanced up and down the street, then checked his chronos. He strolled back and sat down next to Mike. Perfectly normal—a guy waiting for someone on a Saturday night.

"He's lying on the floor. He's not moving."

"You don't mean . . . he can't be . . . I didn't hit him that hard."

"Maybe you did," Wei said. "We should call my parents."

"No," Sal said. "If the GC had your dad questioned in Greenland, that means they're already suspicious about Nina's visits to your house. I'll get in touch with Aunt Rita. Let me go take another look."

"The hotel's DZ." My voice was shaking and my insides were roiling like a pond full of carp at feeding time.

Sal reached behind the bushes and took my hand. "It'll be okay, Nina." Then he crossed the street and disappeared down the alley.

Two seconds later I doubled over. Wei held my hair back while Mike diplomatically looked the other way. I felt as though I was turning inside out.

By the time Sal returned it was pitch-black outside. "Come on, let's get going. Derek's probably wondering where we are. Sandy, too. I'm surprised she hasn't called you."

"Sal . . . is Ed really . . . ?" I didn't want to know, but I needed to.

"Yeah." Sal steadied me. "I checked."

I lurched forward into the bushes and anything left inside me heaved out onto the ground. Soon I was empty, but I couldn't stop retching. Wei took my arm and pressed her thumb above my wrist, hard. In a few moments, the nausea subsided.

I looked at her, bewildered.

"Acupressure. I pay attention to some of what my mom does."

"What do we do now?" I said.

"We go to Soma and see if Sandy's made it there yet," Sal said.

I leaned over and whispered to him, "Ed said he . . ." I couldn't finish the sentence. "Sandy . . ."

"We'll go look for her. Come on," Sal said.

Wei and I must have looked like those wounded soldiers in old End-of-Wars vids. Mike was half carrying her and I was clutching Sal's arm—my legs about as steady as running water.

When we got to Soma, Sandy wasn't there.

"We have to leave," I whispered to Sal. "We have to find her."

"When you're in a DZ, tell Derek what happened," he said to Mike. "I'm taking Nina home."

"Okay. I'll bring Sandy over after the show."

I nodded; the tears were welling up. Then I stumbled outside, Sal right behind me.

***

We ended up at our oasis. Through my sobs I managed to tell him the whole story. Everything Ed had said, about my mother, about Sandy.

Sal rocked me gently in his arms until I couldn't cry anymore.

"What have I done?" I paced back and forth under the muted

lights. "I can't have killed someone—even if it was Ed."

"Nina, it was self-defense. He killed your mother. We don't know what he's done to Sandy, if anything. He was threatening to take Dee and he said he was going to rape and then kill you."

"Courts never believe sixteens," I said. "What will happen to me?"

"Nothing."

I sat down on the bench. "I'll be reassimilated, won't I?"

"No one will ever find out about this. It's been taken care of."

"What? What do you mean, taken care of?"

"Please stop worrying." He took my hands in his.

"Rita. Did she fix it?" I could picture her sending someone like Max to "take care" of things.

Sal put a finger to my lips. "Even if this oasis is DZ, we're out in the open. We need to be careful what we say. Just know that Ed will never hurt you again."

"What about Sandy?" I started to cry again. "It sounded like he . . ." I couldn't bring myself to say the words.

"Nina . . ." Sal twisted it out of my hand. "Stop."

I buried my face in his neck, sobbing.

"Don't worry, we'll find her."

***

It was late when I fell into bed. Sandy hadn't shown up or called. I'd tried to reach her mom, but no one answered. All I wanted to do was sleep and forget, but I couldn't. Ed's words kept running through my mind. *Don't you want to know what happened to your friend? . . . She really was a virgin . . . Bonus for me.* Too much had happened.

My PAV beeped.

"Sandy!"

"No, it's me." It was Wei.

"Wei, are you okay?" I asked.

"Mom doctored me up. I feel a little better."

"Any word about . . . ?" I knew I had to be careful what I said, and Wei did, too. As much as I wanted to know if they'd found Sandy, or Ed, I was afraid I'd wake up Gran if I went and got the scrambler.

"Nothing. I'm sorry."

"And the packet—" I still had the proof Ginnie had stolen from Ed. I didn't want to think about it, not yet, but I knew we had to get the information to my father. This all had to be for a reason.

"Yeah, we'll talk tomorrow." She clicked off.

I lay in bed, scared to close my eyes, scared to see the images that were hiding in the dark.

I rolled over and looked at Ginnie's picture. She'd let all those awful things happen to her, just to keep my dad and Dee and me safe. "Oh, Mom . . . I miss you."

XLIII

The police found Sandy's body three days later, partially buried in a gravel pit outside of Cementville. Media claimed it was sixteen-related and gave lip service to the perils of overt teen sexuality—immediately followed by a vert about how to increase your sex appeal with a pheromone-based body wash. If Ed could have been killed again, Mike would have done it.

Sal borrowed a hire-trannie from his brother and we all went to Cementville for the funeral.

Sandy looked so beautiful—like she was sleeping. Her mother was on a dozen drugs to keep her under control. Even her stepdad looked like he'd been crying. I wanted to think I'd misjudged him, but I don't think I had. I stood at the casket, unable to take my eyes off my best friend. For all of her sex-teen ways, she'd been so naive and trusting. All she'd ever wanted was to get out of her tier, to find someone who loved her. I hoped that somehow she could see or feel just how much I loved her. I leaned over, kissed her forehead, and straightened her bangs. I was so going to miss her.

Mike had offered to be one of the pallbearers. Before they

shut the pod, I saw him place a tiny plasticene cow in her hand. He'd had it since kindergarten—I knew because I'd given it to him. One tear trickled down his cheek. That was the only time he showed any emotion from the funeral home to the burial rocket. He watched as it left on its journey to collect other pods before the final launch into space. Long after everyone else had gone to Sandy's parents' place for the wake, Mike was still standing, staring down the highway.

Sal, Derek, and I finally persuaded him to get in the HT and we drove back to the city in silence.

***

Back at home, I opened the packet again and read the rest of Ginnie's note to my father. It outlined everything that Wei had told me about FeLS. Some of it was on the up-and-up, but most of it had to do with using sixteens as sex slaves for government officials and the ocribundan miners. The chips contained documents, pictures, names, and enough evidence that if it got to the right place, it could not be ignored. My father would know exactly what to do with it. And I would put it and Dee's baby book in his hands myself.

Eventually, what Ginnie'd found would help thousands of girls. But I wondered what would happen to me. My FeLS contract was gone. But at least Ed wasn't around to push a Chooser into taking me. If I was chosen, there was no way of knowing if I'd get sent to the sex-trafficking training or the regular training. Running away was starting to look like a viable option. Except that would mean I'd have to leave Dee and Gran and Pops. And my friends. And Sal. But, I couldn't worry about becoming a fugitive now. I had to get this information to my father first

***

There were still nearly three weeks until Holiday Day break. It was a rare sunny afternoon in Chicago's winter, so Dee and I walked home from school through the park. It was nice not to have to look over my shoulder constantly, worrying about Ed. We stopped by the horse pasture and stood watching the horses pull at mounds of hay. In the distance, I saw the resident herd of cows. I could almost see Sandy leaning over the fence, mooing. I had to turn away.

"Gran says that there's only one way to get to the happy memories. You have to cry out the sad ones," Dee said. "I'm really sorry about Sandy, Nina."

"Yeah; me, too." I swiped a tear away. So much had happened over the past few months. It was going to be a while before I got over losing Sandy. And my mom.

Dee raced up the side of the pasture, petting every horse that would come near the fence. She was safe from Ed. I hadn't told her that Alan was her father. That would remain a secret, at least until I could find him.

***

"We're home." I tossed my gloves on the top shelf of the closet.

Pops thumped into the room. "Checkerheads were here today."

I stopped right in the middle of taking my coat off. "What did they want?"

"It was about that ... uh ... Dee, honey, go see what your gran wants. I heard her call you."

My knees were knocking together as I hung up my coat and sat down across from Pops. "Ed?"

"Yup. Seems he disappeared. Tracked his last PAV signal somewhere around Lincoln and Wells."

"Why did they come here?" I managed to keep my voice normal—suppressing the shriek that wanted to burst out.

"They thought he might have visited Dee." Pops chunked back in his chair. "I told them the deadbeat never bothered before, why would he have been around then? She wasn't anything to him, 'cept by DNA."

I hadn't told Gran or Pops about Dee's parentage either. They were safer not knowing.

"Did the police say anything else?"

"Nah, just to let 'em know if he showed up." Pops snorted. "Like I'd tell them anything. They said his wife hadn't even reported him missing, it was his job that wondered why he wasn't at work."

"I'm not surprised," I muttered.

"Huh?" Pops cupped an ear toward me.

"Nothing, I just wondered if they'd ever find him."

"I hope the miserable SOB dropped off the planet," Pops said.

If only you knew, I thought. Sal had never told me the whole story about who did the cleanup after we'd left Robin's Roost that night. He said the less I knew, the better. I was in full agreement.

XLIV

December 10, 2150. My sixteenth birthday.

I'd left the doctor's office after getting my STD vaccines. They say a girl has to be safe; I was thinking it was more that the guys didn't want to catch anything. Next stop, the government tattoo parlor. I sat in the ID tech's chair, gritting my teeth while she jabbed the needle into my wrist. When she was done, the GC-mandated XVI was etched into my skin—a black stain.

"You're absolutely certain about this?" the tech asked Gran, pointing to a line on the paperwork.

"That's what it says," Gran replied. "The girl's got sense—she doesn't need to be tracked like some animal."

The woman shook her head, but proceeded. I winced as the vac tool penetrated my skin and then sucked the pellet out. She chucked it into the wastebasket. One less GPS to track, I thought.

Gran tucked away my birth certificate, signed the remaining forms, and we left.

Our next stop was the Bureau of Identification and Ranking. More forms, more signatures. I couldn't believe I actually smiled for my photo. The new scan listed all my pertinent information and the box marked *Creative* was checked. All I'd had to do was show them the transcripts from my art classes in Cementville and pay a fee. Now I knew why Ginnie'd sacrificed so much for me to take the classes.

Much as I wanted another tattoo, one like Wei's—the thistles circling the XVI—I knew I couldn't afford one. Besides, when she'd told me about hers, a bit reluctantly as I recalled, it seemed like the tattoo had another meaning, one even beyond its anti-XVI symbolism . Maybe someday I could afford to get my own tattoo, one I would design myself, with special significance for me.

When we stepped outside the bureau, Wei was waiting for us.

"Let's go to Rosie's," she suggested. "I'm dying for a shake."

Gran kissed my cheek. "You go along now. Spend the day with your friends. You deserve some fun."

I didn't argue.

Rosie's was deserted when we got there.

"I'll go in the back and see where Rosie is," Wei said. "Think you can find a table?" We both laughed—since the place was empty.

I sat down and studied my wrist. The zone-out chip had worn off and my arm was throbbing. Mrs. Jenkins had sent along a jar of salve with Wei for me to use on it. I'd just unscrewed the lid when the kitchen door swung open.

"Surprise!"

Rosie came through the door carrying a big cake covered with white icing and chocolate sprinkles. She was flanked by all my friends, and Gran, Pops, and Dee. Even Mr. and Mrs. Jenkins and Miss Gray were there. I burst into tears.

"Hey . . . hey." Sal swept me out of the chair. "No crying today. This is a happy day." He kissed me.

Mike set a bag on the table. "Some stuff from all of us."

I gave him a hug and kissed his cheek. "Thank you," I whispered.

I went through all the presents. There was an antique porcelain horse figurine from Derek and Wei. A bill of sale for a new bed from Gran and Pops; the survivor benefits had finally come through. Dee had made me an old-fashioned picture album with photos of me and her and Ginnie. Mike gave me a digi-frame of me and Sandy that he'd taken at the zoo in the summer. The Jenkinses had paid for the party, and Rosie was giving me a year of Cliste Galad lessons for free. Miss Gray had tucked a real edition of *1984* into a winter cap she'd knitted for me.

"You guys are all so great."

"I think Dad's saving the best for last," Wei said. "Give it to her now, okay?"

"Second best," Mr. Jenkins said. Reaching into his pocket, he pulled out an envelope. "Your FeLS contract, Nina. Signed, sealed, and I recorded them notarizing it. You can never be chosen. You are free."

"Thank you!" I hugged him as hard as if he'd been my own dad. Free. That was how I felt. No FeLS, no two years away from Dee and Gran and Pops, no fear of turning into someone like Joan and no living like a fugitive. Plus, I could apply to the Art Institute now that I had my Creative designation. I felt like someone had lifted a trans off me.

"There is one other thing," he said. "Jade?"

Wei's mother nodded and handed me a special PAV receiver, one that still had a signal in the midst of Rosie's DZ. "I think this is for you. You might want to take it somewhere private."

Rosie directed me into the kitchen.

I held the receiver to my ear. "Hello?"

"Nina?"

"Dad!" I would have known his voice anywhere.

Our conversation lasted for exactly as long as it took for him to say, "Happy birthday."

For me to say, "Thank you."

And for him to say, "I'll see you soon."

That was it. And it was so much more than I'd ever dreamed.

***

After we'd all eaten, the Jenkinses took Gran, Pops, Dee, and all my goodies home. Mike had to go take care of his little sister, and Derek and Wei were working on something special for Holiday Day. I didn't ask what—I knew it was just an excuse for them to be alone together.

Sal and I walked over to the park, to my mountain—that had become "our place."

"Did you know this was DZ?" he asked.

"Really?"

"I'm sure that's why your mom brought you here so often. She could talk to your father without worrying about being heard. No matter, though." He pulled me close. "It's the most special place in the galaxy as far as I'm concerned."

We kissed several times before sitting down.

"Have you read anything else in the book?"

"No, it's personal stuff for my father. Ginnie wanted him to know what she'd been thinking and feeling all those years."

Sal took my hand and kissed my fingertips, which sent a shiver, a really good one, all the way down to my feet. I caressed his cheek, loving the scratchy stubble feeling on my hand. "Right now, though, I don't want to think about the past or tomorrow."

"Me either." He kissed me again.

It was amazing—here we were sitting in the middle of snow, and I was feeling as warm as summertime. Weatherproof jeans notwithstanding—I knew Sal's kisses were the reason.

When we came up for air, Sal said, "Aren't you wondering if I got you anything?"

"No." I laughed. "I guess I was so surprised by everything . . . I never ever imagined a birthday like this one."

He took a small box from his pocket. When I opened it, I found half a silver heart charm. Engraved on it was *I lo*—then there was a jagged break. "What's this?"

He reached up to his neck and pulled a chain from under his sweater. The other half of the heart was dangling there:—*ve you* was written on it.

Blushing, of course, I threw my arms around his neck and whispered, "Me, too."

We spent the next hour kissing, wrestling around in the snow and generally "acting our age," as Gran would say. But no sex. I wasn't a sex-teen. I was just a girl who was sixteen, and that felt pretty good.

When writing XVI *did you have any real-life inspiration for the world and the characters?*
My initial inspiration for *XVI* was an image of a punk rock girl walking down the street in a big city. I chose Chicago, drawing on my memories of the atmosphere, the architecture, the places I used to hang out when I lived there, and the different neighborhoods.

The characters were born exclusively in my imagination. But, as often happens, certain traits and quirks popped up from memories of friends past. There's a little real-life inspiration in quite a few of my characters.

Did you have any reservations/concerns about dealing with such a sexually concentrated topic, particularly in YA fiction?
Honestly, I didn't even think about that when I was writing the book. Sexuality and sexual identity is something that teens deal with on a daily basis. There is a huge disconnect between the vestiges of our country's underlying Puritan mind-set regarding sex and the business of selling teen sexuality through movies, television, and all kinds of advertising. I remember well how it felt as a teen growing up with societal pressures, family expectations, and the struggle for my own identity, of which sexuality is, of course, a part. And, when you're a teenager, it can seem like an overwhelming part.

Dystopian novels are a growing trend. What drew you to the genre?
My mind tends to jump immediately to the what-ifs in discussions about politics, society, and technology. I've found that for pretty much every utopian theme, there's an equally dark dystopian one. And the dystopian ones are much more thrilling!

The characters that you created are very strong, and deal with very mature issues. Whom do you identify with most?
It has to be my protagonist, Nina. Sixteen for me was instant adulthood. I believe that most teens, if thrown into situations requiring them to grow up quickly, will rise to the challenge and discover what they are made of.

Like Nina, your main character, you had a transition at 16 when you moved from Indiana with your grandmother to Chicago with your mother. How did this affect you? Why did you decide to give Nina a similar situation?

It was not a conscious decision to have Nina's situation be similar, but, as the story unfolded, it was impossible not to draw on my own experiences. Moving to Chicago was the single most pivotal event of my life (except for having babies!). My entire world was turned upside-down, in both good and bad ways. However, Nina's choices and her life experiences are not mine, even though remembering my own teen years gave me insights into how she might feel and react to situations.

This is your first young adult novel. Have you been surprised by anything during the writing/publishing process?

Perhaps a better question would be, "What has *not* surprised me?" I think my biggest surprises had to do with time and with the editing process. Publishing time is nothing like real time. There's a lot of hurry up and wait involved every step of the way. And, with editing, I was surprised by how cringeworthy some of my writing was, and even more surprised when I'd read something that was so good I'd have to remind myself that I wrote it.

What books did you enjoy most as a teenager?

I have always been a voracious reader. As a young teen I loved mysteries and read every Nancy Drew at the library. From there I graduated to reading Sherlock Holmes and Agatha Christie. I've also always loved science fiction and fantasy. A couple of favorite sci-fis from my teen years are *More Than Human*, by Theodore Sturgeon, and *Dune*, by Frank Herbert. As far as fantasies go, E. R. Eddison's *The Worm Ouroborous* and his Zimiamvian trilogy, plus many re-readings of *Alice in Wonderland* and *Through the Looking Glass*, by Lewis Carroll. Dystopians that I read then were *1984*, by George Orwell, and *Fahrenheit 451*, by Ray Bradbury.

DISCUSSION QUESTIONS

• Do you think that Nina's mom should have revealed the truth sooner? Why do you think she kept it a secret for so long? Would you have done the same?

• Do you think girls are judged by appearance and gender? Do you think boys are judged in the same manner? What role do you believe the media plays in this? What role do you play in this?

• Despite Nina's concerns, Sandy embraced the media's image of how a girl should look and act when they turn sixteen. Have you ever been in a similar situation? Can you give an example of how you bought into a trend despite your better judgment?

• If you were turning sixteen in this society, how would you feel? Are you a Sandy or a Nina?

• With the recent influx of dystopian literature do you think the plot of *XVI* is plausible? Are we moving toward this type of society?

• Do you see any similarities between our current society and the society that Nina resides in? What distinguishes one from the other? What makes either society undesirable?

• The government's change of legal consent and the unequal treatment of women are left unexplored in *XVI*. What are your theories as to how this happened?

• Teens and sexuality/sexual education is a growing issue in America. The age at which kids are experimenting with sex is getting younger and younger. Discuss the consequences this is having on individuals and on our society in general.